T0195997

Inheriting her late aunt's Massachusetts farm is no gift for app developer Mabel Skinner, who is about to learn that even the best-grown garlic can't ward off murderous intent . . .

Mabel's hope of finding an enthusiastic farmer to buy Stinkin' Stuff Farm is dying a little bit every day. So far, all she's found are double-dealing developers. But after a heated dispute over grass clippings with an obsessive local rhubarb breeder, she discovers something even more distressing—the breeder in question undisputedly dead in his greenhouse. . . .

Uncomfortably aware that she might be a prime suspect, Mabel stops digging in the dirt long enough to dig up more information about the dead man, and anyone else he might have argued with. The list is longer than she imagined, and includes a persnickety neighbor and a rival rhubarb breeder. With all the ingredients for a homegrown mystery, Mabel must unearth a killer—before the next plot to be dug is her grave. . . .

Visit us at www.kensingtonbooks.com

Also by Gin Jones

Garlic Farm Mysteries
Six Cloves Under

Helen Binney Mysteries
A Dose of Death
A Denial of Death
A Draw of Death
"A (Gingerbread) Diorama of Death" (short story in Cozy Christmas Shorts)
A Dawn of Death
A Darling of Death
A Display of Death

Danger Cove Quilting Mysteries
Four Patch of Trouble
Tree of Life and Death
Robbing Peter to Kill Paul
Deadly Thanksgiving Sampler
"Not-So-Bright Hopes" (short story in Pushing Up Daisies)

Danger Cove Farmers' Market Mysteries
"A Killing in the Market" (short story in Killer Beach Reads)
A Death in the Flower Garden
A Slaying in the Orchard
A Secret in the Pumpkin Patch
Two Sleuths Are Better Than One

Rhubarb Pie Before You Die

A Garlic Farm Mystery

Gin Jones

LYRICAL UNDERGROUND
Kensington Publishing Corp.
www.kensingtonbooks.com

LYRICAL UNDERGROUND BOOKS are published by
Kensington Publishing Corp.
119 West 40th Street
New York, NY 10018

All Kensington titles, imprints, and distributed lines are available at special quantity discounts for bulk purchases for sales promotion, premiums, fund-raising, educational, or institutional use.

Special book excerpts or customized printings can also be created to fit specific needs. For details, write or phone the office of the Kensington Sales Manager: Kensington Publishing Corp., 119 West 40th Street, New York, NY 10018. Attn. Sales Department. Phone: 1-800-221-2647.

Lyrical Underground and Lyrical Underground logo Reg. US Pat. & TM Off.

First Electronic Edition: December 2020
ISBN-13: 978-1-5161-0959-3 (ebook)
ISBN-10: 1-5161-0959-7 (ebook)

First Print Edition: December 2020
ISBN-13: 978-1-5161-0962-3
ISBN-10: 1-5161-0962-7

Printed in the United States of America

Chapter 1

"Are you sure this is legal?" Mabel Skinner asked, reluctantly grabbing hold of the nearest yard-waste bag filled with leaves and grass clippings. She'd called her attorney hours ago with the same question, but he hadn't picked up the private line that he shared only with family, friends, and a very few long-term clients like herself. It wasn't like him to ignore her. He'd been representing her since her parents died when she was a young child, and he always either picked up her calls or returned them within an hour or two. Just not today.

"Your aunt and I didn't encounter any problems, and we've been doing it for the past five years," Rory Hansen said, not quite answering the question. She had been one of Aunt Peggy's best friends, and was honoring that friendship by helping Mabel keep the farm going until it could be sold. Rory was in her forties, tanned from her own outdoor work with the local CSA—Community-Supported Agriculture—group, and tall with a solid build.

She casually tossed her own bag full of yard waste into Aunt Peggy's old but well-maintained black Ford F-150 truck. It was Mabel's truck now, she reminded herself, along with everything else at the Stinkin' Stuff Farm, even if she never actually drove the huge truck herself, deferring to Rory or farmhands to do it. Her Mini Cooper was much more her size.

Mabel had always been risk-averse, even as a child, and then her natural inclinations had been exacerbated by losing her parents to a freak accident. Still, she'd let herself be convinced by Rory that their late-night activity couldn't get them into too much trouble. After all, Rory had been married to a local police officer for close to twenty years and would never do anything to embarrass him professionally, the way getting herself arrested for trespassing and theft would.

Mabel got a better grip on her paper bag and managed to get it into the back of the truck, although with a lot more effort than her friend had exerted. She tucked her cold hands into the oversized pockets of her aunt's green barn coat. It was going to be a long night, and a chilly one too. She'd never been much of an outdoor person or a physically active one. She would have much preferred to be back at the farmhouse, in bed, and hunched over her laptop, rather than out here in a neatly manicured subdivision at midnight, collecting bags of what she'd been assured was chemical-free yard waste, perfect for mulching the rows of garlic that would be planted in another couple of weeks at the end of October.

The late-night hour didn't bother her—even if she'd been back at the farmhouse, she wouldn't have been ready to sleep for hours yet. Normally at this time of night, she'd have been working at her job, developing apps for her employer, but she was on hiatus while searching for someone to buy the garlic farm she'd inherited from her aunt. Selling was proving to be much more difficult than she'd anticipated. She'd hoped to be back in Maine before it was time to plant the next season's garlic crop, so the new owner could do it, but that was starting to look unlikely. She'd considered just leaving the fields fallow until the title changed hands, but both Rory and the real estate broker had said that the property would be more valuable if it remained a working farm with a demonstrable stream of income.

"Why can't we just buy some mulch instead of stealing it?" Mabel asked.

"It's not stealing." Rory grabbed another bag. "It's composting. Plus, we're saving the town from having to pick it up and transport it to the landfill. It's win-win for everyone."

Mabel's phone pinged in her pocket, and she took it out to check who had texted her. It was from her boss, Phil Reed. She put the phone away without responding. It wouldn't be fair to make Rory do all the work. Mabel grabbed another bag.

"Who texts you at midnight?" Rory asked. "Is something wrong?"

"No, it's just my boss."

"I thought you were on hiatus until you sell the farm."

"I am, but he likes to check in on me from time to time. He's hoping I'll find a buyer quickly and come back to work soon before the year-end rush."

"I'm not," Rory said, tossing her bag into the pickup. "I'm hoping you change your mind and decide to stay here in West Slocum and continue what Peggy started."

"I won't let Aunt Peggy's legacy be destroyed. I don't have to live here to do that though. I've told the broker that I'll only sell to another farmer. Stinkin' Stuff Farm will continue."

"It's not just the farm's future that I'm concerned about." Rory turned to lean against the black truck's tailgate. "I'll miss you when you leave."

"Me too." Just a few months earlier, Mabel wouldn't have believed she'd feel any regrets about leaving West Slocum. She hadn't wanted to personally oversee her aunt's estate and would have delegated it to an agent if she could have, but Jeff Wright, her friend and lawyer, had insisted she had to do it herself. She'd expected to get in and out in just a few days without any personal entanglement, but Rory and the owner of the goat farm next door, Emily Colter, had quickly dragged Mabel into their circle of friendship. Initially, the two women may have only been honoring her aunt's memory and Mabel had only considered them her aunt's friends, not her own. Over the last three months though, Mabel thought they'd all come to like each other for who they were, not just for their respective connections with Peggy Skinner.

A rusty old beige pickup screeched to a halt behind Mabel's truck on the otherwise deserted street. A bearded man jumped out, leaving the engine running. He wore overalls that were both too short and far too wide for his tall, thin frame, and an equally baggy brown barn coat not unlike the one Mabel was wearing. She'd had to take hers from her aunt's closet, since she hadn't brought any warm-weather clothes with her when she'd come to West Slocum in July.

"Hey!" the man shouted from beside the open driver's side door. "You're stealing my stuff."

That was exactly what Mabel had been afraid of. That one of the home owners would accuse her and Rory of wrongdoing. She knew she should do something to mollify the man, but she'd had never been any good at dealing with emotional people. Or even logical people who disagreed with her, actually, but it was worse when they were angry.

Mabel looked at Rory, who was much better with people. After all, she'd convinced the outdoors-averse and morning-averse Mabel to be a farmer, even if only temporarily. She still didn't quite know how it had happened. Rory was that good. Better to leave this situation to her. Mabel wouldn't be doing her friend any favors by trying to talk to the guy and only making him angrier.

"Relax," Rory whispered. "I'll take care of this. Graham Winthrop doesn't have any more right to the mulch than you do. He lives about the same distance from here and has no direct connection to anyone in this subdivision."

"But if it matters so much to him..." Mabel trailed off.

"It matters to you too," Rory said firmly. "Besides, Graham's got only a tiny parcel of land and doesn't need all this mulch. He grows some rhubarb for the CSA in his back yard, but mostly he's interested in breeding it. He's hoping to develop a new standard for commercial production."

The man from the truck stomped over to the pile of yard-waste bags, and stood in front of it, his legs and arms spread wide, making him look like a live scarecrow in the ill-fitting clothes that Mabel could now see were also torn and frayed from heavy use, not done intentionally as a fashion statement.

"Go away!" he shouted. "These are mine. All the bags in this neighborhood are mine."

Mabel would have told him he could have them, but Rory said, "Settle down, Graham. No need to cause a fuss. There's more than enough here to share. We'll even help you load your half." She picked up the bag just beyond his outspread left arm and took a step toward the man's pickup apparently to show she meant her words.

He grabbed the bag out of her hand, startling a brief, sharp scream out of her. She backed away with her hands raised. "Hey, I was just trying to help you."

"The only help I want is for you to go away."

"We aren't going anywhere," Rory said defiantly, even as porch lights came on at the house that had produced the contested bags of yard waste.

"Maybe we *should* leave." Mabel nodded toward the lights. "I don't want you to get in any trouble over this. I'm sure we can find other sources of mulch."

Graham turned on her, raising his voice. "Other sources? What's your definition of other sources?"

Mabel took an involuntary step backward. The man's voice wasn't just angry, it was loud. The sound had probably carried throughout the entire fifty-lot subdivision. Sure enough, a moment later additional lights went on in nearby houses.

"I don't know what other sources there might be," Mabel said. "But I'm sure we can find some."

"You'd better not be planning to raid any of my other suppliers," Graham said.

"No, of course not."

"I'll be watching you." He glared at her. "And I'll get an injunction if I so much as see your truck in my neighborhood."

"Be reasonable, Graham," Rory said. "You live on the corner of a main street. Mabel has to drive past there to get to the grocery store, the post office, and the library."

"Not my problem," he said. "I'm the innocent party here, so you two will have to be the ones being inconvenienced. It's only fair and equitable."

A man in plaid pajama bottoms, trying unsuccessfully to zip up his hastily thrown-on hoodie as he approached, arrived in time to respond. "Actually, Graham, I'm the one who's being inconvenienced. Along with everyone else in this neighborhood. What the hell are you three doing out here at this hour?"

Mabel heard a slight sigh from Rory before her friend turned to face the newcomer. "Councilor Lambert. I'm sorry you had to get involved."

He snorted. "I bet you are. Does Joe know that you're out at this hour?"

Rory's eyebrows rose halfway up her forehead at the suggestion she needed her husband's permission to go out, but she kept her tone even. "I don't keep any secrets from my husband. But you can't blame him for this situation. Mabel and I were minding our own business, just taking away the unwanted yard waste to put it to good use, keeping it out of the waste stream and saving the town the expense of hauling it away, when Graham showed up and started causing trouble."

Graham started to say something, but the councilor held up a hand for silence. Mabel was surprised when the other man closed his mouth. "Who's she?" Lambert asked, pointing at Mabel.

Mabel answered with her name. Then, thinking that hardly anyone in town knew her yet, but everyone seemed to know and respect her aunt, so it wouldn't hurt to do a little name-dropping, she added, "I'm Peggy Skinner's niece. I inherited her Stinkin' Stuff Farm a few months ago, and Rory's been helping me to keep the farm going until I can find a buyer for it."

"Objection," Graham said. "None of this is relevant, Lambert. You need to tell them that the bags all belong to me, so I can get them picked up and go home. I can't be out here all night. I've got to be in court in the morning."

Getting the threatened injunction? And did that mean she needed to go to court too to stop it? Rory would expect her to defend the farm's right to organic mulch, but Mabel wasn't at her best early in the morning, and it was too late at night to call her lawyer so he could take care of it. He couldn't get from Maine to West Slocum, Massachusetts, in time anyway.

Councilor Lambert wearily ran his hand over his face. "You're waking everyone up over ownership of grass clippings?"

"We didn't wake anyone up," Rory said. "Graham did."

"I wouldn't have had to get loud if they'd been reasonable," Graham denied hotly. "This stuff is valuable. Anyone who knows anything about organic gardening knows that. It's even called black gold once it decomposes a bit."

"He's right about that much," Rory said reluctantly. "Just not about what constitutes reasonableness. We offered to split it evenly, even though he's got a smaller farm than Mabel does."

"I don't care," Lambert said. "I just want to get some sleep. And so do my neighbors. They're going to blame me if I don't take care of this. So, either you three work it out—*quietly*—or you need to leave right now and no one gets the mulch."

"How about we take the bags on the odd-numbered side of the street and Graham takes the ones on the even-numbered side?" Rory suggested.

"That's not fair," Graham shouted. "You're not sacrificing anything, and you're asking me to give up half of what belongs to me."

"The bags aren't all yours," Rory said irritably. "We've been collecting from this neighborhood for years."

"Ha!" Graham scoffed. "I know that's a lie. Mabel just admitted she only recently come to West Slocum. She couldn't have been with you before."

"Enough," Lambert said. "Half and half is a fair split."

Graham grumbled something under his breath, and then said, "All right. But I'm taking the odd-numbered side."

"Fine," Rory agreed.

Graham glared at Mabel. "It's your farm. Do you agree too? Or is Rory authorized to act as your agent?"

Mabel sometimes thought she was Rory's agent, not the other way around, but now wasn't the time to bring that up. "I agree."

Graham peered at her. "You don't sound sure. I don't want to hear anything later about how this contract was entered under duress."

"I'm sure." Mabel tried to project confidence. Her words may still have sounded uncertain, but that was just how she always sounded. Whenever she needed to be tough, she got her attorney to do the talking. "No duress whatsoever."

"Okay," Graham said. "But the agreement is only for tonight's collection. The rest of the season's collections belong to me."

"Wait," Rory said. "We didn't agree to that."

Lambert made a time-out sign with his hands. "Enough. I'll call Darryl Santangelo in the morning. He's not terribly busy managing the farmers' market this late in the season, so he should have time to listen to you present your claims during regular business hours. If he can't help you come up with a solution, let me know and I'll take it up with the town council. Just be warned that if it comes to that, I'll recommend that no one but our trash contractors be allowed to pick up the yard waste, and then neither of you will get it."

"You can't do that," Graham said. "Letting farmers use the yard waste is already an established tradition, like common law."

"I *can* do it," Lambert replied. "Dealing with yard waste wasn't exactly why I joined the town council, but I'm sure my constituents will appreciate that I'm resolving the problem. Almost as much as I'll appreciate going back to bed without you three continuing to keeping me awake. Now go get your agreed-upon bags. And don't make me come back out here again. I'm pretty sure I'm going to have a dozen calls from the neighbors at some ridiculously early time tomorrow, so you'd better hope I've gotten some sleep before then, or you won't like the consequences."

He turned and headed back to his front porch.

Graham didn't seem to know when to shut up. He shouted at Rory, "You won for now, but this isn't over." As he spoke, his barn coat blew open to reveal an orange-handled knife about a foot long in a leather sheath affixed to a belt that cinched in the waist of his baggy overalls. The leather was well worn, but cleaner and in better shape than Graham's clothes, suggesting he both valued it and used it regularly. He rested his hand on the hilt before adding, "I'll get what I need, one way or another."

Rory didn't seem to have noticed the weapon, and waved at him dismissively before starting to cross the dark street for the bags that had been allocated to Stinkin' Stuff Farm.

Mabel caught her by the arm. "Let it go for now, please."

"But your aunt never would have—"

"I'm not my aunt." Mabel used her grip on Rory's arm to tug her over toward the driver's side of the farm's truck. "I'll deal with Graham later, in my own way."

"I heard that," Graham shouted. He turned toward the town councilor's retreating back, which had almost reached the porch. "She threatened me."

Lambert turned around, and even in the dark, even with Mabel's poor people-reading skills, it was obvious he was going to explode if the situation continued. Things could get out of hand pretty quickly. And Graham had a knife. A *big* knife.

Mabel's instincts always called for her to run and hide from situations that involved the risk of even mild confrontation, and they were even more emphatic when there was a risk of violence. Now was not the time to ignore those instincts.

"I did not threaten anyone," Mabel called out from a safe distance, just to set the record straight, while urgently pushing Rory toward the driver's side door of the truck. "But there's no need to argue. We're leaving right now. Graham can have all the yard waste tonight."

"But—" Rory gave her a confused look.

"Get in and drive," Mabel said quietly but firmly. "Or I will. And you really don't want me behind the wheel of a vehicle this big."

Chapter 2

The next morning, Mabel woke to the persistent yowling of her cat, Pixie. She did that whenever a vehicle entered the farm's driveway, but usually settled down after a single warning screech.

Not this time.

After the third howl, Mabel peered blearily at the time. Nine in the morning. And she'd only gone to bed four hours earlier. She'd been too wired to sleep after getting home from the confrontation with Graham, so she'd spent some time reading her aunt's journals, hoping there might be some hints in there for how the farm could be made more marketable.

It had taken a long time before Mabel had been able to stop mentally replaying the confrontation with Graham. On the way home, Rory had tried to convince Mabel that the knife she'd seen on Graham's belt wasn't a weapon, just a standard tool that he probably hadn't even remembered he was wearing. She'd explained that it was a *hori-hori* or "dig-dig" knife that many farmers and dedicated gardeners used for a variety of tasks. In Graham's case, it would be useful for digging holes for planting rhubarb seedlings and then, later in the life cycle, for cutting the poisonous leaves off the harvested stalks.

Mabel deferred to Rory in all things plant-related, but this was a matter of safety and common sense. The knife and the man carrying it were dangerous. There hadn't been any reason, like seedlings to plant or stalks to separate from leaves, to have it on him when they'd been arguing over the mulch. And Mabel was absolutely certain that the security staff wouldn't let Graham into the courthouse while carrying the knife if he went there today as he'd threatened. That made it a weapon.

Pixie continued to yowl, making it impossible for Mabel to go back to sleep. She dragged herself out of bed and headed for her aunt's bedroom to see who was in the parking lot outside the barn. The only person she'd been expecting at all, and not at this early hour, was Rory, who'd offered to come make sure all the supplies and tools were ready for the planting of the following year's garlic crop. Mabel was still hoping against fading hope that she'd find a buyer for the farm before the drop-dead date of Halloween for getting the cloves into the ground. Then the buyer would be responsible for the planting or possibly transforming the fields into beds for a different crop. She didn't care so much about the specific crop the buyer grew, as long as the land remained used for agriculture. That was what her aunt would have wanted. But if Mabel didn't find a buyer soon, she was going to have to plant the garlic for next year, just to maintain the property value.

Mabel made her way through the clutter of her aunt's bedroom and pulled back the curtain. Where she'd expected to see Rory's small green pickup parked next to Aunt Mabel's larger truck was instead a white SUV, with a real estate broker's logo and contact information printed on the hood, trunk, and all four doors. Danny Avila, Jr., was also the town's mayor, so the bumper was plastered with reelection stickers from at least three previous elections. According to Rory, citizens had elected or reelected him—by huge margins—each time. Not so much due to his incredible political skill however, but because no one else was interested in the part-time, low-paying, high-stress job.

Mabel rushed back to her bedroom and the rocking chair where she'd thrown yesterday's jeans and t-shirt. They were reasonably clean, since she hadn't been out in the fields yesterday, and the dirty work of collecting the yard waste had ended almost before it began. Besides, she didn't have time to hunt for something fresher.

She paused before dressing in order to pat the still intermittently screeching orange cat that had moved from her original spot next to the pillows to the bottom of the bed. "It's okay now, Pixie. I'm awake now, and I know who our visitor is. It's someone I want to see. Maybe he's brought a nice, young farmer looking to strike out and buy his own place, and he'll fall madly in love with Stinkin' Stuff Farm. A match made in heaven."

Pixie yowled, and Mabel corrected herself as she stepped into her jeans. "You're right. It would be even better if it were a nice, young farmer looking to buy *her* own place. But either way, we'd be able to sell the farm and get our lives back to normal."

Pixie made it loudly clear that she was not amused and headed for the stairs. Mabel quickly finished tugging on her jeans and t-shirt and followed the cat down to the kitchen where the yowling resumed. At least it was no longer at ear-splitting level, more of a grumble than a yowl.

Mabel raced outside to greet her broker. Danny was of average height and stockily built, with perpetually tanned skin and what looked from a distance to be a thick head of dark, tightly curled hair but which everyone knew was a hairpiece that covered a rapidly balding head. Apparently the hair, like everything else about him, was intended to make him into a replica of his father, from his appearance to his role as the mayor. Rory had once said it was rumored Danny even wore his late father's suits, a tribute to the older man's frugal ways as well as to his habit of always dressing as if he were the head of a much bigger and more important municipality. Danny definitely carried his father's battered old leather legal pad portfolio, the Sr. of the gold-etched name still visible on the front.

Despite his quirks, Danny had done his father proud, since at thirty-eight, he was already a four-term mayor. Of course, according to Rory, it had helped that his father had been the town's quietly competent mayor for the better part of fifty years, so when he'd died and his son was on the ballot to replace him, most residents probably hadn't even noticed the Jr. and had simply voted for the familiar name.

Standing beside Danny was a taller man wearing jeans, polo shirt, and a blazer that fit his broad shoulders and muscular arms so well it must have been custom tailored. He looked to be around the same age as Aunt Peggy had been—fifty—when she'd had her epiphany about the meaninglessness of her accounting career and had jettisoned it for an agricultural one.

"Mabel!" The mayor's excited tone would have been more appropriate for greeting a long-lost friend or relative, but he used it to greet everyone. He usually accompanied it by a hug, but after the time Mabel ran out of patience with reminding him she preferred to maintain a substantial bit of personal space and had stomped on his toes to get him to step back, he'd finally accepted that the most he would get was a handshake. "I know you prefer it if I text you first before showing the property, but I couldn't wait to introduce you to Thomas Porter. He's interested in buying your farm. He's got great plans for it, and he's willing to pay your asking price, cash deal."

Porter reached out eagerly to shake Mabel's hand. "I insisted on Danny bringing me here right away, as soon as he described the property to me." His glance flicked down to her t-shirt, not in a leering way, but in confusion. "I hope I didn't interrupt anything important."

Mabel looked down to see that she'd put her t-shirt on inside out. So much for making a good impression on a potential buyer.

"I was just doing farm things," she said vaguely. Sleeping was part of living on a farm, after all. "You know how it is. The work never ends. No time for me to worry about fashion when there are crops to be planted or weeded or harvested." Not that she'd ever worried about fashion before becoming a farmer either. One of the many nice things about working from home for a long-distance employer was that no one cared what you wore, as long as you did your job.

"I can't wait to shed my office clothes and get to work in the great outdoors." Porter definitely looked like he came from the more traditional office environment where people did care what you wore. His image was all wrong for a farmer, with his form-fitting blazer and his pale, unweathered skin. His muscles suggested he was fit enough to work in the fields, but his clean fingernails and hands that had softer skin than Mabel's had been before she'd come to the farm confirmed that he didn't spend much time digging in the dirt. Of course, she didn't look much like a farmer either— she had no particularly noticeable muscles, and her skin was even paler than his, thanks to a preference for being indoors whenever possible, plus copious amounts of sunscreen whenever she went outside. Yet, here she was, the callused-palmed owner of a farm known for growing the best garlic on the East Coast.

"Have you seen the property already?" Mabel asked. "Or was Danny"— the mayor always insisted on everyone calling him by his first name, just like his father had been addressed, and as long as he respected her personal space, she felt obligated to respect his preference for informality—"just about to give you a tour?"

"I've seen all I need to already," Porter said. "This is the perfect farm for me, the one I've dreamed about for years. I can't wait to put my own stamp on it. Perhaps we could sit down somewhere now and agree on the basic terms of the sale."

Could it really be happening? A sale that would get her back to Maine and her old job before the end of the year? And all she needed to do was provide a table and chairs?

"I've got just the place." Her aunt had loved being surrounded by friends, so she'd expanded the old kitchen area a few years earlier to add a huge dining room and then had filled it with a table large enough to seat at least a dozen people. It seldom got used to capacity now that Mabel owned the property, but it seemed fitting that arrangements for carrying on her aunt's farming legacy would happen at her aunt's table. "Follow me."

Pixie was waiting for them with her tail puffed out in irritation, sitting on the corner of the massive rustic trestle table just to the right of the door. The kitchen, despite the relatively recent work done for the addition, was a throwback to the 1960s, with a harvest-gold stove, an avocado green vintage wall phone, and a pineapple-motif wallpaper that perfectly matched both colors. There was a pineapple-shaped clock that needed a new battery, but other than that, everything was in good condition, if not to Mabel's taste. She wouldn't be living there for much longer, so she hadn't seen any point in redecorating when the new buyer would just change everything to his taste later anyway. The only thing she'd done to the house since arriving in July was to install insulating curtains in her bedroom, more to dampen the sound of inconsiderately noisy early birds, both avian and human, than for any temperature-controlling benefits.

Mabel waved at the table, and the two men took seats next to each other on the long side, across from the irritably tail-swishing Pixie.

Danny unzipped his leather portfolio and said, "I hear you and Rory Hansen got into a bit of mischief last night. Trespassing, breach of the peace, and a dozen other similar misdemeanors."

Mabel had long since accepted that people would talk about her—she'd been the subject of considerable gossip, some true, some not, ever since her parents' deaths in a work-related accident when she was a child—and while she didn't like it, she knew the chatter couldn't hurt her. Especially not if it happened in West Slocum. She'd be leaving soon, so it didn't really matter what people thought of her, and they would forget her soon enough. But Rory had a reputation to uphold. Not just because she was active in the community, running the CSA and volunteering for other local nonprofits but also because her husband was a police officer, whose own reputation could be affected by his family's perceived misbehavior.

"We didn't do anything wrong," Mabel insisted. "We were on a public road, and even the town councilman who lives there said we had equal rights to the yard waste. Graham Winthrop was the one being unreasonable."

"That's not what Graham told me," Danny said. "He called me in the middle of the night to tell me he's planning to seek criminal charges against you two, and he expected me to back him up with the police department. I tried to make him see reason, but you know how he is."

"The facts are on our side."

"Still, you need to be careful with Graham. He's a lawyer, so he knows how to work the system." Danny flipped open his portfolio to reveal the legal pad inside. "But let's not worry about that right now. We've got much more interesting possibilities to consider."

There was something less than inspiring about Danny's forced optimism, unlike the take-it-to-the-bank certainty that emanated from Jeff Wright, her attorney back in Maine. She'd always been able to refer any problem or project whatsoever to him and not give it a second thought, confident he had her best interest in mind, and he would either take care of the matter on her behalf or give her solid advice on what she needed to do. She wished she could feel the same way about entrusting the farm's sale to Danny. She'd only signed with him because Jeff hadn't had anyone better to recommend, and everyone said Danny was the only broker within a hundred miles who knew the West Slocum market inside and out. She hated the feeling that she had to double-check everything he did, but the farm had meant too much to Aunt Peggy to sell it to the wrong person.

"So, we're agreed on the listing price as the selling price, right?" Danny took the pen out of its slot inside the portfolio.

Pixie drowned out Porter's apparent agreement.

Mabel waited for the sound to peter out before saying, "Yes."

Pixie yowled her disagreement again and stalked over to Danny, who was closer to her than the other man. She swiped at the hand that held the pen before continuing over to slash at the sleeve of Porter's blazer.

Mabel hurried over to grab Pixie and drag her away before she could draw blood with another swipe. "I'm sorry. She's not good with people." Which was a bit of an exaggeration. Pixie tended to noisily announce the arrival of visitors, but then she usually retreated to a windowsill to observe what happened next, content with having raised the alarm and not feeling the need to inflict bodily harm on anyone. She hadn't bothered Danny the day he'd come out to get the listing signed, even though he'd sat in the exact same spot at the table then.

Pixie squirmed, but Mabel held on tight. She finally had a buyer to carry out her aunt's vision for the land, and she wasn't going to lose the sale because of a cranky cat who might think she was going to be abandoned when the property changed hands. The barn cats would stay with the farm, and Mabel would make sure the new owner looked after them, but she was bringing Pixie with her to Maine.

Pixie yowled from her position squashed against Mabel's chest. "I'd better put the cat in the other room so we won't be interrupted. I'll be right back."

"Of course," Porter said.

Mabel quickly secured Pixie in the home office in the front of the farmhouse. The cat liked that space, although, as a matter of principle, she never appreciated being forced into a room that wasn't of her choosing. She was certain to make her displeasure known while she was in there, probably by knocking everything off Aunt Peggy's desk, but there wasn't time to cat-proof right now. Having to pick things up later was a small price to pay for not being interrupted during the all-important negotiations to sell the farm.

When she returned, Danny was staring at a row of tiny droplets of blood welling up on his finger. Mabel detoured to get a paper towel and handed it to him to sop up the blood.

He dabbed at his finger. "So, the price is agreed upon," he said as if nothing untoward had happened. "What about a closing date?"

"The sooner the better," Mabel said.

"That works for me," Porter said. "I can't wait to get my hands in the dirt. Let's say the end of next week. Or earlier if the lawyers can do their part before then."

"Anything else we need to address?" Danny asked.

Mabel still wasn't entirely awake and prepared to study the intricacies of a real estate contract. To buy some time, she said, "I'm parched. Would anyone else like a glass of iced tea? I make it myself."

"No thanks," they said in unison. Danny added, "But go ahead if you need something."

"I do." Mabel opened the refrigerator door to grab the pitcher. She still hadn't had any caffeine this morning, and she needed something to wake her up after too little sleep. She couldn't go back to bed after they left, not when she was expecting Rory to show up as promised to help prepare for the fall planting. Of course, if the property changed hands next week, Mabel wouldn't be responsible for the planting, but it wouldn't hurt to keep everything on schedule, just in case.

Danny waited until she'd returned to the table with her drink before saying, "Have either of you thought of anything else you need to include?"

Porter shook his head. "I just want to make my dream of farming come true at last."

"I just thought of one thing," Mabel said. "There are some feral cats in the barn that my aunt rescued and I've been caring for. I need to know that they'll be fed and vetted, going forward."

"Of course. I like cats." Porter chuckled and glanced toward the hallway where Mabel had taken Pixie. "Even the ones who don't like me. And they're a great selling point for customers visiting the property, I bet."

"I don't know about that." Mabel hadn't ever thought of the cats as an attraction. She never wanted to attract visitors, and as far as she knew, of all the people who used to visit her aunt, only one had been particularly interested in the cats. "They do keep the barn free of vermin though."

Unfortunately, the cats continued to disappoint her by not being as good about dealing with the noisy birds as they were with mice, but most people seemed to think that was a good thing.

"Ah, working animals." Porter nodded. "Every farm should have them."

That reminded her of something she'd read in her aunt's journals about diversifying her streams of income as the key to small farm sustainability. "Are you planning to bring in more animals? My aunt was thinking about adding a flock of chickens."

"No, I'm more about the crops," Porter said. "The garlic, of course. And other things."

"There's a lavender bed too," Mabel said. "I don't know if you've seen it. And we mix winter squash in with the garlic so we have two harvests from each field. There's room for another field to be cultivated, but my aunt hadn't decided what to put there before she died."

"I'm still considering my options for what to plant," Porter said. "I only found out about the property being available a few days ago. I've been looking forever, so I can't wait to get this done."

"Well," Danny said. "I think we've got a deal."

"It needs to be in writing first," Mabel said. "And my lawyer needs to review it."

Danny closed his portfolio. "The same one who handled your aunt's estate? Quon Liang? I can have it delivered to him later this morning."

"No." The local lawyer was doing a fine job on Aunt Peggy's estate, but small-town probate work was, from what she'd been told, largely a simple matter of shuffling paperwork and waiting for notice periods to run out. For something as major as the sale of her aunt's farm, Mabel would only trust her lawyer back in Maine. She'd come to depend on his advice, not just on legal matters, but also more general decisions, especially after the grandparents who'd raised her had died. He would tell her if he thought it was a bad deal, even if the contract itself was legally sound. She had to be sure she wasn't letting her emotions—especially her desire to sell the farm as quickly as possible, preferably before the next year's garlic crop had to be planted—affect her judgment.

Mabel continued, "I'd like to have someone else review the big picture first. Then the local attorney can go over the finer points of state law."

Porter frowned. "How long will that take? I really want to close on this deal right away."

"It won't take long for my attorney to review it. I've known him for years," Mabel said. "I want to get the sale done quickly too. Otherwise, there's a lot of work for me to do on the farm in the next few weeks."

"Don't worry about the farm maintenance," Porter said. "I'll take care of everything as soon as the contract is signed."

"I have to warn you that there's a big project coming up right away," Mabel said. "Next year's garlic crop needs to be planted by the end of the month."

"Still not a problem," Porter said. "As soon as we close, I'll be spending all my time here."

"As long as you understand that you're up against a deadline by Mother Nature, which isn't the sort of thing you can get an extension on. I learned that the hard way this summer."

"Trust me, I know all about farms," Porter said, standing. He held his hand out for a farewell shake. "So we've got a deal?"

"Assuming my lawyer approves." Mabel took his hand and then shook Danny's too. She couldn't help noticing again how soft Porter's skin was. Even Danny had a few rough spots on his palm and fingers, perhaps from lugging the town's old archive books around, since studying the town's history was his real passion in life. Politics and real estate only paid the bills.

The men left, and Mabel released Pixie from the office. A dozen pencils, a sticky-note pad and the contents of the paper-clip holder were scattered around the floor, clear evidence of Pixie's displeasure. Probably from being confined in a room she hadn't chosen, but Mabel couldn't help thinking the cat also disapproved of the proposed deal with Porter.

Pixie didn't have a say in the deal, any more than Mabel's friends did, although they would probably find some reason to declare Porter an inadequate successor to Aunt Peggy. Mabel, however, was relieved to finally have a bona fide buyer, someone who would carry on her aunt's legacy at Stinkin' Stuff Farm. She couldn't wait to return to the quiet isolation of her home in Maine, sharing it with only Pixie. No more noisy birds to disrupt her sleep, no more early mornings dragging herself out of bed after only four hours' sleep, and no more constant stream of visitors to annoy both Pixie and herself.

Still, Mabel was left with the nagging worry that Porter didn't know what he was getting into. When Aunt Peggy had pursued her dream of farming, she'd gone about it in an efficient, organized, and well-researched way. Despite Porter's casual assurance that he knew all about farming, Mabel had to wonder if it was unfounded confidence gained perhaps from reading an idyllic story about living as one with nature. Probably without inconvenient weather patterns, crop thieves, or noisy birds. If Porter was as unprepared as she herself had been, the farm would fail, destroying Aunt Peggy's legacy in the process. Mabel couldn't let that happen.

Chapter 3

After the men left, Mabel poured herself another glass of iced tea and filled a bowl with the granola she'd become addicted to since moving to West Slocum. It was made locally and sold at the farmers' market where Mabel sold her garlic. She was going to have to see about getting her fix shipped to her in the future.

She left her breakfast on the kitchen table temporarily while she fetched her aunt's journal from the bedroom, so she could read it while she waited for Rory.

On the way down the stairs, she noticed that a few pages were loose. She'd already known it was deteriorating over time. In places, the ink of her aunt's otherwise clear handwriting had faded where drinks or food had been spilled on the page. It might be a good idea to scan the whole journal before anything else could happen to her beloved aunt's words.

Mabel hadn't brought her scanner with her from Maine when she'd come to deal with her aunt's estate. Normally, she'd have asked her attorney, Jeff, to have someone pack it up from her house in Maine, and send it to her, but she still hadn't heard back from him after her text asking him about possible criminal charges for the midnight mulch-gathering expedition. He must have been busy with some more serious crisis or he'd have responded by now. If so, the scanner was too minor a matter to bother him with. It would probably be cheaper to buy a new one anyway, with less risk of it being damaged en route. She could stop by the local electronics store later in the day to pick one up.

The thought caused her to pause at the bottom of the stairs. Before she'd come to West Slocum, if she'd needed something like a scanner, she'd have gone straight to an online vendor and bought it there without a second thought. Now, as a local vendor herself, she'd come to appreciate the benefits of buying from her neighbors whenever possible. Would she go back to her old ways once she returned to Maine? It might not be as easy to leave West Slocum behind—mentally as well as physically—as she'd expected.

Mabel settled at the head of the kitchen table to study her aunt's words while eating her breakfast and occasionally making notes about possible ways to improve the farm's profitability. She didn't need to implement them herself if the sale to Porter went through, but she could pass the ideas on to the buyer in the hope of increasing the odds of her aunt's legacy surviving over the long term.

Mabel got lost in her reading, so it was almost two hours later before she looked up from her empty granola bowl to wonder where Rory was. Mabel had been expecting her to arrive with a lecture about the importance of lining up an alternate source of mulch to cover the soon-to-be-planted garlic for next year's harvest, and a plan for doing just that. Maybe there was another neighborhood with chemical-free lawns. Or, given the circumstances, maybe Rory would concede that the mulch could be purchased. Mabel was certain she'd seen it advertised for sale somewhere. What she didn't know, and needed to ask Rory about, was whether there was something special about the midnight-raid type of mulch that had contributed to her aunt's being able to say she grew the best garlic on the East Coast.

Mabel carried her empty bowl over to the sink. Rory had probably slept in this morning after what was for her an extremely late night out. Rory was an actual morning person, something totally inconceivable to Mabel, although she didn't hold it against her friend. Not for long anyway. Just some sleepy grumbling under her breath whenever Rory was all perky while rousting Mabel out of bed at dawn for some CSA activity or another.

She was rinsing out her bowl when the back door opened behind her. She turned to see her next-door neighbor, Emily Colter. She looked like a trophy wife—young and blonde and thin, with a model's pronounced cheekbones—who'd been caught without her fancy wardrobe and make-up, although Mabel had never seen her all dressed up. Emily always wore essentially the same outfit she had on today—a long-sleeved t-shirt under white painters' overalls with the name of her goat farm, CAPRICORNUCOPIA, embroidered across the bib. A chunk of the fabric had been ripped away near her hip, presumably by one of the goats she raised for their milk. She made and marketed artisanal cheeses, including a garlic-flavored version in collaboration with Stinkin' Stuff Farm.

Emily also kept a few chickens and brought Mabel fresh eggs once or twice a week. She had a wire basket with her today and went straight to the harvest-gold refrigerator.

"You haven't been eating your eggs." Emily was almost the same age as Mabel, but she mothered everyone. "Is there a problem with them? Or have you been forgetting to eat again?"

"No, I've just been busy and getting takeout instead of cooking," Mabel said. "But you can skip today's egg delivery, and I'll let you know when I've finished the ones I have. It'll be soon, I promise."

"All right. I can use the extra eggs to make a pound cake for the Friends of the Library meeting later this week." Emily set her wire basket on the counter and helped herself to a glass of iced tea from the pitcher in the refrigerator.

Mabel might not be much of a cook, but she could make the perfect pitcher of iced tea. Of course, her skill was mostly in choosing high-quality leaves. It was one of the few things she still ordered online without feeling guilty about not buying locally. There weren't any tea farmers in the CSA, and none of the shops in town carried the variety she preferred. There were plenty of coffee options in town—at the diner, the coffee shop, and even the organic grocery store—but no one in West Slocum seemed to care about tea as much as she did.

Emily added an ice cube and a spoonful of honey to her drink before plopping herself at the kitchen table across from where Aunt Peggy's journal was still open. She pointed at it. "What have you been working on? Maybe I can help. I need something to do to distract myself from my husband's latest business trip. Ed's going to be gone another ten days, and it's making me restless."

"Running a goat farm isn't keeping you busy enough?"

Emily shrugged. "There's always something that needs doing on the farm, but nothing's all that critical right now. I got tired of moping about how much he's been gone lately, so I thought I'd come see what the mayor was doing here this morning. I saw his car turn into your driveway earlier."

"He was here as a broker, not the mayor. He's found someone who wants to buy Stinkin' Stuff Farm. His name is Thomas Porter, and he wants to close next week."

"Next week?" Emily frowned. "What's the rush?"

"He said he's been dreaming of a place like this for years, and he's anxious to get started," Mabel said. "I'd rather not have to plant next year's crop, so the sooner the sale happens, the better as far as I'm concerned."

"I don't know," Emily said, swirling the ice in her glass. "Buying a farm shouldn't be something you do on a whim. And it takes more than a week or two to get financing. If he doesn't know that, he's not ready to own a farm."

"He's paying cash."

At that, Emily's frown deepened and her eyebrows lowered. "The biggest obstacle for most aspiring farmers is coming up with the money to buy the land. Where'd he get all that cash?"

"He didn't say, and it's none of my business," Mabel said. "Aunt Peggy bought this place with her savings. I think this guy's doing the same thing. He's about the same age she was when she changed careers. He looks like some sort of businessman who made enough to retire on and is ready for a change."

"Have you checked him out to make sure he's who he says he is?"

"My attorney will do that," Mabel said.

"I still don't like it."

"You're just being emotional about it, because we've become friends," Mabel said. "I'll miss you and Rory too, but I don't belong here. I'm not a farmer."

"I don't think your buyer is either," Emily said. "It just doesn't feel right, between the ready cash and the rush to close. He probably wants to develop the land into condos, and it will disturb my goats, and they'll stop producing milk, and I won't be able to keep them, and I promised each one of them that they'd have an absolutely wonderful life with me. Can you imagine the karma I'd experience for letting them down?"

Mabel didn't believe in karma, but she did understand that breaking a promise to the goats would upset her friend. "I'd never sell to a developer. You know that."

"Not intentionally," Emily said, "but you know you're not the best at reading other people. That makes you vulnerable to lies."

She had a point, but Mabel's attorney would protect her. "I appreciate your concern. I'll definitely get Porter checked out before I sign anything."

After a deep drink from her tea, Emily said, "If he is a developer, Charlie Durbin might know him. You should ask him."

"I will." Charlie was a developer himself, and Mabel had gotten off on the wrong foot with him, assuming he'd befriended first her aunt and then her in order to get his hands on Stinkin' Stuff Farm to develop it. Fortunately, he hadn't held her rudeness against her as far as she could tell. He definitely wouldn't do anything to hurt her aunt's legacy, since they'd truly been good friends before her untimely death. "If Charlie says the buyer isn't a developer, will you be okay with the sale?"

"I know it's what you want"—Emily's disappointment showed in her face—"and I'll try to be happy for you. But I don't want you to leave. I think you'll be good for the farm and the town, and they'll be good for you. It just feels right to me."

"But I don't know what I'm doing when it comes to growing things."

"You could rent out the fields if you wanted to," Emily said. "You need to open yourself to all the possibilities of the universe. You're just stuck in a rut that leads back to Maine. It's not where you belong though. You don't have friends there, people who care about you, like you have here."

"I have my home in Maine," Mabel said. "And Jeff Wright. He's a friend as well as my lawyer. And I'll be taking Pixie with me for companionship."

Emily grunted skeptically. "Still, that's not a lot of ties. You have a home here, too, and more than one friend. And a dozen cats."

Mabel looked around the green and gold, pineapple-themed kitchen. "This is my aunt's home, not mine."

"You could make it yours," Emily suggested. "Some paint, new wallpaper and fresh curtains, and it would be totally different."

Mabel didn't want different. She liked the reliability of things that didn't change, surroundings that were familiar. Then she could concentrate on her work without distractions. "I already have a home that doesn't need paint or wallpaper or fresh curtains."

Emily sighed. "All right. But I still don't think you should be in such a rush to sell the farm. Or make any big life decisions. Things are always unsettled between the fall equinox and the winter solstice, and it doesn't take much to throw your life forces out of balance. You should wait until January before you do anything you can't easily undo."

"Nothing's final until my attorney has had a chance to review the agreement and give me his opinion," Mabel said, although she hoped she and Pixie would be settled comfortably back in Maine by January at the very latest. "He won't let me do anything foolish."

Emily jumped up from the table and carried her empty glass over to the sink. She turned to lean against the counter. "I know you rely on your attorney and have for a long time, but you need to ask yourself if he's got your best interests at heart in this matter. It's convenient for him if you return to Maine. But it's not necessarily good for you. You belong here. On the farm. Where Peggy always dreamed of you carrying on her work."

Mabel knew that wasn't true. Her aunt had only wanted Mabel to be happy, and had known that they didn't share the love of farming, with its early mornings, physical labor, and too many people stopping by. Still, Mabel felt a small pang of guilt. Not enough to change her mind about selling the farm, just enough to keep her motivated to protect her aunt's legacy by ensuring the land would continue to be a successful small farm.

To keep from upsetting Emily, Mabel changed the subject. "Rory should be here soon, and I bet she'll have projects to keep you busy if you really need a distraction. She said she'd be picking up the butternut squashes allocated for this week's CSA deliveries. You're welcome to join us loading them up if you want."

"Might as well," Emily said. "A little hard work might help me forget how much I miss my husband. And how I'll be missing you too before long."

* * * *

Rory's truck pulled up just as Mabel and Emily were approaching the barn. Rory backed as close as she could get to the barn doors before parking. She leaned out of the driver's side window. "Hi, Emily. What are you two up to?"

"Just waiting for you," Mabel said.

Rory turned off the engine and climbed out of the truck. Emily put a hand on Rory's arm. "Brace yourself. Mabel's got some bad news for you."

"Oh?"

Mabel didn't know how Emily knew about the fallout from last night's encounter, but gossip did travel fast in a small town. "Yes. Graham told the mayor about what happened last night. It sounds like he's serious about getting criminal charges filed against us."

"That wasn't the bad news I meant," Emily muttered. "You've got to tell her about why the mayor was here this morning."

Mabel pretended not to hear her, and Rory apparently really didn't hear her, since she'd gone around the back of the truck to drop the tailgate.

Rory waved her hand dismissively. "I already knew about the threats, and it won't be a problem."

"What about your husband?" Mabel asked. "Won't it cause him trouble if his wife is arrested?"

"I won't be arrested, and Joe can take care of himself." Rory grabbed a stack of plastic crates to be filled with squash, and Emily hurried over to get a second stack. "Besides, everyone in town knows that Graham has been... unreliable lately. Half the time, he's fine, and the other half, no one knows what he's talking about. I'm sure last night was one of the confused periods. He'll be better today, probably forget that last night even happened."

"I'm not so sure about that," Mabel said. "Danny told me he tried to talk Graham out of pressing charges, but didn't think he was successful."

"Danny couldn't talk a cat out of going for a swim," Rory said. "But don't worry, Graham will come to his senses eventually."

"That might be too late." Retractions never made their way around the grapevine the way the initial scandal did. There were still some people back in Maine who thought Mabel's parents had died in some sort of murder-suicide pact instead of a fluke accident.

"It will be fine." Rory headed into the barn with her crates, but from behind her, Emily shook her head at Mabel.

"It won't be fine." Emily could be a little superstitious and illogical about some things, but she was good at reading people, especially someone she knew as well as she did Rory. "I think Graham may have completely broken with reality recently, and he's never going to have any more lucid moments. There's a rumor going around that Graham's been telling people that rhubarb leaves are going to be the new kale. A super-food that will cure everything that ails them."

"What's so bad about that?" Mabel asked, following the other women into the barn with the final stack of crates. "Nutritionists say we should eat more green leafy vegetables."

"But not rhubarb." Emily dropped her crates next to where the squash was stored. "Their leaves are highly toxic."

"I wonder if Graham decided to see if he could change that with his breeding program," Rory said. "Perhaps he thought he'd created a variety that has edible leaves, and he's been testing the theory on himself, and it's made him crazy. That would explain a lot about his recent behavior."

"He's too smart to take that kind of risk." Emily turned to Mabel. "You'd have liked him if you met him before he got quite so out of touch with reality. You should see how detailed his records are for his breeding program. You could have bonded over your shared love of spreadsheets."

"Much as I love spreadsheets," Mabel said, "I'm not going to risk getting attacked in order to view them. Graham had a knife with him last night."

"Of course he did," Rory said. "It was a *gardening* knife. I carry one myself more often than not, and you're not afraid of me. Graham's harmless. Really."

"I don't know about that," Emily said. "He wouldn't hurt anyone physically, but that doesn't make him harmless. He can use the law and his status as a lawyer as deadly weapons against people. If he does get criminal charges filed, it would hurt Rory's reputation. Possibly scare off some of the CSA's customers too. People don't like to buy from criminals."

"It won't come to that," Rory insisted, but she didn't sound as confident as she usually did.

And Emily was frowning. She was better at reading people than Mabel was, so if she wasn't convinced by Rory's nonchalance either, then there really was a problem.

It was Mabel's fault that Rory was in trouble. Aunt Peggy wouldn't have let Rory take the blame for something that had been done for the benefit of Stinkin' Stuff Farm, and neither would Mabel. She'd have to go talk to Graham. Perhaps if she apologized, he would drop his plans to get charges filed against them. Or she could offer to plead guilty to some misdemeanor, if he'd just leave Rory out of it.

She wasn't good at talking to strangers, but someone had to protect Rory. Jeff Wright would do a better job of it—almost anyone would be better at confronting a stranger than Mabel was—but he still hadn't returned her call and as he would have said, time was of the essence. In any event, it would be better done in person than long-distance by phone.

The memory of the knife at Graham's waist made her anxious, but she couldn't let her fear stop her. Emily had agreed with Rory that he wasn't likely to be physically violent, just legally troublesome.

It wasn't like she'd be going there completely unprepared. She'd be ready to dial 911 if necessary, and she'd tell him she'd set her phone to record their conversation. Surely he wasn't so lost to reason that he would attack her when he knew he was being recorded.

Chapter 4

Mabel slowed as her GPS told her Graham's home was only a few hundred feet away on her left. At least, she hoped that was his home. She'd tried calling his law office to talk to him there, but the receptionist had said he was taking the day off. He wasn't at the courthouse either, despite having claimed he'd planned to be there early in the morning. According to his receptionist, the local court didn't have a session on Mondays.

Mabel hadn't dared wait another day to talk to him, for fear it would be too late to prevent him from taking legal action against Rory, so she'd searched the internet for his home address. It would have been quicker and easier if she could have asked Rory, who would definitely know where he lived, but that hadn't been an option. Rory's willingness to ask people to help each other didn't seem to extend to asking for help for herself, so she would have tried to talk Mabel out of confronting Graham. Fortunately, finding information online was one of Mabel's skills, and she'd quickly found his home address in a directory of New England plant breeders.

She drove around a curve and caught sight of a farmhouse that had to be her destination. It looked a great deal like her Aunt Peggy's—white, two-storied, and with several additions that weren't particularly well integrated into the architecture. Unlike her aunt's house, however, this one was in rough shape. It desperately needed a coat of paint, some of the front porch steps looked rotten, and the front yard's landscaping had gone native.

The rustic stone wall that ran the length of the property's front yard was overgrown with weeds, hardly the sign of a conscientious farmer. She recalled Rory mentioning that the rhubarb plot was small and located in the back yard, which Mabel couldn't see from the main street, so maybe Graham spent all his time and energy out there instead of on curb appeal.

The farmhouse was on a corner lot, with a rustic stone wall along the frontage. Its unkempt condition was in marked contrast with the property on the opposite corner on the same side of the street, where the matching stone wall was lined with daylilies instead of weeds, and the lawn around it was neatly mowed. That other lot also featured an elegant wooden sign that marked the road as the entrance to the Robinson Woods subdivision. The houses, for as far as Mabel could see, were bland and oversized colonial-style homes that were much newer than Graham's antique farmhouse, probably no more than ten years old. They were also in pristine condition with perfectly manicured lawns, small trees, and neatly pruned bushes.

Mabel turned left into the subdivision, looking for Graham's driveway, since there wasn't one in the front yard. She found it, but it was short—a greenhouse took up much of the side yard between the house and the driveway—and the paved space was completely filled with an SUV, a lawn tractor, and a pickup that looked like the one Graham had been driving the night before. She had to be in the right place, and, judging by the packed driveway, it looked like he was home. She made a U-turn to park on the street near the foot of the driveway.

Mabel turned off the engine, but didn't get out of her Mini Cooper. Her brain was telling her this was a mistake. She should leave, Graham was dangerous and unpredictable, and she wasn't any good at being nice to people.

She gripped the steering wheel and took a deep breath. She had to do this. She owed it to Rory. She reminded herself of all the reasons why she was perfectly safe. Everyone said that Graham wasn't violent. And he hadn't actually gotten his knife out of the sheath during the confrontation the night before. All he'd done was yell and be unreasonable. If he did that today, she could just leave.

Still, she hesitated, trying to convince herself that talking to him could wait until the next day when she could visit him at his law office. He wouldn't have any reason to carry a knife with him there. But she couldn't wait that long, not if he might get charges filed first thing the next morning before she could talk to him. She had to act while she still had a chance to protect Rory's reputation.

Mabel climbed out of the Mini Cooper, and as she did, a tall, blonde woman in an expensive-looking beige skirt suit appeared from behind an eight-foot fence that separated Graham's back yard from the side of his neighbor's property. The roof of the abutting house, another one of the massive modern pseudo-colonials, was visible beyond the fence.

The woman was carrying a compact video camera as she stalked toward Mabel. She stayed to the outermost edge of the sidewalk as if to avoid any possibility of contact with the overgrown, eight-foot-high hedge that hid Graham's back yard from view. It did need pruning, but the branches only stuck out an inch or two at the most, not the two feet of space that she kept between her and the greenery.

If the woman lived next door, she might know if Graham was home. "Hello," Mabel said.

The woman raised the video camera to eye level and began recording. She pointed it first toward where Mabel's Mini Cooper was and then back to Mabel. "You can't park there."

Mabel obviously could park there, since she'd just done it. "I didn't see any *no parking* signs."

The woman continued recording the conversation. "It's against the homeowners' association rules. Visitors have to park entirely on the resident's property, not on the street."

Mabel gestured at the completely filled driveway. "There's no room."

"It's still against the rules to park on the street. Your car is blocking an entire lane, so I could have your car towed for interfering with the free flow of traffic."

"There isn't any traffic for me to block, and I promise I won't be long," Mabel said. "I just need to talk to Graham briefly. Do you know if he's home?"

The woman pushed something on the video camera, presumably to stop the recording, and lowered it to her side. "Why would you want to talk to him? He's crazy."

"We had a bit of an argument last night, and I want to apologize before the situation gets blown out of proportion."

The woman shook her head. "Once he's upset, there's no point in trying to make amends. He never listens to reason. I should know. I'm Lena Shaw, and I've been living next door to him for eight years now. I'm also the president of the homeowners' association. I haven't been able to get him to follow any of our rules."

"I guess you can't exactly have his house towed away."

Lena shook her head irritably as if she'd once considered trying exactly that. "I can't even fine him. Technically, he's not subject to the HOA rules. He used to own all the land around here, and when he sold off most of it to a developer, he made sure to exclude his place from the rules."

"Then why the video camera?" Mabel asked.

"He may not be subject to HOA rules, but he still has to follow town health and safety regulations." Lena gestured at the overgrown hedges.

"Just look at that mess. Some of the branches are obstructing the sidewalk. I came out to gather proof, and then I saw your illegally parked car."

The hedges were messy, but it was a stretch to suggest that they would prevent people from using the sidewalk safely. It was pretty clear though that Lena was as unlikely to listen to reason as she claimed Graham was.

Lena continued, "The rest of the property is even worse. The rusty vehicles in his driveway are an eyesore, the front yard is a jungle, and the front porch steps are a clear danger to anyone visiting the property."

Judging by the lack of a visible path through the front yard's weeds to the front porch, Mabel thought it was unlikely Graham had any visitors who used that entrance. Presumably the back door that he used for himself was in better condition.

"What about the yard behind the house?" Mabel asked. "I'm told he breeds rhubarb there. He must keep that in good shape."

"He does," Lena said. "That's why I know he could do better with the rest of the property if he wanted to. He's just refusing to maintain the visible areas to spite me."

"At least I'll be safe if I stick to his back yard then."

"If you're absolutely determined to talk to him, you'll probably find him in the greenhouse," Lena said. "That's where he always is. Probably because his living quarters are as unhealthy as the front yard. All he cares about is those stupid plants. Who likes rhubarb anyway?"

"I don't know," Mabel said. She'd wondered much the same thing herself, but she also knew just how varied people's interests could be. Over the years, she'd developed apps for some of the strangest subjects, and the more obscure they were, the more passionate the clients had been about them. She'd quickly learned that the apps she'd thought didn't stand a chance of finding a market because they were for such niche subjects, were often among the most commercially successful. "I can think of worse things for someone to be interested in than growing rhubarb."

Lena snorted delicately. "You must be as crazy as he is. Don't let me stop you from wasting your time. I'll cut you some slack this one time while I finish getting my video evidence on the dangerous condition of Graham's property. It'll probably be another ten minutes before I'm done and can get home to call the tow company, so you'd best finish your business by then. I may not be able to apply the HOA rules to Graham, but I *can* get *your* car towed."

* * * *

Mabel hurried up the driveway, squeezing between the vehicles and past a pile of discarded broken pots, rotted pieces of potting benches and several lengths of broken metal sidewall supports to the entrance of the thirty-foot-long commercial greenhouse. The door was propped open with a bucket of what looked like potting soil, so she stepped inside and called out, "Hello, Mr. Winthrop. It's Mabel Skinner. Could we talk?"

There was no response.

"Hello?"

Again, nothing but silence. Graham had to be nearby, though, given the way the door was propped open. People in a small town might leave their back doors unlocked, like her Aunt Peggy had done, but they didn't leave them wide open in locations visible from the street. The greenhouse was attached to the side of the farmhouse, and apparently served as an oversized mudroom, leading to the kitchen, which Mabel could see through another propped-open door into the house itself. The air was heavy and humid, presumably both virtues for growing, if not for human comfort. The exterior shingles of the wall to the left of the entry into the house itself were entirely covered with pegboard, and hanging from them were hoes, rakes, trowels, dibbles, and several sizes of clippers, along with a set of keys and a car remote. Next to it on the ground was a pair of pet dishes and another plastic bucket like the one at the entrance, except that this one had a lid, and KIBBLE was neatly handwritten on the side in precise block letters.

If Graham wasn't answering her, it was most likely because he didn't want to talk to her. Mabel had ignored unwanted visitors herself in the past, and after a few minutes, they'd gone away. At least when she'd lived in Maine. It hadn't worked as well here in West Slocum, because all of Aunt Peggy's friends knew the trick to opening the kitchen door, even when it was locked. Mabel had grown accustomed to Emily and Rory wandering in with only a perfunctory greeting, but she wouldn't have been as understanding if a stranger showed up and couldn't take a hint when she refused to answer the door. The last thing she wanted to do was annoy Graham even more than he'd been the night before.

As she was turning to leave, she heard a small, rough engine starting, followed immediately by a high-pitched squeal that sounded human, not mechanical. What if instead of ignoring her, Graham was injured, and that was the only noise he could make to call for help?

The noises seemed to have come from the far right corner of the greenhouse, near the door into the kitchen. Mabel took a few tentative steps deeper into the greenhouse.

"Mr. Winthrop? Are you all right?"

There was no response, just a soft scrabbling sound from where she'd heard the prior noises, like fingers digging in the dirt. Graham wouldn't do that if he was trying to pretend he wasn't there so she'd go away. She continued down the center aisle of the greenhouse to see what was making the noise. The ground was covered with wood chips that had been smoothed and tamped down so thoroughly, they almost looked like a sheet of fiberboard. To each side of the aisle were low tables holding flat after flat filled with two-inch-diameter pots. Each pot held a single seedling, presumably rhubarb, judging by the tiny red stems, and a wooden marker with a five-digit number in handwriting that was almost as precise as if it had been done by a laser printer.

Once she was halfway down the center aisle, she could see that the greenhouse, like the farmhouse, had been added onto over the years. In the far corner, where the sounds had come from, the main growing space opened into a smaller, hobby-sized greenhouse that jutted out toward the back yard.

Mabel continued down the path, keeping a wary eye out for hoses or abandoned tools that might trip her, but unlike the unkempt state of Graham's front yard, everything inside the greenhouse was orderly and well maintained, more like a scientist's lab than anything to do with messy Mother Nature. The glass walls and roof looked freshly washed and dried, with no water spots or specks of dirt. Hoses were all coiled and hung on the lower half of the pegboard, beneath the smaller tools. She noticed then that the pegboard had been painted with outlines to indicate what went where. A trowel was missing, but everything else appeared to be in its assigned place.

The engine sound clicked off just as she reached the end of the seedling tables where the wood-chip-lined path turned right toward the secondary greenhouse. Mabel paused, waiting for any indication that she wasn't alone. She thought she heard a light rustling in the greenhouse, but it might have been her imagination. Or perhaps just some leaves brushing against each other in the breeze that ran through the greenhouses.

Steeling herself, Mabel turned the corner to look inside the smaller greenhouse. As she did, a fat little tortoiseshell cat came racing at her, startling her into taking a step back and setting her pulse to racing. The cat skidded to avoid a collision with Mabel's legs, and then shot past her on the way to the exit.

Mabel shook her head in bemusement. It had been weeks since a barn cat—or in this case, a greenhouse cat—had startled her. She'd grown used to them appearing without warning in the most unexpected spots, peeking out from crevices in the barn, peering down from the rafters, or leaping out of piles of hay.

As her adrenaline settled down, Mabel realized that the cat's presence would explain both the squeal she'd heard before and the brushing sound. The engine was probably something automated for the greenhouse. She'd been letting her anxieties get the best of her, and Graham was either hiding inside the farmhouse, waiting for her to leave, or possibly out in the back yard, working in his rhubarb bed and oblivious to her presence. There was no reason to be nervous. Or to stay. She should just go home and try again the next day at his office.

Mabel's attention was caught by the antique library card catalogue directly to her left on the inside of the short wall next to the smaller greenhouse's doorway. Each drawer was labeled with the same precision she'd seen on the pot labels. It reminded her of the tidy labels Aunt Peggy had used for her seed stock. Had the two farmers known each other? They'd both participated in the same CSA and farmers' market, so they might have run into each other. Mabel couldn't recall any mention of the rhubarb breeder in her aunt's journal pages but she hadn't read the entire thing yet. She'd been too busy just keeping the farm in top condition for attracting a buyer.

Mabel would have loved to peek inside the catalogue drawers, but if Graham caught her being nosy, she'd never be able to convince him to forget about what had happened the night before. Reluctantly, she turned away and gave the smaller greenhouse a quick once-over, just in case it hadn't been the cat making the little noises earlier. Nothing seemed to be out of place, and she started to turn back to the main greenhouse and leave.

Something niggled at her brain though, and she gave the space another look, starting with the card catalogue to her left and moving along the tables with larger pots than in the main greenhouse, filled with full-grown rhubarb plants instead of seedlings, and across the other short end.

There. She looked again. On the floor at the far end of the greenhouse, the neatly compacted wood chips gave way to a disheveled pile of shredded leaves that had been pulled from a half-dozen or so nearby plants, leaving only bare stalks.

That was odd. The naked stalks looked unhealthy without their green tops, and it didn't seem like something that would be done to anything except weeds. Even if harvesting the leaves didn't harm the rest of the plants, dropping them on the ground didn't seem like something Graham would do. Someone else might compost them, but Graham reportedly believed they were edible, so if he'd harvested them, he would have put them in some sort of container, not where they might be exposed to unhealthy pathogens that would outweigh the anticipated benefits from eating the leaves. No matter how neatly the place was maintained, the paths were still made of dirt and wood chips, and definitely weren't clean enough to eat off of. So why would he go to the trouble of collecting relatively clean leaves and then put them somewhere that would make them dirty and difficult to transport?

It had taken all Mabel's willpower to resist peeking in the card catalogue, so she had none left to keep her away from this new puzzle. She took a cautious step closer to the pile of shredded leaves. Maybe it was a farming thing that only another grower would understand. Perhaps if she could get a close-up look at it, she could describe it to Rory and Emily and they would know why the leaves had been shredded and then tossed on the ground. A picture would be even better.

Mabel took out her phone and glanced behind her, half expecting Graham to appear suddenly, waving his knife and claiming she was trying to steal his pile of rhubarb leaves. One good thing about going farther into the small greenhouse was that if he did show up to threaten her, she wouldn't be trapped, but would be close to the other exit just beyond the shredded leaves.

Reminded that time was of the essence, not just because Graham might catch her snooping but because the ten minutes to move her car was rapidly running out, she hurried over to get her picture. After snapping one from about six feet away, she moved closer to get a better shot. As she moved her phone to center the image, she caught a glimpse of a rubber boot almost the same color as the leaves. It was lying on the back of its shaft, the toe sticking up out of the leaves, right next to the glass door.

Mabel froze, convinced now that something was seriously wrong. She could believe that the shredded leaves were some farming thing she didn't understand, but there was no reason for a boot to be abandoned on the greenhouse floor, half buried in shredded leaves, right where someone would trip over it on the way in or out of the back door. Especially not when the rest of the growing space had been so obsessively tidy.

Mabel moved closer. As she did, it became apparent there was more than just a boot and a few shredded leaves on the ground. To the right of the back door, in the space between the glass wall and the potting tables, was the body of Graham Winthrop. He lay on his back, his eyes opened sightlessly, with more shredded rhubarb leaves jutting out from between his still, dead lips.

Chapter 5

An hour after Lena had threatened to have Mabel's Mini Cooper towed, the car was still parked in the street. Of course, it was now penned in by an ambulance, a fire truck, three police cruisers, and a detective's unmarked SUV. Even Lena wouldn't dare try to have all of those vehicles towed.

Mabel had long since given her statement to a detective, who'd introduced himself as Frank O'Connor. He was a short, thin man about her own age, with dark hair. While he was getting her contact information and a basic description of how she'd found the body, he'd accompanied each question with a nervous laugh that made her wonder how effective he would be while interviewing actual suspects.

Apparently his department knew his limitations and wouldn't let him investigate a homicide alone, because he'd told her she couldn't leave until he'd heard back from a state police detective who would be consulting on the case and might want to talk to Mabel. O'Connor said she could wait in her car, but as she was turning away she thought of the cat that had run out of the greenhouse right before she found the body. It would need to be cared for, now that Graham couldn't do it any longer. Lena didn't seem like the sort who'd make sure the animal was fed and watered, and she'd probably consider anyone doing it to be in breach of the HOA rules. Mabel turned back to O'Connor and told him about the cat. He promised to pass the information along to the animal control officer.

Mabel went over to her car to wait for the state police detective. The weather was clear and warm enough, at least while wearing her aunt's barn coat, that she chose not to climb inside. Instead, she leaned against the driver's side door and checked her phone to see if Danny had sent her a proposed contract for the sale of the farm yet. He had, so she forwarded it to Jeff Wright in Maine, and began making a list on her phone of things she needed to do to prepare for the sale. Mostly, it involved packing and figuring out what she wanted to take with her back to Maine. Pixie, of course, and all of her food and toys. Plus the farm journals and the pineapple clock that was Mabel's favorite of all her aunt's kitschy items. She couldn't think of anything else she wanted to keep. She didn't have room for any of her aunt's knickknacks or other personal belongings in her cottage in Maine, even if they were to her taste. Perhaps the buyer would be able to use the larger items like the appliances and basic furniture.

Mabel looked up from her phone and noticed Lena zeroing in on the young detective. She must have come outside earlier in response to all the sirens and been held back until just then by the uniformed officers controlling the scene.

Mabel couldn't hear the words clearly due to the rumbling noise of a fire engine idling on the street, but judging by Lena's emphatic hand gestures in the direction of the various parked vehicles and the nervous laughter of the junior detective, she had jumped straight into lecturing him about the HOA parking restrictions. Maybe Lena was really that determined to enforce the association's rules and was threatening to tow the police and emergency vehicles after all. If Lena had considered the tiny Mini Cooper to be a dangerous obstruction of local traffic, then she had to be in a total panic over the way the subdivision's entrance was completely blocked by the emergency and police vehicles.

After about five minutes, Detective O'Connor was saved by the arrival of the mayor, who'd had to wait while the fire truck, which was no longer needed, left to make room for his SUV to enter the subdivision. He'd eventually parked in front of Lena's house, perhaps because it was out of her current line of sight. If she had seen it, she'd likely have embarked on another lecture about the rules, not just because of the traffic issues, but because of the advertising on the vehicle, which was probably prohibited by the HOA too.

When Danny came up from behind Lena to talk to the young detective, the woman didn't give him a chance. She rounded on him, her words carrying clearly now that the idling fire truck had left. "I told you that someone needed to deal with the Graham Winthrop situation before something bad happened. Your father would have listened to me. No one was murdered in West Slocum while he was mayor. But now there have been two just this year. That's what happens when you let the little things slide. They turn into bigger problems."

"I'm sorry, Lena," Danny said. "I had a talk with Graham every time you came to me about it, but there was nothing more I could do. In any event, we don't know that he was murdered yet. It could have been natural causes. You know Graham wasn't in the best of health recently. He'd been going downhill for months, in fact."

"There's no way Graham died of natural causes. He was too stubborn for that." Lena turned toward Mabel and gestured imperiously for her to join them.

She decided she'd better go see what the woman wanted before Lena decided to ask one of the uniformed officers to give the Mini Cooper a parking ticket.

"Well?" Lena demanded. "Am I right? Was Graham murdered?"

"I'm not qualified to answer that." Even if Mabel had been, she wouldn't have wanted to get dragged into the middle of something that wasn't any of her business, especially with the detective, whose business it was to figure out if it was murder, standing right there. Mabel just wanted to get back to the farm and start preparing for its sale. "I'm not a medical examiner or a detective."

"No, but you saw the body," Lena said impatiently. "Did it look natural?"

Mabel glanced at the detective, who nodded his permission to answer. "It depends on what you mean by 'natural.' There wasn't any blood or obvious injury, but Graham had a bunch of rhubarb leaves sticking out of his mouth. I don't know if that counts as a natural death, but it's definitely not normal, even for someone who advocated eating them. It's possible that he killed himself with the leaves, either intentionally or because he truly believed they were safe to eat."

Lena focused on the mayor again. "See? I knew it wouldn't be something as simple as a heart attack with Graham. He's been determined to make my life miserable for the last eight years, and I bet he's laughing right now about how much trouble he's causing me even when he's dead. Now there's going to have to be an autopsy, and an investigation, and it's going to take forever to resolve, and meanwhile, this property, which is already an eyesore, is going to get worse and worse with no one to care for it."

"What about his family, or heirs?" Mabel said. "Won't they step in to take care of the property?"

"Not likely," Lena said shortly. "I'll probably have to end up buying it myself so I can raze the buildings and get it properly landscaped. It may be the only way to finally rid the town of this blight on the neighborhood. No one else seems to care about it."

"Graham doesn't have any remaining family that I know of," Danny explained. "He wasn't from here originally, and I've never heard him talk about any family other than his wife. He only moved here when they married. His wife was born and raised in West Slocum—her family owned the farmhouse and all the land around it before it was sold to the subdivision's developer. She inherited it before she married Graham. They never had kids, and I believe he was an only child."

Lena snapped, "Well, you'd better figure out who his heirs are, and let them know that they need to do something about this property before someone gets hurt." After a brief pause, Lena added, "Before *someone else* gets hurt, I mean."

"That's not really my job," Danny said.

Lena raised her eyebrows. "Then why did I donate to your campaign last election? You promised me you'd work in the best interest of the town."

"I do that. Always. But"—he waved one arm in the direction of the emergency and police vehicles—"there's still a limit to what I can do. I can't do the detective's job or be a private investigator who finds long-lost heirs."

Lena huffed her exasperation. "Maybe not, but you'd better make yourself useful if you expect me or anyone else to support your next campaign."

"I'm always working for this town," Danny insisted.

"Don't get me started," Lena said. "You start your days early enough, speed-walking around town before the residents are even awake, but then you spend the rest of the day studying the town's archives for historical tidbits that don't do anything to help present-day people."

"That's not fair. I have lots of meetings, and I'm always on call. For things like this." He waved at the various emergency vehicles in the road.

"Just sitting through a meeting and pretending to listen won't help this situation," Lena said. "At the very least, you should have a serious talk with this young detective to make sure he does his job properly. He was extremely rude to me, you know. He laughed at everything I had to say. That's no way to get to the bottom of things quickly."

"I will talk to him," Danny said, obviously glad to have an excuse to end the conversation. He took the detective's arm. "I'll do it right now, if you'll excuse us so we can do this in private. We'll just go on over to the cruiser."

"Of course." Lena made a shooing motion toward the two men.

Uh-oh, Mabel thought. Now she was the only one for Lena to complain to. Probably about moving the Mini Cooper.

To head her off, Mabel tried to steer the conversation to something more productive. "What do you think will happen to Graham's rhubarb breeding program now? He may not have maintained the outside of his property very well, but he was amazingly conscientious about caring for his plants."

"It hardly matters," Lena said. "If it were up to me, I'd bulldoze everything. Getting rid of the house would make the whole subdivision so much more attractive. I may have to do just that."

"What if someone else buys the property to live in?"

Lena shrugged. "They'll still probably bulldoze everything so they can start fresh."

It was probably for the best, Mabel thought, looking at the poor state of the farmhouse and front yard. The greenhouse might be sold and transported for use elsewhere though. According to the assessors' map she'd found online when she was looking up Graham's address, the property was only an acre and a half, and that was pretty small for any kind of sustainable commercial growing. Her aunt's farm was barely profitable with about ten acres in cultivation.

Graham's property wasn't worth saving as a farm, but the rhubarb plants and seeds were another matter. Mabel hadn't known Graham well, but she'd seen how well he'd cared for his plants. He would have been heartbroken by the wanton destruction of all of the hard work that must have gone into the neat rows of rhubarb seedlings. It was immediately obvious that Graham had put a lot of time and energy into his breeding program. There might even be a real breakthrough for the species stored in his records or seedlings.

Maybe there was another rhubarb breeder or farmer who would continue the work or at least buy the plants, separate from the land and buildings. Rory or Emily would know if there were any likely buyers. She'd ask them as soon as O'Connor let her go home.

* * * *

The state police detective kept everyone waiting for two hours, and then called to tell O'Connor that Mabel could leave without any further questioning as long as she promised not to leave town until further notice. She'd agreed, since even in the best-case scenario, it would be another week before ownership of the farm could be transferred, and in the meantime, she'd get Jeff Wright to talk to the detectives about lifting the restriction on her travel.

On her way home, she stopped at the home repair store to pick up packing boxes. Back at Stinkin' Stuff Farm, she carried them up to her aunt's room, but the sight of all the clutter there was overwhelming. She decided it could wait and instead went out to the barn where, inspired by Graham's organization of his greenhouse, she dug out the labels her aunt had used in the past and made sure all the shelves of garlic stock were marked so that their contents could be identified at a glance, without checking the individual mesh bags. She'd also added the recommended planting dates and projected harvest dates to the labels. That way, the farm's buyer—whether it was Thomas Porter or someone else—would have all the information he'd need to keep the farm successful. Her handwriting wasn't as precise as Graham's or her aunt's—Mabel was just relieved she could still write by hand after doing everything on a keyboard pretty much since the day she got her first laptop—but it was legible enough.

That task completed, Mabel started over to the farmhouse, so she could begin sorting its much more extensive contents to decide what to keep and what to get rid of before the sale of the property. On the way, she noticed a friendly black-and-white tuxedo cat, a regular resident of the barn, in the driveway, rolling on the ground in a bid for attention, and paused to pet him.

He made her think of the tortoiseshell cat she'd seen racing out of Graham's greenhouse. She wondered if it was feral like most of the other cats who lived in the barn or if it was Graham's pet. She wasn't at all confident that O'Connor would follow through on making sure it was cared for, and if it was left to Lena Shaw, the poor creature wouldn't stand a chance. Perhaps Mabel should ask the high school student she'd hired to feed and water her barn cats every morning to go out and check on Graham's cat.

It struck her that the barn-cat-feeder would likely lose her job when the farm was sold. Paying someone to do such simple work only made sense for a night owl like Mabel. She'd quickly learned that cats whose crack-of-dawn breakfast was delayed were even noisier than early-morning birds were, and hiring a cat-feeder had been cheaper than fully soundproofing her bedroom, especially since she wouldn't be staying long enough to justify the construction costs. Most farmers were morning people, and feeding the cats only took a few minutes, making the employee an unnecessary expense.

That was something else she needed to ask Rory and Emily about. They might know where the cat-feeder could get another part-time job when the one at Stinkin' Stuff Farm ended.

She gave the tuxie a final pat. On her way back to the kitchen entrance, she heard a faint feline screech from inside the farmhouse. She stopped to wait for whoever the Pixie alarm was indicating had entered the driveway. She wasn't expecting anyone, but she'd grown cautiously accustomed to people dropping in unannounced.

A moment later, the pickup belonging to Charlie Durbin came into sight and then parked outside the barn, next to Aunt Peggy's truck.

She couldn't imagine what he might want. They weren't exactly best friends, but she had at least stopped thinking of him as an evil developer. He was a property developer, just not a particularly evil one, stooping to lies and deceit to make deals. She hadn't trusted him at first, but he'd been a true friend to Aunt Peggy, helping to make sure the farm didn't fail after her death by helping Mabel bring in the recent garlic crop when it was at risk of being ruined by bad weather.

Her initial distrust hadn't been solely because of his work as a developer. In her experience, whenever men who were as good-looking as he was were nice to her, it was generally because they wanted free help on an idea for an app they were sure would be wildly successful, even though they didn't know anything about apps or entrepreneurship.

It was still possible he wanted something from her. He was definitely the best-looking man she'd ever met—over six feet tall and muscular in a natural way, from physical work, rather than from a gym. He had brown hair that was just long and thick enough to get noticeable creases where his hard hat's inner straps had flattened it. At the moment, he was wearing his usual jeans and a blue sport shirt with his company's logo embroidered on the left upper chest. He often wore a blazer, especially if he was meeting with vendors or prospective purchasers of his homes, but he'd skipped it today.

As soon as Charlie emerged from the pickup, he said, "I heard about this morning. You should call your lawyer."

"I already did, but he isn't returning my calls. Must be in the middle of a trial or on vacation or something." Although, as time passed, that wasn't a completely satisfactory explanation for his silence. He usually texted ahead of time to let her know if he'd be incommunicado for more than a day. Still, she trusted him to respond as soon as he could. "There's no real rush for him to review the purchase and sale agreement. It can wait a few days."

"What purchase and sale agreement?"

"The one for the farm," Mabel said. "I figured you'd have heard about it by now. The mayor was certainly excited about the deal, and I assume you interact with him regularly, when it comes to getting building permits and the like."

He shook his head. "No one said anything to me. I must be losing my connection to the grapevine. Have you told Rory? She's convinced you're not really going to sell."

"Not yet." It hadn't come up while they were loading the squashes for the CSA this morning. And Mabel hadn't gone looking for an opening. She wanted to wait until the deal was official before having what she knew would be a difficult conversation, especially since Emily seemed willing to hold off on spilling the beans to Rory until Mabel was ready. "I haven't signed anything yet and won't until my lawyer reviews the contract. All I did was agree to the basic terms, and there's no guarantee the deal will ever be finalized. If it does, though, it could happen fast. Closing next week, because the buyer is paying cash."

"Interesting." Charlie folded his arms and leaned against the driver's side door. "Not many farmers these days have land-acquisition money ready at hand. It's part of why developers can often buy farms more easily than farmers can. We can pay more, and even pay cash from a line of credit if speed is what the seller cares about."

"Emily said it was odd too. But I think she's just looking for reasons to discourage me from selling. She thinks the buyer might actually be a developer and not a farmer like he claims. His name is Thomas Porter. I don't suppose you've heard of him?"

"I don't recognize the name, but I'll ask around," Charlie said. "But I'm not done talking about your lawyer yet. I meant you should call him about Graham's murder. That can't wait."

"He doesn't need to do anything about that," Mabel said. "Although I would like to know how I can go about making sure Graham's seeds and plants don't get destroyed. I was planning to ask my lawyer how the probate process will work, but there's no major rush on that either."

"There's a bigger legal issue for you to worry about than the probate process," Charlie said. "As the person who found the body, you're going to be a suspect in the murder."

"That's ridiculous," Mabel said. "I didn't even know Graham. Not really."

"I heard you had an argument with him the night before."

"Sounds like you're still pretty well connected to the grapevine."

"And so are the cops. They're going to hear about the argument too."

"It wasn't a big deal," Mabel said. "And I didn't care that he got the mulch in the end. I'd been telling Rory we could get it somewhere else even before Graham showed up."

"Then why'd you go see him today? The police are going to assume it was to continue the argument."

"If there was going to be an ongoing serious argument over the mulch, I'd have sicced Jeff Wright on Graham instead of confronting him myself," Mabel said. "I only went because I couldn't wait for Jeff to get back to me, because I was afraid Graham was going to get criminal charges filed against Rory for trespassing. She was with me when we ran into Graham. And you know how bad it would look for the wife of a police officer to be charged with a crime. I went to see if I could talk him into letting the matter drop if I promised to let him have all the mulch he wanted without any interference from me."

Charlie nodded. "That makes sense. Did you tell anyone before you went?"

"No," Mabel said. "You know Rory. She would have insisted she could take care of herself, and that it wouldn't matter all that much if the charges were filed."

"Still, it would have been better if someone could confirm what you were doing there."

"I talked to Lena Shaw right before I went into the greenhouse," Mabel said. "She knew why I was there. Would that help?"

Charlie shook his head. "Probably not. She never listens to anyone about anything, so she won't even remember what you told her unless it was something that violated the subdivision's rules."

"I did park illegally," Mabel said. "That's not inconsistent with my going there to kill someone though. Especially since Lena seems to think breach of the HOA rules is almost as bad as murder."

"That's the other thing about Lena speaking on your behalf," Charlie said. "No one would pay her any attention, because she's taught them to ignore her. She complains to anyone who will listen about all sorts of trivial matters, acting as if, like you say, they were as big a deal as murder is."

"Still," Mabel said. "I'm sure the whole matter will all be resolved without involving her or me. There can't possibly be any evidence against me. All I did was find the body. I don't know for sure how he died, but it looked like he'd eaten a bunch of rhubarb leaves. If someone forced him to do that, and it's what killed him, I couldn't possibly have done it. He was a lot bigger than I am. And he had a knife to defend himself. All he had to do was show it to me last night, and I ran away."

"I still think you should talk to a lawyer." Charlie took his phone out of the back pocket of his jeans. "If not the one in Maine, then someone here."

"I'll mention it to Jeff when he returns my call," Mabel said.

"Good." Charlie glanced at his phone and then back up at Mabel again. "Sorry. I just stopped by to make sure you were okay, and now I've got to go. I'll look into this Thomas Porter person for you, see if any of my contractors knows him."

"Thanks."

As Charlie climbed into the truck and drove off, Mabel realized she was going to miss him when she got back to Maine. She'd known she'd miss Rory and Emily and her field hands from the local university, and even the girl who fed the barn cats. But Charlie? She hadn't expected that.

Chapter 6

After Charlie left, Mabel began looking through the contents of the farmhouse to get a better idea of exactly how much there was to get rid of or offer to the buyer. She started in the kitchen, where Pixie sat on the windowsill over the sink and occasionally meowed for attention, which came as welcome invitations to take a break from digging through all of the clutter.

She'd just finished the last of the kitchen cabinets when she received a text from her boss, Phil Reed. *Interested in hot new project?*

Mabel was looking forward to getting back to her usual work, and it was nice to know her boss was anxious to have her back earlier than the six months she'd estimated for her leave of absence, but she needed a little more time to wrap up the sale of the farm before taking on a new work challenge. It helped to know Phil wasn't likely to fire her if she turned down this offer. He'd always been as flexible as possible with her work assignments, since she'd been a reliable employee, and he knew that she could earn more as a freelancer if he pushed her too hard and she quit. The relationship was generally good for both of them, since she gladly gave up any extra money she could earn on her own in return for her boss dealing with all the work she was no good at, like selling their services and being nice to clients even when they asked for impossible things in their apps.

Not yet, she responded. *Might be able to do it next month*

When next month? Big new contract. Really need you

I'll let you know. Can't commit yet

There was no further response, so Mabel started for her aunt's home office to see what needed to be dealt with in there. Halfway there, Pixie yowled a warning that someone had entered the driveway. Had Rory heard about the possible sale of the farm and come to talk Mabel out of it? Might as well get it over with, she thought. She gave Pixie a pat on the way through the kitchen and headed outside. A white van marked with the West Slocum town seal had pulled up next to the barn. The animal control officer—a man in his fifties, at least six and a half feet tall, with intensely red hair—climbed out of the van. She'd met Chris Vance a few months earlier, when he'd convinced her to give Pixie a home after other volunteers had given up trying to get the cat to stop her persistent yowling at traffic.

Vance made his way to the back of the van. "I got her for you."

"Got who?"

"Your cat," he said. "From Graham Winthrop's yard. The police said you wanted her. You're lucky I was able to catch her so quickly. I found the spot where Graham had been feeding her, so I could set the trap right where she's used to finding food. She must not have been fed this morning, so she was hungry enough to go after the bait right away."

"Wait," Mabel said as her phone pinged to let her know she'd received a text. She hoped it was from Jeff Wright, but she needed to deal with Graham's cat first. "I didn't say I wanted the cat, just that someone ought to look after it."

"Guess that someone is you." Vance paused in the middle of pulling the trap closer to the van's doors. "You will take her, right? She's pregnant. Kind of late in the season, but all the usual foster homes are overwhelmed or burned out after all the kittens they've dealt with for the last six months and they're not taking any new placements. You're my last option."

"I thought she was a barn cat. Don't they usually get neutered so they can't reproduce? All of Aunt Peggy's were fixed before I got here."

"This one wasn't a working cat," he said. "Can't tell for sure, but she seems feral, although it could just be the hormones of pregnancy. She's in good health overall though. I stopped by the vet and had her tested. She's negative for the most serious contagious diseases so she won't be a danger to your barn cats once she's released. You'll need to keep her contained though until the kittens are born. And then for a couple of months afterwards, until her kittens are weaned and socialized for adoption."

"I can't do all that," Mabel said. "I won't even be here that long. I'm leaving town soon."

Vance laughed. "What? You're planning to go on the lam? I bet you killed Graham so you could steal his cat, and now you're just pretending not to want her."

"I don't want the cat," Mabel said. "And I'm not going on the lam. I'm selling the farm. I agreed to the deal shortly before I found Graham's body."

"I was just kidding," he said, but Mabel couldn't help thinking that jokes often hid a great deal of truth. If even the animal control officer thought she might have had a reason to kill Graham, absurd as it was, then maybe Charlie had been right in thinking that the homicide detective—the one she hadn't met yet from the state police, if not the local one—would certainly have her on the list of suspects. She had to nip this in the bud.

"I didn't kill Graham, and I didn't have any reason to."

"Good to know." Vance reached inside the van to bring the trap closer, until the tortoiseshell cat inside was visible. "Since you're not going to be arrested in the next few days, you can take her. Just until the kittens are born. It'll only be a couple of weeks, max, according to the vet. In the meantime, I'll work on finding a foster home for the whole family once they're born. I've got to say though that we're stretched pretty thin when it comes to placing cats. Nothing we do ever seems to cut down on the feral population. They're incredibly prolific breeders."

Mabel tried not to look at the trap or its occupant, but knowing she shouldn't risk getting attached to another cat only added to the temptation to inspect it. She gave in, and confirmed that it was the same cat she'd seen racing out of the greenhouse. She was tiny, except for her bowling-ball-sized belly.

"What will happen if I don't take her in?"

"She'd have to stay at the shelter," he said. "And if she's feral, well, they don't do well in that setting. The stress could cause her to miscarry the kittens."

Mabel looked into the cat's golden eyes, which glared back with obvious, lethal hatred. Mabel had to admire the simple honesty. At least with cats, unlike with human beings, there was never any doubt about what they were thinking. This cat was plotting escape. Followed by murder. Although she'd settle for the other way around if necessary.

"She hates me."

"It's nothing personal," Vance said without disagreeing with Mabel's assessment. "You'd hate anyone who locked you up in a cage too."

Was that another joke about getting arrested? Mabel wasn't sure. Another reason to like cats. They didn't make obscure jokes.

"I'm really busy right now, with the farm's sale and all."

"It won't take much time at all," he said. "And you won't be doing this all alone. I can give you a crate to keep her in until the birth if that will help. She'll know what to do when she goes into labor. And then once the kittens are born, I can arrange for the mom to be spayed, and the shelter will help spread the word about kittens available for adoption. All you have to do is give them a little space in your house and feed the momcat." Mabel sighed. She knew it wouldn't actually be that easy, but she also knew what Vance was going to say if she argued with him, because he'd done it before. He was going to say that her aunt would have taken in the cat and her soon-to-be kittens without a second thought. It was true. And Aunt Peggy would have wanted Mabel to do it too.

There really wasn't any solid reason to say no. If all she had to do for the cat was let it stay in a crate somewhere, it could stay in her aunt's bedroom. Mabel had been sleeping in the smaller, second bedroom, the one she'd stayed in when she'd visited as a child. It was something of a stretch to call her aunt's room a "master" bedroom anyway, since the two rooms were the exact same size and layout. The main difference was just how much furniture and odds and ends each room held. Mabel's room held nothing but the bare necessities, while her aunt's room was stuffed to capacity with barely a clear path between the door and the various pieces of furniture. Mabel hadn't been able to face sorting through it before now, but the clutter was going to have to be removed soon for the farm's sale, and having to make space for the cat's crate would help motivate her to deal with her aunt's possessions.

"Two weeks," Mabel said finally, ignoring another ping from her phone. Porter had said he could close in just a week, but she didn't think he'd withdraw the offer if she asked for another week to finish packing everything. Even if the cat weren't an issue, she'd need that long to sort out the contents of the house. Porter would have to understand that she needed a little extra time, especially if she showed him the clutter hidden behind the kitchen cabinet doors. "I can keep her for exactly two weeks. Not one minute more."

"I'll start looking for a foster home right away," Vance promised, pulling the trap the rest of the way out of the van and handing it to her. "You take this, and I'll bring the crate into the house for you."

* * * *

The animal control officer carried the crate up to Aunt Peggy's bedroom with Pixie at his heels. Vance stayed long enough to help move a pair of reading chairs and small table to clear a space in the corner to set up the crate. After it was installed and the cat released into it from the trap, he'd gone back to the van twice and brought in the basic supplies she'd need, from a litter box and litter to a special brand of kibble for pregnant or nursing cats. Mabel couldn't help thinking that she was supposed to be getting things *out* of the farmhouse in preparation for the sale, not bringing more things *in*. As it was, she'd had to toss the moving boxes out into the hallway. Even folded flat, they took up too much space in the crowded room.

Finally, Vance covered the crate with a canvas drop cloth, explaining that cats, especially feral ones, felt safer when they were tucked into a cozy spot, unable to see humans. "Or other cats," he added, gently moving Pixie away from where she was trying to pull back the cloth to peer inside. "It's best to keep them separated, at least until the kittens are born and weaned. Momcats can get aggressive due to hormones."

Mabel picked up Pixie and followed Vance out of the bedroom, closing the door behind her before she put down the cat and went downstairs. After the animal control officer left, she gave Pixie a handful of treats to apologize for evicting her from a portion of her territory.

She checked her phone to see who'd been pinging her, hoping it was Jeff Wright, but it was just a spam call. Her thoughts returned to Vance's joke about her having killed Graham. She'd thought Charlie was being paranoid on her behalf, but now that a second person suggested she might be a suspect, she had to take it seriously. She'd been the object of curiosity before, but she'd never been the focus of suspicion. This time, it seemed as if everyone in town might be wondering if she'd just killed someone.

She definitely needed to divert attention elsewhere. Except she had no idea who might be a better suspect than herself. Lena was a possibility, but no matter how seriously the woman took her role as president of the homeowners' association, would she really have killed Graham over some messy hedges? And would she have used rhubarb leaves as the murder weapon?

If not Lena, then who?

Mabel needed more information, and she knew exactly where to get it. She gave Pixie a pat and a warning to stay away from the pregnant cat's room, grabbed her phone and headed for the library. She could always count on Josefina Marshall, everyone's favorite librarian, according to both Josefina herself and if not quite literally "everyone," at least the vast majority of the local residents.

When Mabel walked inside the main lobby shortly after five o'clock, Josefina was in her usual spot behind the checkout counter. In her late seventies, she had white hair with a jagged streak of hot pink on top, just off-center, and she generally wore clothes in assorted coordinating shades of pink. At the moment, she wore a white blouse topped with a neon pink cardigan.

Josefina was looking down at her computer's keyboard while her hands, bent and swollen with arthritis, hunted and pecked at the keys. Mabel always cringed at the librarian's typing and had to fight the urge to offer to take over for her, not so much because it was so slow and inefficient, which would be irritating in other circumstances, but because it looked so painful.

When she finally looked up and caught sight of Mabel, Josefina squealed like a teenager and raced around the checkout counter much faster than her age should have allowed to engulf Mabel in a hug.

Mabel had been counting on finding Josefina here, since she seemed to work around the clock, seven days a week. When Mabel had first arrived in West Slocum, she'd needed to use the library's public internet and phones quite frequently until the access at the farm was upgraded, and Josefina had always been at the checkout counter.

Mabel still wasn't ever completely prepared for dealing with the librarian. She liked Josefina, who would undoubtedly have all the information for coming up with a list of suspects in Graham's death, but there was a price. Hugs. Josefina hugged everyone, especially if they were new to the library or a long-time patron she hadn't seen for a while or she'd heard something sad or distressing about their lives. Or, really, just because it was a Monday afternoon.

Mabel had grown accustomed to it, and was careful to tamp down on her automatic urge to push the frail librarian away, but it still felt like an eternity before she was released.

Josefina stepped back and peered at Mabel. "Are you all right?"

"I'm fine."

"I wouldn't be if I were you." Josefina headed back to her spot behind the checkout counter. "What's the world coming to, with dead bodies in greenhouses?"

"Just one body."

"It's still shocking," Josefina said. "I always thought Graham would die of grief, just sort of fade away. He's been getting more and more detached from reality ever since his wife died about ten years ago. She was so young, and he took it hard. She had some kind of cancer, although I don't know all the details."

"What about his rhubarb obsession?" Mabel thought it had to have something to do with Graham's death, possibly giving rise to the killer's motive. It just didn't make sense that someone would force-feed him the leaves—assuming he hadn't eaten them intentionally—unless they were trying to send some sort of message. "His breeding work seemed to give him a purpose for living. Did he ever talk to you about that?"

Josefina looked down at her keyboard for a moment as if it held all the answers and then looked up again. "He wasn't a regular patron, but he did come in occasionally. He asked for my help two or three years ago, when he was researching the use of rhubarb leaves to cure cancer. He said he'd just discovered their potential, and they might have saved his wife if he'd known earlier."

"That's odd," Mabel said. "Rory told me they're highly poisonous."

"Oh, they are," Josefina said. "I did some background research when Graham first mentioned his theory. I thought it was interesting that he wasn't the first person to think the leaves might be edible. Perhaps because both the roots and the stalks have some purported medicinal benefits, so they assumed the leaves must too. During a food shortage in England in the midst of World War I, people were mistakenly advised to supplement their vegetables with rhubarb leaves. Fortunately, it takes a lot of them to kill you, or the consequences would have been worse. I warned Graham to be careful, but I don't know if he listened."

"What if his breeding program had produced a variety where the leaves were non-poisonous?"

"That would be remarkable, but I doubt it happened," Josefina said. "From what I read, scientists don't even know what it is that makes the leaves so toxic, so they wouldn't know what to breed out of them. There's a relatively large amount of something called oxalic acid that's not good for you, but they suspect there's a second, unidentified element that's even more toxic. In any event, you'd probably have to eat a huge amount of the leaves, a whole bushel basket of them, not just a regular half-cup serving of greens, for a lethal dose. Even a few bites can make you good and sick, but it's hard to imagine anyone would eat enough for the oxalic acid to be fatal. At least not without first going to the hospital for treatment."

"Maybe he did go, but no one figured out he'd been poisoning himself by testing his theory," Mabel said. "Do you know what the symptoms are?"

"Not offhand." She keyed a few painful-looking words into her terminal's search engine. "Ah, here it is. The symptoms are mostly gastrointestinal, and then if it progresses to damaging the kidneys, there could be fatigue, faintness and weakness. Oh, and this is interesting. One symptom of kidney failure is trouble thinking clearly. That could explain a lot about Graham's recent behavior. He was usually confused, rather than aggressive."

"He wasn't very logical at all last night. I was surprised to find out he was a lawyer."

"Maybe he had been experimenting on himself," Josefina said sadly. "I've been hearing rumors that he'd been making mistakes in court for the last couple of years. I figured any mistakes he'd made were due to being distracted by his hobby. Now, I have to wonder if he was sick and deteriorating mentally."

Mabel was going to ask about the clients who'd been upset with Graham, but Josefina pulled her pink cardigan around her more closely and said, "Enough about Graham. How are you doing? It must have been terrible to find his body."

"I'm fine," Mabel said. "But I'm worried that people think I killed Graham."

Josefina waved a hand dismissively. "It's nothing personal. They don't know you yet, but they'll realize how silly they're being once the real killer is caught."

"What if he's never caught?" Mabel said. "Detective O'Connor seemed a little green to be handling a homicide case."

"He's getting help from an experienced homicide detective, but I know what you mean. It would be more reassuring if someone who was both local and experienced were in charge. O'Connor knows the people around here and has access to the local grapevine, but he might not know what clues to pay attention to or what information he should pass along to the more experienced detective."

"What's the grapevine saying about the murder?" Mabel braced herself for confirmation that people were betting on her as the culprit.

"Not a whole lot yet," Josefina said. "All I know for sure is that he was stabbed in the back."

"Literally?" Mabel sometimes had trouble telling when statements were meant metaphorically. "Or do you mean they think he was betrayed by someone he trusted?"

"Both." Josefina sounded certain.

"But there was no blood," Mabel said. "At least none that I saw. Of course, he was lying on his back when I found him, so his body might have hidden it."

"I heard the cops were surprised too. Apparently the blood seeped into the dirt floor of the greenhouse, so no one noticed until the body was moved."

"I really thought he'd been poisoned. He had rhubarb leaves sticking out of his mouth when I found him."

"Oooh, I hadn't heard about that," Josefina said with a little too much relish. "Someone must have put them there after he died then."

"It wasn't me."

"I know," Josefina said without hesitation. "And I'm sure you didn't stab him either."

"Definitely not." Mabel said. "Do you know anything about what he was stabbed with?"

"It was his own gardening knife." Josefina shook her head at the irony. "He really loved that knife. I sort of feel responsible. He came to me shortly after his wife died, wanting to know what the best tools were for planting and harvesting. My research suggested a *hori-hori* knife was indispensable. It's multipurpose, with a serrated edge that's good for cutting the leaves off stalks, and a beveled tip so it can be used as a dibble for transplanting the seedlings."

That wasn't what Mabel wanted to hear. The police might be able to identify a suspect by way of the murder weapon if the killer had brought it to the greenhouse. But if it had already been there, then anyone would have had access to the first of the three elements for identifying a suspect: means by which the murder could be done. And looking just at motive and opportunity, Mabel was, at least logically, a prime suspect. It could be argued she was desperate to keep him from filing charges against Rory, which created motive, and by finding and reporting the body, she'd identified herself as someone who had been at the crime scene and, depending on the time of death, could have had the opportunity to kill.

"Does the grapevine have any suspects?" Mabel asked. "Besides me, I mean."

"No one in particular," Josefina said. "Graham was a lawyer though, so I'm sure he'd made a few enemies over the years. I had a few patrons ask me for help with looking up how to report lawyers to the Board of Bar Overseers, and I'm pretty sure they were all represented by Graham. A few were pretty vocal about it, and not just in private with me."

"Anyone in particular?"

"Well, I heard Sam Trent was really angry," Josefina said. "He claimed that Graham revealed something confidential to opposing counsel. I know Sam threatened to get Graham disbarred a year ago, but I don't know if he carried through with it."

"He couldn't have been successful with it," Mabel said, "since Graham was still practicing law. The client might have decided to take things into his own hands to get his justice."

"Or he could have done what the other clients did," Josefina said. "Most of them just fired him and moved on."

"Still, looking into angry clients seems like a good avenue of inquiry for the police."

"That could be difficult," Josefina said. "The detectives would have to get past attorney-client privilege in order to search Graham's office, and even if they did, I'm not sure what they'll find in his records. His last employee, not counting the answering service, quit about six months ago. Given how he'd been going in and out of coherence lately, who knows what he was doing with his office paperwork?"

"His greenhouse was perfectly organized," Mabel said. "I didn't look inside the seed drawers, but judging by the precise labels, I suspect his records there are in good shape."

"I'm sure you're right," Josefina said. "But he cared passionately about the breeding program. I'm not sure he ever cared all that much about being a lawyer. It was just something to generate the money he spent on his rhubarb plants."

"If you hear anything more about Graham's death or who might have wanted him dead, will you let me know so I can make sure the police aren't spending too much time trying to prove I did it?"

"Of course," Josefina said, coming around the counter to give her a farewell hug. "I'll always do whatever I can to make sure the police don't even think about arresting Peggy Skinner's niece."

Mabel let the hug go on longer than usual, as an unspoken apology for not having told Josefina about the sale of the farm yet. One way or another, Mabel would be leaving West Slocum in the next few weeks. If she wanted her destination to be her home back in Maine rather than a prison cell, she needed to figure out who else had wanted Graham Winthrop dead. She'd hit a dead end with Josefina, but Rory might have some ideas about where to start, since she knew everything about everyone in town.

Chapter 7

Mabel took care of a few errands after she left the library, picking up some groceries so Emily couldn't fuss about the empty refrigerator and then getting the scanner she needed to copy her aunt's journal. Maybe it was just her imagination, but it felt like people were staring at her wherever she went, more so than they had in the past, even when she'd first come to West Slocum and they'd been curious about Aunt Peggy's niece. And they accompanied their stares with whispered comments she couldn't quite make out. Were they all thinking that she had killed Graham Winthrop? She wished she were more like Rory, who would have gone up to them and asked them what they were saying about her, but that wasn't Mabel's way. She just made her purchases and left.

By the time Mabel got home, it was dark. Too late to call Rory, who went to bed around nine o'clock. Or was that just an excuse to delay the inevitable? The next time she talked to Rory, Mabel would have to confess about the pending sale of the farm, and she wasn't in a rush to have that conversation. Getting some leads on who might have killed Graham could wait until morning. Late morning, when Mabel was fully alert.

Until then, Mabel had work to do. She loved being inside the farmhouse at night. The birds were asleep, no one was likely to set Pixie to yowling, and she could work without interruption during her most productive hours. Not that she had any paid work right now, but she would soon. She just needed to sell the farm and get back to Maine first.

Mabel went upstairs to check on the pregnant cat. It was hiding in the farthest corner of the crate, cowering inside a cardboard box the animal control officer had tossed inside for that purpose. Water had been splashed all over the front half of the crate, and the kibble bowl was half empty, despite having been filled just a couple of hours earlier. She probably needed to eat more than normal during the pregnancy. Graham must have been feeding the cat regularly, since he'd had the food and water bowls, along with a bucket of kibble, near the back door of the house, but it seemed likely she hadn't been fed the morning of the murder. The animal control officer had said she'd been ravenous when he'd caught her, making her easier to catch than if she'd been fed shortly before the trap had been set.

Too bad the cat couldn't testify to when her human had been killed, since an exact time of death should exonerate Mabel. She hadn't arrived until late morning, and it seemed likely that Graham's schedule would usually call for him leaving for his office and feeding the cat before nine at the very latest, around three hours before she'd arrived. If she was right about that as the estimated time of death, she might even find herself grateful for the nosy neighbor whose video, if time-stamped, would establish Mabel had entered the greenhouse well after whatever time the autopsy would reveal was when Graham had died.

Mabel cleaned up the water on the floor of the crate and refilled both bowls while Pixie scratched at the bedroom door to be let inside. With the pregnant cat taken care of, Mabel contemplated the contents of the rest of the room. The reading chairs and side table that the animal control officer had moved to make room for the crate were stacked with several loads of laundry that had been washed and folded but not put away before Aunt Peggy had died. The bed was even more covered with stuff, now that a box of canned cat food and bags of kibble and kitten-safe litter had joined the dozen lacy pillows, three paperback books, and a breakfast tray with an e-reader and an empty mug that had been on the bed since before Aunt Peggy had died. The closet door and the dresser drawers didn't shut completely because of their overflowing contents.

It was going to take hours to inventory everything, and her presence was going to irritate the feral cat who, whenever she paused in munching on the kibble, threw angry looks at Mabel. Virtually all of the room's contents, other than the cat supplies, would be either thrown out or donated to charity, so she might as well just mark it all down as not coming to Maine with her, and give the cat some privacy.

Satisfied that she was done with the bedroom for now, Mabel glanced into the crate and found that the pregnant cat had already eaten about half of the kibble and retreated to her box in the back corner. Mabel topped off the food bowl again and left the room, careful not to let Pixie inside before shutting the door behind her.

She went downstairs to hard-boil the eggs she'd promised Emily she'd eat before the next delivery. Pixie joined her, eating her own dinner and then perching on the windowsill to stare in the direction of the barn as if communicating telepathically with the other cats.

After dinner, Mabel settled at the desk in her aunt's home office to inventory its contents. The small room was Spartan compared to the rest of the house, with none of the pineapple decor and clutter-topped furniture, just an antique wood desk, an ergonomic chair, and a wall of floor-to-ceiling bookshelves. Many of the books were on farming and especially about the economics of agriculture. Once an accountant, always an accountant, Mabel thought.

She spent the next few hours sorting through the desk drawers and books for anything she might want to keep. Ultimately, all she wanted was the series of journals her aunt had written about the farm and her life since moving to West Slocum. There were ten of them in all, one for each of the years Aunt Peggy had owned Stinkin' Stuff Farm.

There were only nine on the shelves, since she'd taken the most recent one up to her bedroom the night before. She hadn't gotten far, and she was convinced it would contain useful information for the new owner of the farm.

It was almost midnight by then, so she headed upstairs to resume her reading. After a final check on the pregnant cat and another refill of the food bowl, Mabel settled in bed with the heavy, leather-bound journal on her lap and Pixie curled up at her side.

She was almost ready to turn out the lights an hour later when she came across a passage where her aunt had been considering adding a field of rhubarb to her farm. There was even a diagram showing where it could be sited for best sun and soil conditions.

She bookmarked the page with a note to scan it in the morning to share with Thomas Porter. Perhaps he'd find it useful, and he might even be interested in buying some of Graham Winthrop's plants so they wouldn't be plowed under. He'd obviously put a great deal of time and energy into their propagation, and no matter what she'd thought of Graham as a person, it would be a shame to waste all of his painstaking work.

* * * *

The next morning, before getting out of bed, Mabel checked her phone for a message from Jeff Wright, but he hadn't replied. Not a text, not a voicemail, nothing at all. While she mulled over why she still hadn't heard from him and whether she should contact him again, she refilled the pregnant cat's bowls and then went downstairs to peel two of the hard-boiled eggs for breakfast. Maybe Jeff was waiting until he'd had a chance to review the purchase and sale agreement. She'd give him until the end of the day before she bothered him again.

While she ate, she found an app to organize her move and installed it on her phone. After breakfast, she resumed inventorying the contents of the farmhouse, starting with her own bedroom, which had the least number of things to deal with. Even so, filling in the basic information for the app made her aware of just how much work she had to do in the next few weeks to get ready to leave. And there was nothing in the app about saying goodbye to friends.

Mabel took a break at noon. She needed to get some *Help Wanted* flyers made and posted them around town. With the planting season starting in just a week, she couldn't wait any longer to collect potential farmhands in case the sale fell through. Even if she no longer owned the farm then, Thomas Porter would need help, and she could pass along the information on potential employees to make the transition go more smoothly.

Mabel updated the flyer she'd used for the summer harvest and sent it to the local printer, who promised to have them ready whenever she got there to pick them up. After checking on the pregnant cat in her aunt's bedroom and giving Pixie a treat and a quick pat so she wouldn't get jealous, Mabel headed out of the farmhouse to go into town. She made it as far as her car outside the barn before Rory arrived and accosted her with a hug and a worried, "Are you all right?"

Mabel almost blurted out that she was feeling stressed about how much she needed to do before the sale of the farm, but stopped herself in time. That wouldn't be the way to break the news to Rory about the sale. Assuming she hadn't already heard about it from the grapevine.

"Why wouldn't I be all right?" Mabel asked cautiously as she pulled away from the hug.

"You found a dead body. My husband told me everything. It's all anyone can talk about at the police station."

"Does that mean the police have found the killer?"

"Not yet," Rory said. "All Joe knew was that Graham had been stabbed and you were the one who found him in his greenhouse."

"That's all I know too," Mabel said. "Except that everyone in town has been looking at me funny, like I was the one who killed him."

"You wouldn't be my first choice for a suspect." Rory went over to the back of her truck to lower the tailgate.

Mabel followed her. "Who would be?"

"There are too many possibilities to choose just one." Rory pulled a stack of empty bins toward her. They were the ones she'd helped fill with squashes the day before, but that had apparently been transferred to the delivery boxes for CSA members. She hefted her bins and carried them into the barn.

Mabel grabbed her own stack and hurried to follow. "Like who?"

Rory dropped her bins near the back wall. "Like his clients. Most of them were mad at him. Then there's the local judge who's been threatening to throw him into jail for contempt, and another rhubarb breeder Graham was feuding with."

"I never realized rhubarb was that big a deal. Was there really another breeder who lived close enough to have had in-person dealings with Graham? Close enough to have come here to kill him?"

"Definitely," Rory said. "I suppose it is surprising there were two of them in the same little corner of Massachusetts, considering how small a niche rhubarb is. Perhaps she inspired him. Or vice versa. All I know is that her name's Sandy Faitakis, she's a professor at the local university, and her breeding program is part of her academic work. Her trial field is about half an hour's drive from here."

"Do you think she might have killed Graham?" Mabel leaned against the shelves she'd labeled the day before. "The local detective doesn't seem to have a lot of experience, so I want to be sure he's got some suspects other than me."

"I don't know her at all. I've just heard that the two of them didn't get along, and they both thought the other one was either stupid or malicious."

"I suppose it's not too likely that a university professor would kill a rival breeder." Mabel laughed. "Actually, I never would have thought anyone would kill over a few not-very-popular plants, but then I saw Graham's greenhouse and how much work he'd put into this breeding program. There must have been thousands of seedlings in there, and that's not even counting what was growing in the back yard. I wonder what's going to happen to them."

"They'll probably die," Rory said. "The ones growing outside can fend for themselves, but the ones in the greenhouse are dependent on human watering and temperature control. Even this time of year, it can get pretty hot in the greenhouse on a sunny day."

"What if someone bought them from the estate?" Mabel asked. "Aunt Peggy was thinking about adding a rhubarb field. She even drew up plans for where the plants would grow best. Maybe Graham's seedlings could find a home here."

"I thought you were looking for less responsibility at the farm, not more," Rory said, taking a closer look at the newly affixed labels. "Preparing and planting a new field of perennials is a lot of work."

"Actually," Mabel said, steeling herself for what was to come. "It wouldn't be me doing that work. I have a buyer for the farm."

Rory continued silently inspecting the labels for a long moment before finally saying, "Is it anyone I know?"

"Probably." As far as Mabel could tell, Rory didn't just know everyone in West Slocum, she knew everyone in New England who had any connection whatsoever to agriculture. "He says he knows a lot about farming, so I'm guessing you've run into him at some point. His name's Thomas Porter."

"Doesn't sound familiar. I'll ask around, see if anyone else knows anything about him." Rory headed for the barn doors. "What kind of time frame are you looking at for the sale?"

Mabel followed. "I've already sent the contract to my lawyer, but I haven't heard back from him yet. Once it's signed though, the closing will happen pretty fast. He's paying cash."

Rory slammed the tailgate of her truck with more force than necessary, but her voice remained unemotional. "You shouldn't rush into things."

"It's been months already without any offers," Mabel said. "You know I'm no farmer, and I can't keep relying on you to tell me what needs doing. You've got your own life to live. You should be as anxious as I am to see the place turned over to someone who knows how to grow things before I destroy the farm."

"There are other options, you know," Rory said, her tone turning earnest. "You could hire a farm manager and split your time between here and Maine."

"But Maine is my home." The closet thing she had to family—her attorney, Jeff Wright—was there, her cottage was there, and all of her backup electronics were there.

"Maine *used to be* your home," Rory said. "West Slocum is now. I'm sure of it, and I'm afraid you're not going to figure it out until it's too late."

"Why don't we see what my attorney has to say about the sale of the farm before we start worrying?" Mabel suggested. "He advises me on more than purely legal issues, and he won't let me do anything rash."

"All right," Rory said. "But I want to talk to him before he makes up his mind about whether the sale is a good idea."

"Sure." Mabel texted Jeff to give him permission to talk to Rory about things that would otherwise be confidential, and then texted the attorney's office number to Rory so she could call him. "He may be out of town or something though. He hasn't responded to my recent texts."

"I'm not in any rush," Rory said. "I've got plenty to do while I wait to hear back from him. I promised to help out with a school project for my daughter's class, and Joe's wearing his last clean uniform today, so I need to do some laundry. I may not be all that domestic generally, but I do try to support his career at least a little."

And yet, Mabel thought guiltily, Rory had risked criminal trespassing charges, which wouldn't reflect well on her husband, just to help out a friend. "That's another reason why I really need to sell the farm as soon as possible. So you aren't busy with me when you've got more important things to do."

"Don't be silly." Rory waved away Mabel's concern with a flip of her hand. "I love helping you, and you won't need me much longer. You've come a long way in just a few months. Once you've overseen the planting of next year's crop, you'll have gone through the full growing cycle for garlic. At least the parts that require intense work."

Mabel refrained from mentioning that it would most likely be Porter doing that planting, not her.

"I'll take your silence as recognition of how amazing it is to be a farmer." Rory moved to the truck's door. "I'm heading out now, and I'll leave you to your work. You know what needs to be done to prepare for the garlic planting, right?"

She nodded. She knew exactly what needed to be done. Get Jeff's approval on the purchase and sale agreement, so the farm could be sold next week and Porter could do the planting. That answer would only upset Rory though, so Mabel said, "I made up flyers for hiring field hands. I was just going into town to pick them up and then post them."

"You can count on my daughter to work at least a few hours. Especially if you get Terry Earley to work for you again. Dawn can't wait to see him again."

Terry was an agriculture student at the local university, and he'd been a huge help with the summer's harvest. "I still have his number, so I'll text him to make sure he knows about the work."

"Good." Rory climbed into the truck. Through the open window, she said, "Are you sure you're all right after yesterday? You're not afraid to be alone or anything?"

"Of course not," Mabel said. "The only thing I'm afraid of is that everyone will assume I'm responsible for Graham's death. The sooner the police arrest someone for the murder, the sooner I'll be able to go home to Maine."

"In that case," Rory said with a grin, "don't tell my husband I said so, but I hope they never find Graham's killer."

Chapter 8

The announcements board at town hall was just inside the main entrance, above an ancient steam radiator that hadn't been turned on yet due to ongoing warm daytime weather. If the temperatures didn't drop soon, the ground might be too warm for planting the garlic in October. The cloves had to develop some roots but not sprout so much that the energy went into green shoots and not into surviving the winter. The Halloween deadline was a judgment call apparently, and a balancing act based on weather, not a hard-and-fast rule. Which Mabel thought was one more reason why selling the farm was the right thing to do. She much preferred set-in-stone rules, especially in situations like farming, where she didn't have enough experience to make a judgment call.

Mabel pinned her *Help Wanted* notice between a smaller ad for an apartment for rent and a dozen index cards offering free kittens to a good home. She'd already left some flyers at the office of the farmers' market manager, but she still had to give some to the university's job placement office.

She turned to see Charlie Durbin carrying a set of rolled-up architectural plans as he left the building inspector's office at the far end of the main corridor. He came over to read her flyer and then pointed his paper cylinder at it. "Does that mean your sale fell through?"

"I'm just making sure I'm prepared for whoever does the planting, whether it's me or the buyer."

"Your aunt was always an advance planner too," he said. "She'd have been proud of how you've managed her farm so far."

"Does that mean you think she wouldn't approve of my selling it?"

"I didn't say that." He paused for a moment before saying, "I think she'd have approved of whatever you chose to do with the farm as long as it made you happy. She loved you even more than the farm."

Which was exactly why Mabel couldn't let anything happen to the farm. She had to be as good a person as her aunt had been, doing what was right rather than what was convenient. "I don't suppose you've found out anything about Thomas Porter yet, have you?"

"I have, but you're not going to like it, and I need more confirmation to be absolutely sure."

Mabel sighed. "So he's a developer like you?"

"A developer, yes," Charlie said, "but not like me. He's the kind who gives the rest of us a bad name by doing things like what he's done to you apparently. He's lied before about what he's going to use property for in order to make a deal. A friend is sending me a court order from when Porter promised that a historic building on land he was buying for condominiums would be moved to another site for preservation, and then after the deed was signed, he demolished the old house instead of saving it."

"It could have been a single instance and he's changed his ways," Mabel said desperately.

"I doubt it." Charlie twisted the rolled-up plans, tightening them into a narrower cylinder. "The seller sued and won, but it was too late to save the historical building. The money judgment was just a small fraction of the profit Porter made, so he probably considered it a cost of doing business rather than a reason to behave more ethically. My guess is that example is just the tip of the iceberg, and his other victims didn't have the resources to sue him."

"Do you think my broker knows?" I asked. "Danny's supposed to be representing me, doing what I want, and I told him right up front that I wouldn't sell to a developer."

"I don't think Danny would intentionally mislead you," Charlie said. "He probably didn't know the guy since he's not local. Danny wouldn't think to look into the man's background like I did, since he tends to see the best in everyone. I've learned not to trust anyone, especially when it comes to real estate."

Mabel hugged the remaining flyers to her chest. "I'll let my attorney know the deal is off."

"You trust me that much?"

Mabel nodded. "I'd hoped for better news, but you don't have any reason to lie to me about this. It's not like you're planning to buy Aunt

Peggy's farm if Porter's deal doesn't go through, so it shouldn't matter to you whether I sell it to him or not."

"Maybe I just don't want you to leave town, and I'd say anything that might keep you from selling."

"Have Rory and Emily drafted you into their campaign to keep me here?"

"I didn't know there was a campaign, or they wouldn't have had to draft me. I'd have volunteered."

Mabel wasn't sure what to make of his statement. Why would he care if she left town? He'd asked her to have lunch with him a few times, but she'd been too busy to accept and he hadn't pushed the issue. She'd assumed he'd just been being kind to her out of respect for her aunt, who'd been a close friend for a number of years. Had he actually been flirting with her and she hadn't realized it? She'd have to ask Emily later. Until she understood what Charlie meant, it was better not to risk making a fool of herself.

"Careful. If Rory hears the word 'volunteer,' you'll never have time to do your actual work." Mabel nodded at his rolled-up plans. "Is that a new project?"

He shook his head. "Just a minor amendment that I wanted to get the building department's comments on."

"Have you considered buying Graham Winthrop's property to develop?"

"Would you hate me if I did?"

"No," she said. "Graham's situation is different. It's too small for a sustainable farm, and I'm pretty sure he didn't care about the land itself all that much, just his breeding program. That can be moved to another location fairly easily. It's not like Aunt Peggy's farm, where the thing she cared about was the place as a whole. I'd like to find a way to save Graham's rhubarb plants if I can, but the land itself might be better used for residential purposes. I was just wondering what you thought of its development potential."

"I can't see a professional developer being interested in it. I'm certainly not. It's too small for more than one or two houses, so it's not worth the time I'd have to spend on it."

That was disappointing. Mabel had been hoping that the value of the land might have provided a possible motive that would refocus the police's inquiries to someone other than herself.

Charlie continued, "Even if it were a bigger lot, it wouldn't be worth the hassle of dealing with Lena Shaw and her homeowners' association. She's going to make life hell for whoever buys the property. Assuming she doesn't buy it herself. She's tried to buy it in the past, but Graham wasn't interested in selling."

"She mentioned possibly buying it now." Lena had made it seem like an altruistic thing, intending to tidy up the property, but she had as much incentive to lie about her intentions as Thomas Porter did. Mabel needed to have another talk with Lena. It seemed unlikely that she'd have killed Graham simply because he was making her look bad as the president of the homeowners' association, but if she could have gotten rid of the eyesore that clearly annoyed her, while at the same time making money for herself by flipping the property, that seemed like a more credible motive for murder. "Do you know what Lena had planned to do with the property if Graham had been willing to sell?"

"I heard she wanted to tear down the house and build a small guest cottage for when family members visit. Not a bad idea actually, from a land use point of view."

"Doesn't she live in the house right next to Graham's?" Mabel hadn't gotten a good look at it because of the fence that obscured the view of the first floor, but she assumed it was a close match to the identical homes across the street from it. "If it's like everything else in the subdivision, it must have six bedrooms and parking for ten cars. That's not enough for her family to visit?"

"Apparently not," Charlie said. "Although, I remember someone saying her plan seemed odd, that they'd never met any of her family members in the ten or so years Lena has lived in West Slocum, and no one could recall her even talking about any relatives. And she's not married, so it can't be for a spouse's family."

"What else could she want Graham's land for?"

"Probably to flip it. It's not worth my time, but it's a good location, surrounded by houses on the high end of the price range for West Slocum. And if she lost a few bucks on it, she might consider it a reasonable investment to have a better neighbor, especially since she'd probably make up the difference with the increase in her own property's value once Graham's house stops bringing down the values for the whole subdivision."

"Sounds like a possible motive for murder to me," Mabel said, wondering if anyone had developed an app for investigating homicides. The user could key in the names of suspects, with their motives and whether they had an alibi, and have the app calculate the odds that each person was the killer. Even without doing the math, it looked like Lena would have been high on the list of suspects. "I hope the police are taking a close look at Lena. Not just because of her motive, but means and opportunity too. Graham was killed with his own knife, so no one had to bring their own murder weapon or have any special skills to use it. I'm pretty sure he died hours before I got there, and as the closest neighbor, Lena could have slipped into the unlocked greenhouse and confronted him about the poor upkeep of the property, then killed him and left without anyone noticing."

"I'm sure the police are looking into whether she's got an alibi."

"I'm not that optimistic," Mabel said. "I haven't met the detective the state is sending out to help, but the local one seems extremely new to murder investigations."

"And you think you can do a better job?"

"I probably have more experience than Frank O'Connor has," Mabel said. "I did solve my aunt's murder when no one even thought she'd been killed. That's more experience than O'Connor seems to have. He might decide I'm the best suspect, since I found the body. People are already looking askance at me."

"It's just your fifteen minutes of infamy," Charlie said. "The gossips will move on to something new soon enough."

"Not if the real killer isn't arrested," Mabel said. "Until then, people will suspect me, and I won't be able to leave town without everyone thinking I'm running away from justice. Even Rory and Emily don't want me to be *forced* to stay. They want me to *choose* to live on the farm."

"Me too," Charlie said. "I'll keep an ear out for anything that might be useful to clear your name."

"Thanks." Mabel remembered the flyers she'd been posting. She held out a handful of them. "If you know anyone looking for some seasonal work, the garlic needs to be planted soon, and it doesn't look like I'll be able to hand the workers off to a new owner. I can use all the help I can get."

Charlie held out a hand to take the flyers. "I'll share it with my crew. I might even be able to put in a few hours at the farm if it's the only way I can spend some time with you. I was hoping we might be able to do something together that didn't involve digging in the dirt sometime."

Before Mabel could decide whether Charlie had really been flirting with her, a man in a jacket with the town seal on it came through a nearby doorway and called Charlie's name, insisting they needed to talk.

It was probably just as well, she decided. Planting the garlic and keeping herself out of jail was going to keep her busy for the foreseeable future. And both projects were less stressful than the thought of Charlie being interested in her for herself, not just as her aunt's niece.

* * * *

Mabel left Charlie to his work and headed outside. On the way to her car, she texted Jeffrey Wright to ask him to hold off on reviewing the contract with Porter, just in case the lawyer was planning to start work on it before contacting her. She didn't tell him the deal was dead, hoping against hope that Charlie's evidence would turn out to be incorrect, and simply said she needed to talk to him before he spent time reading the contract.

She put her phone away, only then remembering that the police station was right next to town hall. It was a simple, single-story brick building, easy to miss in the shadow of the imposing, three-story, stone-exterior town hall. She wondered if Frank O'Connor was working at his desk or had gone out to interview suspects. Assuming he had any in mind other than herself. She doubted he would tell her anything about the investigation if she asked him directly, but he might let something slip if she talked to him about other things.

Easier said than done, Mabel thought, at least for her. She'd never been any good at small talk or conversational subtlety, so she needed to plan out a seemingly impromptu conversation that included a plausible reason for visiting him.

After several minutes of pacing the sidewalk outside the police station, she was as ready as she'd ever be. A person's heirs were always suspects, and she could ask who they were in the context of the risk to the rhubarb plants if they weren't cared for right away.

Once inside, she was asked to wait while O'Connor was notified she was there. The lobby was only about ten feet square, with bare, off-white walls, equally bland commercial carpeting, and a dozen metal chairs. There were no tables with reading material to pass the time, like most waiting areas had, or even a window to look out of. Big signs on the walls asked visitors not to use their phones, and the last thing she wanted to do right now was give the police any more reasons to view her with suspicion.

O'Connor kept her waiting for about half an hour, plenty of time for her to have second, third, and even fifteenth thoughts about what she was going to say to him. Eventually, he appeared and escorted her back to a room that was as devoid of decoration and comfort as the lobby had been. The only difference was that there was a sturdy metal table in addition to the four chairs that matched the ones in the lobby.

O'Connor tossed a legal pad on the table and took a seat, gesturing for her to sit across from him. "Did you think of something you wanted to add to your statement?"

"No," Mabel said, pulling out the chair but remaining on her feet behind it. After half an hour in the matching, unpadded chair in the lobby, she wasn't in a rush to add to the numbness of her rear end. "But I wanted to thank you for arranging for animal control to catch Graham's cat."

"You're welcome," he said, although he looked irritated by her brilliant conversational gambit. "Is that all? I've got a homicide to investigate, you know."

"I do know." Mabel reluctantly sat down. "I was wondering if I could ask you for another favor."

"I can't tell you anything about the investigation." O'Connor giggled nervously as he grabbed his legal pad in preparation for leaving.

"Of course not," Mabel said quickly. "I wouldn't ask you about that. I'm here about the plants in the greenhouse. They need a caretaker, too, like the cat has, and I want to be sure someone is responsible for keeping the seedlings alive. It would be a shame for Mr. Winthrop's life's work to die with him."

"And you're volunteering to adopt the plants as well as the cat?"

"I just want to make sure they survive until the estate gets settled. The plants will die before then if they're not watered and monitored. Perhaps you could let Mr. Winthrop's heirs know that they need to send someone to check on them?"

"Perhaps," O'Connor said. "But it may be a while before we find them. No one seems to know who they are. Graham was a loner after his wife died, no new girlfriend or even close friends that we know of. He and his wife didn't have kids, he was an only child, and her sister moved away from West Slocum decades ago. There's no one left in town who can give us any information about his heirs."

"He was a lawyer," Mabel said. "He must have had a will with information about his heirs."

"He probably did, but we haven't found it yet," O'Connor said. "It's not in the farmhouse, and searching a lawyer's office is tricky because of client confidentiality. We have to get someone appointed to protect Graham's clients' privacy during the search. The state police detective who's helping me is going to court tomorrow to deal with it, so it won't be long before we have the will."

"Good luck," Mabel said, not entirely convinced it would be as simple as O'Connor believed. By all accounts, Graham hadn't been interested in anything except his rhubarb since his wife had died. What if he'd left all his assets to the plants, like some people did with their pets?

"Don't worry," O'Connor said, clearly unconcerned, since his nervous laughter was absent. "It will all work out."

Mabel had been expecting him to be more anxious, like Rory's husband would have been. Maybe it was the difference in perspective between a beat cop and a detective, but Joe Hansen always anticipated the worst when it came to crime and fretted over how often things didn't work out. It worried her that O'Connor seemed more inclined to believe that justice would happen without any real work on his part. With that attitude, he would be more comfortable with arresting the easiest suspect he could come up with—herself—rather than one he had to struggle to find.

"It won't work out for the rhubarb plants if someone doesn't do something to help them soon," Mabel said.

O'Connor shrugged. "Not my responsibility. I've got a killer to catch. The plants will just have to fend for themselves."

Except they couldn't. They would die. Much like Aunt Peggy's farm would have died if it were sold to Thomas Porter. Now that the deal was off and the packing could wait, Mabel had some spare time over the next couple of weeks before the garlic needed to be planted. If O'Connor wasn't going to do anything about Graham's work, and the heirs didn't even know that they needed to take action, then she was the only one left to act.

"What if I volunteered to water the plants?" Mabel asked. "Would I get into trouble for trespassing?"

"Not from me. As of this morning, we're done with the crime scene. I'd suggest staying away from the immediate area where Graham died in case the technicians want to recheck it, but other than that, I don't care if you want to be a Good Samaritan." O'Connor stood up and laughed before adding, "Lena Shaw might care, though, so make sure you don't upset her. We're too busy right now to deal with more of her petty grievances."

"I'll talk to her before I do anything," Mabel said as if she hadn't already been planning to. Now she could honestly tell Lena that the police had suggested talking to her. Leading with that might give her an opening to ask about Lena's whereabouts at the time of Graham's death, although Mabel wasn't quite sure how to work that into the conversation. Too bad she couldn't just create an app with the questions she needed answers to about motives and alibis, and then just ask people to respond to the app. It would be so much easier than dealing with people face-to-face. Perhaps she could appeal to Lena's obvious pride about how she watched over the subdivision. Even if she hadn't seen Graham the morning he died, she might know his daily routine, including when he usually fed the cat.

"Wait here and I'll get you a key to the greenhouse," O'Connor said. "The house itself is also locked, but you won't need to go in there."

"Thanks."

Gin Jones

She would have liked to ask him whether they'd confirmed the time of death yet since it might exonerate her. O'Connor wasn't likely to share something like that though, despite his inexperience. He might get suspicious, and if he mentioned it to his colleague from the state police they would definitely think she was showing too much interest in the crime itself, rather than the rhubarb.

Mabel expected O'Connor to dally, but he returned after only two or three minutes. He dangled the key in front of her before abruptly pulling it back into his closed fist. "Just one thing first." He was facing Mabel but didn't look her in the eyes. He giggled nervously before saying, "I, uh, heard you were thinking of leaving town soon. We need you to stick around until the murder investigation is wrapped up. Just in case we have questions."

Or in case he wanted to arrest her, she thought. It was probably a good thing the sale of the farmhouse had fallen apart, so she could focus on proving she hadn't killed Graham instead of preparing to move. "I'm not going anywhere until I sell the farm, and it looks like that's going to take a while longer."

"Good to know." He giggled again as he handed over the key. "I'd appreciate it if you'd let me know if anything changes."

"I will." Mabel grabbed the key before he could change his mind again, anxious to leave before he restricted her freedom even further. What would it be like to always need permission before leaving a room? She'd rather not find out. "Just how long do you think the investigation is going to take?"

O'Connor shrugged, assuming a world-weary expression that he couldn't possibly have enough experience to justify, and that was odds with the accompanying laugh. "Hard to tell when there aren't any obvious suspects, like in this case."

"What about Graham's clients?" Mabel asked. "I heard some of them were upset with him."

"Yeah, we'll be talking to them," O'Connor said. "But first we need to get the court order to search his office. Not just for his will, but also so we can put together a list of who he represented. They're our best leads so far, but it'll take time to sort everything out. Any time you don't have a clear suspect in the first day or so, you know it's going to be a real challenge. The investigation could take weeks before we have solid answers. Months even."

Her heart sank. There wasn't anything she could do to help compile a list of Graham's clients, so she was dependent on the police doing it and following up diligently, which she wasn't sure would happen. "How many months?"

"A couple," O'Connor said. "Or more. The state police detective told me it once took her ten years to catch her man, but she never gave up."

"Let's hope her perseverance won't be quite so necessary in this case."

Chapter 9

On the way to her car, Mabel got a text from Charlie Durbin with a link to the court order in the fraud case against Thomas Porter. She sat behind the wheel, with the engine off, and read the whole thing, just in case there was some mistake. Unfortunately, it didn't take a lawyer's training to know that Thomas Porter was definitely a real estate developer, and not an ethical one like Charlie who would honor a no-development provision in the contract. She could no longer hope that the rumors had been wrong or there was someone else with a similar name who'd been sued for lying to a seller.

Mabel texted Jeff Wright to let him know the sale was definitely off. Then she decided it was time to send another message asking him to call her to let her know he was okay. She'd been planning to wait until the end of the day, but she was starting to worry about him. Members of the legal profession generally had a reputation for not responding to calls and texts, but Jeff had never been that way with her. She was a long-time client of course, and that got her some special consideration, but she'd heard from some of his other clients who said he always got back to them quickly too. So why hadn't she heard from him in close to two whole business days since she'd first texted him about the legality of collecting yard waste from other people's property?

Mabel decided it was time to try something else to contact him. She called his regular office number, the one she'd given to Rory but hadn't ever used herself, since she had his direct number. All she got was a recording inviting her to leave a message. That, too, was worrisome. Even if Jeff was on vacation, his administrative assistant should still be in the office and answering the phone at four in the afternoon.

Mabel left a message, asking for a call back, but wished there was something more she could do. If she'd been at home in Maine, she'd have driven to his office, just to be sure it was still there. She couldn't do that right now, not with the murder investigation hanging over her head. All she could do was wait for him to get back to her and hope that he'd been on vacation, and his assistant had perhaps taken a sick day or had been running an errand when Mabel called.

If she didn't hear from Jeff or his assistant by the next morning, she was going to do whatever it took to get answers, even if she had to call every single person who lived in her hometown to find one who'd go over to Jeff's office and ask him why he hadn't responded to Mabel's texts and calls.

Mabel was about to start her car when she saw the mayor park in his reserved space outside the main entrance to town hall. She needed to have a talk with Danny about buyers who weren't farmers.

She caught up with him at the base of the front stairs. "Thomas Porter is a real estate developer, not a farmer," she said. She'd never liked small talk, and he didn't deserve any social niceties in the circumstances.

Danny gave her a broad smile, as if she'd just complimented his work instead of criticizing it. "Come on inside where we can talk in private."

"I don't have time for that," Mabel said. "I just wanted to let you know the deal with Porter is off. I won't accept any offer from him. He's a developer, and I won't sell to anyone who isn't going to use the land for farming. You know that. It's even in your listing contract." Jeff Wright had given her the language to insert before she'd signed the document.

Danny glanced around furtively, obviously checking to see if anyone might overhear the conversation. The only people in sight were about half a dozen teenagers walking home from the local Catholic school in their distinctive uniforms. She doubted they would care about adult issues like property ownership.

Still, Danny lowered his voice. "I didn't know Porter was a developer. All I knew was what he told you, that he'd always wanted to be a farmer and now he was ready to make his dreams come true. He sounded just like I did when I was dreaming about following in my father's footsteps as mayor. I didn't expect it to happen when I was so young, and I'd rather my dad was still alive, even if I'd be out of a job, but I definitely know what it's like to have a passion for something."

"I don't care how much you have in common with Porter." Mabel didn't even believe the mayor was passionate about his job. From what she'd heard, Danny's real obsession was with writing about local history, rather than either of his actual jobs. Aunt Peggy had a couple of the books he'd written about West Slocum in her home office, because they'd focused on agriculture rather than prominent citizens or architecture like the rest of his books apparently did. "You represent me, not Porter. And I'm not going to sell to him."

"But he really wants the property," Danny said. "I've got to advise you that he's probably the best buyer you're going to find any time soon. A cash deal doesn't come along very often, and I bet Porter would pay even more than the listing price if you make a counteroffer."

"I'm not interested at any price," Mabel said. "It's not about the money. I will only sell to someone who will continue using the property as a farm."

"Okay, okay." Danny raised his hands defensively. "I'm just doing my job here. I have to be sure you know your options."

"I do." Mabel had originally intended to list the farm herself online, but Jeff Wright had insisted she hire a broker. She didn't always follow her lawyer's advice, but he'd reminded her that if she sold it herself, she would have to personally show potential buyers around during their viewing of the property. And that meant engaging in small talk. Not her best skill. Or any kind of skill at all. With a broker, she could make herself scarce when strangers were on the site. "The only thing that matters to me is finding someone who will carry on Aunt Peggy's work."

"All right, all right," Danny said. "I'll do what I can. Just keep in mind that it will take some time to find the right person, and you might have to lower the price."

Mabel didn't care so much about getting top price, but she was anxious to get back to Maine as soon as possible. Although, now that she thought of it, waiting until spring to go back home wouldn't be too much of a hardship. Especially since, while West Slocum wasn't anywhere near tropical, the weather was a little less extreme than in her part of Maine. And it would give her more time to watch her foster kittens be born and grow up to adoption age. A spring deadline would give Danny another five or six months to find a buyer. She could wait a bit, just not indefinitely. "How long do you think it will take to find a buyer who's a real farmer?"

Danny shrugged. "Could be years if you insist on keeping the land agricultural."

He was about as optimistic as O'Connor was about when she'd finally be able to go home to Maine, she thought. In Danny's case, though, he was probably exaggerating the situation to convince her to give up and accept the quick sale. It was a little tempting, especially as she thought about the imminent heavy labor to plant the garlic, but she owed it to her aunt to care for her legacy.

"I can wait," Mabel said, as much to remind herself as to answer Danny.

"Perhaps we'll get lucky. Hobby farms are popular these days, and Peggy's place is the right size for that." Danny's attempt at an enthusiastic expression faded, and he asked, "You're not so fussy that the buyer has to be a full-time grower, are you?"

Mabel didn't have anything against hobby farmers, and as far as she could tell, neither had her aunt. The next-door neighbor, Emily, was a hobby farmer, with her husband's high-powered job providing enough income to purchase the land and maintain it, while the goats barely paid for their direct expenses by producing the milk that was made into cheese. Aunt Peggy had been close friends with Emily and had partnered with her on the production of garlic-flavored goat cheese. That wouldn't have happened if Aunt Peggy had looked down on hobby farms.

"Any kind of farmer would be fine," Mabel agreed. "Just not a real estate developer who will destroy the fields my aunt worked so hard to establish."

Danny's enthusiasm resumed, looking more real. "I'll do my best."

That didn't exactly reassure her. On the other hand, there really wasn't any other broker who worked in West Slocum and knew the community. Even Graham's heirs would probably end up hiring him to sell his property. From what Detective O'Connor had said, it seemed unlikely that there was a local heir who might want to move into the house, so the property would have to be sold and the proceeds distributed according to his will.

"There's one other thing you could do for me in the meantime." Mabel needed to think about what could make the farm more interesting to buyers, and maybe having an even more diversified crop would do it. She already had a blueprint in her aunt's journals for adding a rhubarb field, and maybe that would entice a buyer. "I might be interested in buying the rhubarb plants from Graham's estate. If you get the listing to sell the property, would you ask the heirs if they'd be willing to sell me some of the plants?"

"They'd be as crazy as Graham was if they didn't sell someone the plants. The best price they'll get for the property is as a building lot, with the buyer tearing down the house. No one is going to want that much rhubarb in their yard." Danny's face fell. "But I doubt I'll get the listing. I expect Lena will jump in and make an offer the moment the heirs are identified. She'll sweeten the deal by telling them they can save the broker's fee by selling direct to her, so they'll get to keep more of the proceeds."

"I heard she might buy it, but I don't understand why," Mabel said. "It seems like a lot of work for her and a lot of money to invest, when she could just sit back and let someone else build something new there. Whoever buys it is likely to care more than Graham did about maintenance and even about the homeowners' association's rules."

"Lena likes to be in control," Danny said. "She won't want to take the risk that the next owner will fall short of her standards. She tried to buy it plenty of times before, but Graham wouldn't sell. She was a friend of the man who developed the subdivision, and she got some sort of sweetheart deal on her house in return for being the broker on the other houses. I've heard she later had a falling-out with the developer, and I suspect it was over his failure to buy Graham's farmhouse when the rest of the land was purchased."

Mabel thought he was probably right. Lena didn't seem like the sort to accept defeat gracefully. Or to accept no as an answer. Just how far would she have gone to get the title to Graham's land? More than just nagging, all the way to stabbing?

* * * *

Mabel found Lena in her yard, a few feet in from the sidewalk, raking a smattering of leaves that had blown onto her property from Graham's overgrown hedges.

"Hello," Mabel called out as she entered the yard. "Do you have a moment to talk?"

"What are you doing here?" Lena demanded. "You aren't parked illegally again, are you?"

Mabel had made sure to park out on the main street, outside the subdivision, just so she wouldn't upset Lena over something so innocuous. "Now that I know what the rules are, I'm following them."

"Good." Lena put her hands on top of the rake's handle and propped her chin on them. "What do you want?"

"I was wondering about the cat that lived in the greenhouse," Mabel said.

"Ugh," Lena said with a shudder. "I hate cats. They're such a nuisance. All they do is eat the beautiful birds and poop in our gardens. We have a rule against free-range animals here, you know, but of course Graham didn't care, and there was nothing I could do as long as the cat stayed on his property."

"You don't have to worry about the cat any longer," Mabel said. "She's at my place now. I was wondering if you knew what time of day Graham usually fed her. I'm trying to keep her routine as normal as possible."

"I didn't even know he had a cat," Lena said. "But he was always an early riser, up by five o'clock most days, working in the greenhouse until he left for the office. At least he was quiet about it, since I'm definitely not a morning person. I'd see him finishing up in the greenhouse so he could get ready for work when I got up at eight o'clock. I assume he fed the cat before then, when I wouldn't see it happening."

If the cat was usually fed by eight, but hadn't eaten the morning of the murder, then it did seem mostly likely that Graham had been dead for several hours before Mabel had found him. That was good news, since once the police figured out the time of death with their own investigation, it should rule her out as a suspect. Anyone could tell them that she didn't leave her bed, let alone the farm, before nine o'clock in the morning.

"What's the big deal about the cat anyway? It should be glad it was fed at all."

"Cats tend not to express gratitude as well as they express their demands for food," Mabel said. "I'm not a morning person either, so I have to hope Graham's cat will adjust to my time schedule, at least until she can join the ones in the barn after she's had her kittens and they're weaned."

"Kittens?" Lena shuddered. "If I'd known Graham was breeding invasive wildlife along with his rhubarb, I'd have killed him myself."

Mabel was shocked into silence.

"Too soon for jokes, I suppose," Lena said, adjusting her grip on the rake and stabbing at a single leaf near her foot. "But I'm not going to pretend I cared about the man. Everyone knows I hated him. The only person who hated him more than I did was his brother-in-law. And really, if there'd been kittens running all over Graham's property, it would have been the last straw. I'd have had to call animal control to trap them, and everyone would hate me, when they should have blamed Graham for making it necessary. I know people already think I'm heartless, because I have to enforce the rules, but someone has to do it."

"At least now you don't have to worry about the kittens," Mabel said. "The animal shelter will find homes for them."

"I'm grateful for that, and for your taking responsibility for them. No one ever takes responsibility for anything these days."

"I do," Mabel said. "In fact, I'm planning to come over and take care of the rhubarb plants until things get sorted out. O'Connor said I should let you know, in case you see me and wonder why I'm here."

"You're wasting your time," Lena said. "Everything will be bulldozed flat in a few months."

"I hope not," Mabel said. "Graham put a lot of work into his plants. I might even be interested in buying them, once the heirs are identified. For now, I just want to keep them alive. You wouldn't know anything about who might inherit the house, do you?"

"Probably his brother-in-law, Rob Robinson." Lena said.

"I thought you said Graham hated him."

"Oh, he did." Lena stopped raking. "But from what I've heard, his wife, Carolina, adored her brother. She inherited the land from her parents before she married Graham, and since they didn't have children, I expect that she would have wanted to keep the land, or at least the profits from it, in her family. Her grandparents started the farm that used to be here, and passed it down to her parents and then to Carolina, since she'd worked the farm for a while, and her brother had never been interested in it."

"Did you tell the police about the brother-in-law? I was talking to Detective O'Connor earlier today, and he didn't seem to have any idea about who the possible heirs were."

"He didn't ask, and I didn't think it was my place," Lena said. "I always have to get involved with the police to enforce the homeowners' association rules, but as Graham was so fond of saying, his property is outside the subdivision, so it's not my responsibility. Besides, I can only share what I've heard, not what I witnessed personally, and I've learned that the police won't do anything without a firsthand account. I never met Carolina Robinson-Winthrop. She died before the subdivision was built and I moved to town. In fact, her death was why the bulk of the land had to be sold. To pay off her medical bills. Only the main farmhouse was left."

Mabel didn't have any direct attachment to her aunt's farm, but she was still determined not to let it be destroyed. It would have been far worse for Carolina to know her family's farm was going to be erased. Had her brother blamed the sale of the land on Graham somehow? Even if he hadn't wanted to work the farm, he might still have been upset by the prospect of his family's legacy being lost to development. "Did the sale of the land have anything to do with why Robinson hated Graham?"

"I doubt it," Lena said. "When I first moved here, they seemed okay, with Rob visiting once a year around the anniversary of his sister's death. But this last year or so, Rob must have been here half a dozen times, and there were always loud arguments. I couldn't hear what they said, but it got bad enough once that I had to call the cops when I thought the shouting might turn into a brawl in the greenhouse."

Lena was willing to call the cops on cats and parked cars, so Mabel wasn't sure how big a deal the argument was. "Did they ever actually get physical?"

"Not as far as I know," Lena said. "The time I called the cops was the worst, and they calmed down before the cops arrived."

"Do you have Rob's contact information?"

Lena narrowed her eyes suspiciously. "What do you want it for?"

Because Mabel wanted to ask him where he'd been on Monday between five and eight or nine in the morning. But given Lena's tendency to go running to the cops about every little thing, it would be better not to mention Mabel's plan to do a little snooping or she might end up under arrest instead of simply being advised not to leave town.

Mabel scrambled for a more acceptable reason, one that Lena would accept but not consider worth passing along to the police. "If you're right and Rob's the heir, I'd like to find out if he'd be willing to sell me the rhubarb before I waste a lot of time caring for it."

"I've got a call in to him myself already," Lena said. "If you give me your number, I'll ask him to call you."

Lena's reluctance to share the information with either the police or anyone else seemed out of character, considering how few qualms she had about gossiping in other circumstances. Perhaps she just wanted to be the first to make an offer to buy the land and finalize the deal before a competitor even figured out who would inherit it. If that was the reason, Mabel didn't care who talked to him first.

"Thanks." Mabel rattled off her number while Lena keyed it into her phone.

It was only as Mabel was heading back to Graham's yard that she thought of another reason for Lena to want to talk to Rob first. What if she had seen something on Monday morning that she hadn't told the police about, something that would implicate Rob in the death of his brother-in-law, and she was blackmailing him in order to get the property? If Lena helped Rob get away with murder, Mabel might never be able to clear herself of suspicion.

Now she was even more determined to talk to Rob than when Lena had first mentioned him. There were other ways to find him than to get the information from Lena. The internet was a rich source of information, and she was far more at home in the digital world than the agricultural one.

Chapter 10

Mabel propped the greenhouse door open the way she'd seen it before. The heavy bucket was still nearby, along with the broken pots and discarded sidewall supports. Inside, the rich scent of earth and growing things enveloped her as it had done before. This time, she wasn't worried about running into Graham, alive or dead, but the sheer number of plants she'd agreed to oversee was daunting. How could she tell if it was too hot in there or whether the plants needed more water? She looked up to see a few sections of the roof were tilted open, providing ventilation in the late-afternoon sunshine, and they seemed to be mechanized. That just left watering and feeding for her to take care of, much like she was doing with the pregnant cat. Unfortunately, she knew even less about the care of rhubarb than about cats.

Then she remembered the neatly labeled card catalogue drawers she'd seen the last time she'd been there, just inside the second greenhouse. Perhaps Graham had some records in there that would tell her what she needed to know. She made her way past the farmhouse's back door and the no-longer-needed cat supplies, but then hesitated in the opening. She wasn't supposed to get too near the crime scene, and the police might consider the entire second greenhouse to fall under that label, even though Graham's body had been at the far end from where she stood. The only crime scene tape was over there. It didn't create a barrier, consisting as it did of just a few yellow and black scraps that hadn't come away when the bulk of the tape was removed.

In the absence of a clear signal to stay away, Mabel's need to know what was in the card catalogue overcame her natural caution. She tiptoed across the short distance into the smaller greenhouse and peered at the drawers, hoping they were as organized on the inside as outside. Most of the labels had neatly handwritten alphanumeric codes, starting with AA01001 to AZ01100 in the upper-left corner, and then continuing through the alphabet, ending with a row of blank drawers along the floor. She peeked inside one at waist height to find packets labeled consecutively within the range marked on the drawer. Somewhere, there had to be a spreadsheet that would translate those codes into more information about the seeds, presumably identifying the parent plants that had produced each packet of seeds and possibly when they'd been collected. All fascinating, but not helpful in deciding what the already germinated seeds needed to thrive.

Mabel gave up on the card catalogue and returned to the main greenhouse, looking for where else Graham might have kept his growing records. To her right was the back door of the farmhouse. He might have an office inside, like her aunt did, but she wasn't ready to see if she could get to it. The detective had said she could go into the greenhouse, but he'd also made it clear that the house itself was off-limits, even assuming she could pick the lock. If O'Connor was already considering her a murder suspect, catching her trespassing would only make him more suspicious.

To her left, a two-drawer metal file cabinet supported the end of a growing bench that was covered with seedling trays. She crouched to pull out the top drawer and found a stack of quad-ruled notebooks instead of file folders. She pulled the top one out and flipped it open. The first page had Graham's name and address on it, with a listing of his initial purchase of stock plants on the next few pages and then, finally, page after page of spreadsheets with the alphanumeric codes on the card catalogue drawers matched up with the parent stock, year the seed had been collected, a new code for any seeds he'd germinated from crossing the original plants, and a few brief comments about anything else he'd found noteworthy. Nothing, however, about how he'd grown the plants or how much water, light, or fertilizer they needed.

Mabel put it back and pulled out the second notebook. It was dated January of the current year, and it contained a mix of prose and charts, much like her aunt's journals. She assumed he'd written about his breeding efforts, but she couldn't actually read it, because everything was encrypted. She might be able to crack it, but it had been years since she'd done that kind of puzzle, so it would take some time, and she needed to get the plants taken care of first. She stuck it in one of the oversized pockets of her barn coat to look at later and resumed her search.

The rest of the notebooks in the top drawer were blank, and the bottom drawer contained more of the quad-ruled books filled with journal entries, and all battered from use and age. She dug through them, looking for any basic information Graham might have recorded without encryption. They were stored in reverse chronological order, and about halfway down the stack, going back three years, the information was a little more accessible, with only a few sections encrypted. By the time she reached the very bottom, the very oldest journal contained no encryption.

Mabel's excitement quickly turned to disappointment, since a quick skim proved that there was no useful information in it for maintaining the plants in the greenhouse. The contents seemed to be more of a therapeutic exercise, before he'd fully immersed himself in breeding. The first pages focused on his grief over his wife's death and how he'd turned to rhubarb, a plant she'd been particularly fond of, to work through his depression. Mabel flipped to the end, and it was still all about how much he missed his wife and how much she would have loved having the many varieties of rhubarb that were growing in the yard after he'd taken a trip to the USDA repository of rhubarb varieties in Washington state to get plant stock.

Reading the early portions of the journal, even just skimming the pages filled with Graham's grief, felt like too much of an invasion of his privacy to keep going, so Mabel put it back on the bottom of the stack of journals. She was still bent over the drawer when she heard a vehicle door slam nearby. It sounded like it was at the end of Graham's driveway where it was going to cause Lena to have a conniption and probably blame it on Mabel if she didn't get it moved right away.

Mabel hurried out of the greenhouse. The corner of a black sedan was visible just beyond Graham's hedges. Coming up the driveway was a petite woman in a black pantsuit with a white blouse. Even in three-inch heels, she was barely above five feet tall. She was talking on her phone as she squeezed between Graham's truck and tractor that were parked so close together Mabel hadn't even considered trying to fit between them and had always gone around.

"I'll let you know when I have it." The woman looked in Mabel's direction as she cleared the confines of the two vehicles, apparently only then noticing there was someone else nearby, and added, "I've got to go now." She disconnected the call but kept the phone in her hand as she crossed her arms over her chest.

"Hello," Mabel said. "If you're parked on the street near the driveway, you might want to move your car before the local homeowners' association president has it towed. She lives next door, and she's a bit of a stickler for the rules."

"Who are you?" The woman's voice was confident and radiated authority much larger than her physical size. She sounded like she at least thought she had a right to be on Graham's property, and maybe she did. For all Mabel knew, this could be the state police detective consulting on the case. "I'm Mabel Skinner. Detective O'Connor said it would be okay if I watered the rhubarb plants in the greenhouse so they wouldn't die before the heirs could see to them. And you are..."

"Sandy Faitakis," she said. "I'm here for the same reason. I didn't expect anyone to have the forethought to hire someone to take care of the plants."

"I'm more of a volunteer than an employee."

"A friend of Graham's?"

"I only met him recently," Mabel said. "What about you?"

"More of a colleague," Sandy said. "We were in a race to breed a new standard in rhubarb."

She didn't look like a farmer, any more than the developer trying to buy Stinkin' Stuff Farm had. Thomas Porter at least had the size and strength associated with agricultural work, even if he hadn't had the hands of a physical laborer. Sandy looked too small to drive a tractor or lug heavy supplies, and her wardrobe and neatly manicured hands were more suited to an office than the outdoors. After the experience with the lying Porter, Mabel wasn't about to accept another person's word on their love of farming.

"I don't mind doing the watering today." Mabel nodded at the other woman's outfit. "Working in the greenhouse will make a mess of your clothes, and the paths aren't really designed for supporting high heels."

"I only found out about Graham's death after I got to my office, and I didn't have a spare set of clothes at my office to change into there. My breeding project is a personal interest, not my day job. I work in the agriculture and life sciences department over at the university, which, unlike the outdoors, is conducive to suits and high heels."

"Do you know my field hand, Terry Earley?" Mabel asked. "He's majoring in agricultural sciences there."

"I'm afraid not," Sandy said. "I specialize in the business of agriculture, which, sadly, too many farmers don't pay enough attention to. I've chosen rhubarb to test my theories about the economics of farming."

"Is rhubarb that valuable a crop?"

"It could be," Sandy said. "Unfortunately, it's not one of the miracle crops that can save small farms, so it's hard to get funding for research. There's never enough grant money for all the work that needs to be done, and the less popular plants often suffer from that scarcity. I still believe in rhubarb, and I'm fortunate not to need to make a profit from my breeding program, so I do the research on my own time, with my own funds. It's slower that way, without any of the shortcuts or hired help that grant money could facilitate, but I'm making progress. It's really a pity that I couldn't get more funding, though. Farmers could really benefit from growing rhubarb. It's easy, with few pests or viruses, and it's a great source of calcium for people who don't eat dairy foods, as well as several important vitamins."

"I think my aunt knew about the nutritional benefits. She served it in stewed form as a side dish with lunch most days when I visited her. Claimed it was good for regularity, as well as being nutritious. I was a bratty teen at the time and refused to even try it. I know it's foolish to judge it on appearance, but I couldn't get past how disgusting it looked."

"That kind of bad first impressions is exactly what I'm trying to overcome with my breeding program." Sandy dropped her phone into her jacket pocket, freeing her hands to gesture as she spoke, revealing the previously hidden calluses on her palms. "The currently marketed varieties don't appeal to the buyers' senses. The stalks either look too much like celery for people to associate it with fruits, or if the color is nice and red all the way through so they look pretty, they're too small to be appreciated in a world where bigger is automatically considered better. Graham and I were both convinced that if we could breed a variety that has both solid red color and a consistently large size, it could become the new super-food. At least as long as we didn't breed out all the flavor and nutrition the way commercial breeders have done with tomatoes."

Mabel decided that Sandy was definitely a real farmer. Not just because of the calluses on her hands, but because she was every bit as knowledgeable and passionate about her rhubarb as Emily was about her goats and Rory was about community-supported agriculture. It wasn't something that could be faked.

"We should work together to save Graham's rhubarb," Mabel said. "I'm willing to take care of the seedlings until the heirs decide what to do with them, but I'm not much of a farmer. I need you to tell me what I need to do."

"He didn't leave any records that you could refer to?" Sandy's brow furrowed. "I'm sure he had some. He used to brag about how he had reams of data."

"I found his journals easily enough, and there's probably data in them," Mabel said. "Just not the basic information I need."

Her eyes lit up. "I'd be glad to take them to my office for safekeeping if you'd like." The words sounded casual, but Mabel thought the woman was more eager to look at the journals than she let on.

"You'd have to check with the police before anything is removed from here," Mabel said. "Besides, from what I've seen, they don't have the basic information, like how often to water and fertilize things and how to tell if it's too hot in the greenhouse. I don't even know if rhubarb does best in warm or cool temperatures."

"Then you shouldn't be in charge."

Sandy moved to go around Mabel and into the greenhouse, but Mabel blocked her. Collaboration was all fine and good, but not with someone who wasn't willing to be part of a team. If Sandy didn't want to help, then she could leave.

"I'm the only person available. The police entrusted the key to me, and they didn't authorize anyone else to go inside." That would probably change if Sandy contacted Detective O'Connor, but she didn't know that. "Besides, the longer you stay, the more likely the neighbor will have your car towed."

Sandy glanced over her shoulder before shrugging. "It'll still take another ten or fifteen minutes for a tow truck to get here, assuming they were called right away. Before I leave, I'd really like to see what Graham accomplished. He talked a good game, but he isn't a trained scientist. Some amateurs can do amazing work, while others, not so much."

She tried to go around Mabel, who blocked her again. "Maybe another time. After I check with the police."

Sandy grimaced. "At least let me look through the doorway. I've never even seen his setup."

Mabel relented. "Okay. It really is impressive. At least, I think so. I know more about coding than about plants. But it looks like he had meticulous organizational skills that would have served him well in any kind of work."

Sandy stopped just outside the entrance and slowly inspected the long benches of neatly labeled seedlings. "Hunh."

"Impressive, isn't it?"

"It's not what I was expecting." Sandy leaned forward as if trying to study the alphanumeric code on the nearest label. After a moment, she straightened and shook her head. "Not up to my standards of course, but not bad for an amateur. If you ever want to see what a professional setup looks like, I'd be glad to show you my plantings and greenhouse."

"I'd like that."

"Just text me to set up a time." Sandy recited her phone number and Mabel keyed it into her own phone's contacts.

Sandy looked into the greenhouse again. "I'm surprised he could keep his plants alive, let alone collect any data. Especially the last year or so. He came to me for advice something like five or ten years ago when he purchased his initial rootstock and the main greenhouse. I gave him some books to study, but I never thought he'd actually read them, let alone follow their procedures. He seems to have at least tried."

"Why wouldn't he?" Mabel asked. "If he was willing to learn from an expert, why wouldn't he do what you recommended?"

"Originally, I thought his interest in breeding was just a phase he was going through. Part of grieving after his wife died," she said. "He'd started reading about the plant just because his wife had liked rhubarb so much, and he wanted to plant some in her memory. That wouldn't have been so bad. But then he stumbled across the various medical uses it's been put to. Mostly the roots for digestive issues, but there's a lot of speculation about the stalks too. They contain vitamins and minerals, of course, which is part of why I want to make it more attractive to consumers. But Graham saw even greater benefits than that. He came up with this theory that some of the compounds in rhubarb might have cured his wife. Totally baseless, of course, but he wouldn't listen to anyone who told him he was wrong."

"It sounds like you followed his work closely."

"Not really," Sandy said, turning to leave. "We lost touch over the years, so most of what I know about him is what I've heard from others. He'd become convinced that the leaves weren't just safe to eat—which they're not, if you don't know—but were actually an overlooked resource for curing cancer."

Mabel escorted the professor down the driveway, taking the slightly longer way around instead of squeezing between the vehicles. "Is there any chance Graham could have been right? Or at least had the germ of an idea for further research?"

Sandy shook her head. "He wrote to the chairman of my department once about his theory that rhubarb could cure metastatic breast cancer, and I had to explain that there just wasn't any reason to justify the research, much as I'd love to think my chosen crop could get more attention. There's still a lot to learn about cancer and about the various compounds in all plants, but there's absolutely no reason to think rhubarb would have any cancer-treating properties whatsoever, and there's far more promising cancer research happening that has actual scientific merit."

"You said you lost touch with him," Mabel said. "Why was that?"

"He stole some of my breeding stock," Sandy said shortly. "I wouldn't have minded if it was one of the varieties already on the market, but he took some of my hybrids, things I'd been working on for years."

That sounded like a good reason to dislike Graham and even a potential motive for murder. "When did that happen?"

"About three years ago."

Maybe not such a likely motive then, since enough time had passed to get over the initial anger. Still, Mabel needed to establish that she wasn't the only person who might have wanted Graham dead, so she wasn't ready yet to give up on the rivalry as a motive. "Did you call the police about the theft?"

By then, they'd arrived at the sidewalk, and the car, fortunately, was still there, and not attached to a tow truck. She almost wished it had been, since then she'd have had more time to grill Sandy.

"I considered calling the police, but my colleagues talked me out of it. Graham denied stealing the plants, and it would have been complicated proving they were mine. I could have done it, of course, but not in a way that a non-scientist like a judge would easily understand." She went around to the driver's side door. "Besides, everyone said it would reflect badly on my professional reputation when the matter went public, and it came out that I hadn't been able to keep my work secure. It might have encouraged others to steal from me or, worse, from other researchers at the university, even though this was my personal project, not a school-funded one."

"Are there really that many breeders of rhubarb who might want to steal your work?"

She laughed. "I almost wish there were, and then I'd have handed off what I had to someone who had more time and resources to work on it. I was more concerned about my paid work for the university. Then I could choose to work with a more popular plant that would increase the chances of my getting grants. And tenure."

"Do you think Graham still has your plants, or the descendants of them?" Mabel asked.

"You think that's why I'm here? To steal them back? The thought did cross my mind, but I'd lose my job if I got caught, and I didn't expect all of this." Sandy looked back longingly at the greenhouse. "I just wanted to see what he'd accomplished and if anything could be salvaged. Legally. I could buy them from the estate. The data too. You did say there were records, right? And they're as tidy as the labels are?"

Sandy obviously intended it to sound like idle curiosity, but she sounded a little too eager for the information for Mabel to believe there wasn't more to it. What if Sandy had indeed been willing to risk her professional career and even her freedom to get the results of Graham's work that used her original stock? She'd said herself that she didn't have the labor she needed to expedite her research. Perhaps she'd let Graham steal her stock—or even gave it to him and only pretended that he'd stolen it—so he would invest his time into it, and she could claim it down the road, after he'd made a breakthrough or at least had put enough time into it to have advanced the research beyond what Sandy could have done alone. Then if he'd refused to work with her, she'd have a motive for murder.

Mabel wasn't a fan of irony, especially not here, where the irony would be squared, if his death was all wrapped up in his beloved breeding program. She already knew that the means of the murder was the knife he'd bought to use on his rhubarb, and it was possible that the motive was also related to his breeding program.

"The data looks good to me," Mabel confirmed. "But it could be all gibberish. I'm just keeping it safe until the estate can take over."

"What if—"

She was interrupted by the roar of a tow truck turning into the subdivision.

"I did warn you." Mabel shrugged. "The next-door neighbor sees everything that goes on over here, from parking to trespassing."

Sandy didn't answer, hurrying as she was to get into her car and start the engine before the tow truck could get in place. Still, Mabel thought the professor had gotten the message: Don't even think about coming back later and stealing Graham's data. Sandy was a smart woman. She had to know she couldn't get away with it, not with Mabel knowing of its existence, and the neighbor keeping an eagle eye out for visitors.

Chapter 11

It took Mabel a couple of hours to fumble her way around the greenhouse, dragging hoses and searching for faucets and guessing at how much water was enough without being too much. It would have been easier and probably quicker if Sandy had been more willing to share some basic agricultural information, but all things considered, Mabel had done as well as she could, and it had to be better than if no one had acted.

On her way out of the greenhouse, she took a series of pictures of the interior, including the drawer full of journals and a shot of the smaller building, being careful not to get too close to where the dead body had been. It seemed like something Jeff Wright would have advised her to do, just in case someone later accused her of stealing or damaging any of the plants. By the time she locked the door behind her, she had a record of all the plants and how they'd looked when she'd started taking care of them. And if someone else stole anything later on, whether it was data or plants, the pictures would help to establish what was missing.

Back at the farmhouse, Mabel went upstairs to check on the pregnant cat and refill the water and kibble bowls. There was no rush to pack up Aunt Peggy's belongings now that the sale of the farmhouse wasn't likely to happen for months, but Mabel was going to need more space for the cat and her eventual kittens. She might as well go ahead with packing up the contents of the room. She had the boxes already, and she'd need to do it eventually.

Before she could get started, Pixie meowed from the kitchen. Not the warning yowl of someone on the property, fortunately, but the cry that signified it was dinnertime and her bowl was empty. The packing could wait until after everyone had eaten. Mabel had forgotten to have lunch, and now it was after eight o'clock, and there was nothing in the fridge except the last of Emily's eggs. Fortunately, her two favorite restaurants in town, Jeanne's Country Diner and Maison Becker, both delivered. The number for Jeanne's was busy, so she ordered the daily special from the other place before fixing Pixie's dinner.

Mabel was unwrapping the delivery half an hour later when Emily knocked on the kitchen door and let herself in. "I saw Maison Becker's delivery girl as she was leaving. Is there enough to share? I brought dessert. Cheesecake bars made with goat cheese." She raised a cupcake carrier in front of her chest. "I've been thinking of adding them to my farmers' market offerings."

Mabel always ordered too much from Maison Becker because the food was so good, and even when she tried not to, the portions were huge, so she always ended up with leftovers. Usually saved for the next day's lunch, but she didn't mind sharing. Emily was probably lonely with her husband gone on a longer-than-usual business trip. Besides, Mabel had been meaning to ask Emily if it was possible Charlie had been flirting with her.

"Have a seat. You're always welcome." It struck Mabel that it was true. She'd grown accustomed to the unannounced visits, and even Pixie didn't seem to feel Emily presented any risk that needed to be warned against.

Emily settled at the table and peered eagerly into the delivery box. "Is that chili? Perfect for a fall evening."

"I didn't ask, just ordered the special." Mabel got an extra plate and silverware, along with bowls for both of them.

"I could never let them choose for me. I don't like surprises."

"What about good ones?" Mabel took her own seat on the other side of the table.

"It depends." Emily looked up from the chili she was dividing between two bowls. "The last 'good' surprise I got was when my husband said he had a new contract, and it was going to pay for a trip when he got back. Turned out, he forgot to tell me that it would mean his being away for six weeks in order to earn the big bonus."

"I'm sorry," Mabel said. "But this one's all good. No downside for either of us. The deal to sell the farm is off. You were right about Porter being a developer who would destroy my aunt's legacy."

"I'm sorry," Emily said, licking her finger where some of the chili had spilled. "Not that the deal fell apart, but that you had your hopes raised for nothing."

"I'm sure someone will want the farm eventually," Mabel said. "I've still got a little time to look for the right buyer. I told my boss I'd probably need six months of leave, and that gets me to the new year. Then the next few months should be pretty quiet here when the fields are covered with snow, and I work virtually anyway, so I could go back to work then and hope for a sale before the spring squash planting starts."

"What about the newest addition to your household? I heard you'd taken in a pregnant cat that was found at Graham's property."

"She'll have her kittens soon, and they'll be ready for adoption by next spring," Mabel said, although it dawned on her that she didn't know what the gestation period or time to weaning was. "Won't they?"

Emily nodded. "Kittens are born about two months after conception, and they can be weaned at about eight weeks. It's a lot faster than with goats."

"Plenty of time for the kittens to not need me or their mother before I sell the farm," Mabel said.

"I wonder where the kittens' father is," Emily said.

"Probably pooping in Lena's flowerbeds," Mabel said. "She said pets weren't allowed to be out loose in that subdivision, so the father is probably as wild as the mother is. All I know for sure is that he didn't stick around to take responsibility for his kittens."

Emily laughed. "You should call her Billie Jean then. Like the song."

"Thanks a lot. I'm going to be singing that in my head forever now." Mabel stood to get some water for both of them, and as she brushed against the barn jacket draped over the back of her chair, Graham's journal fell out of a pocket.

"What's that?" Emily asked.

Mabel bent to pick it up. "One of Graham's gardening notebooks. It looks a lot like my aunt's journal, except that it's encrypted."

"Really?" Emily held out her hand. "What do you think he was hiding?"

"Secrets of his breeding program, I assume." Mabel handed over the journal and continued over to the sink to get the water. "Did you know there's another rhubarb breeder nearby? She works at the university."

"You must mean Sandy Faitakis. She wouldn't consider herself 'another' breeder, someone in Graham's league. She would call him a mere hobbyist, while *she's* a scientist. She once claimed that if he actually came up with a better variety than the current standards, it would be a matter of luck rather than science. She would really have hated it if he'd lucked his way into a breakthrough. She's staking her entire career on the scientific method and her application of it to rhubarb."

"I think Graham was more of a scientist than anyone ever knew," Mabel said, returning with two glasses of water. "He definitely kept extensive spreadsheets with detailed information on all his plants. I wouldn't understand most of the data even if it weren't encrypted, but he interspersed it with narrative sections that look more like a diary. I was thinking there might be some information in there that I would understand about his current crop of seedlings."

"It might say something about why he was killed too." Emily flipped through the pages. "If only you could decode it."

"I may be able to," Mabel said. "I plan to try anyway. I used to be pretty good at cryptograms when I was a kid, before I got into coding. It's probably a fairly simple letter transposition code, nothing fancy. Graham was a lawyer, not some tech guru or international spy."

Emily handed the book back. "See? This is just what I've been telling you. You don't have to leave West Slocum to have interesting work to do."

"Having enough work is never a problem," Mabel said. "In fact, my boss is pressuring me to take on a project for him before I move back to Maine."

"I hope you'll keep an open mind about it. You can work from here as easily as from your home in Maine."

"It's not that," Mabel said. "It's that I don't belong here. I'm not a farmer."

Emily gave an irritated sigh. "You can learn. I wasn't a farmer before I moved here."

"But you *wanted* to be one. I don't. I just want to be sure my aunt's legacy is protected."

"The only way you can be sure that happens is if you stick around and supervise."

"I'll think about it," Mabel said.

"That's all I ask." Emily pushed back her empty bowl. "Now I need you to tell me what you think of the cheesecake bars. You're the only person I know who will tell me the truth, even if they're terrible."

* * * *

The cheesecake bars were not terrible, of course, and in fact were amazingly good, so Mabel was spared having to hurt her friend's feelings. Emily left a few minutes after hearing the verdict, explaining that she expected a call from her too-long-absent husband soon, and wanted to be home for it.

After washing the dishes, Mabel meant to go upstairs and tackle the clutter in her aunt's bedroom, but she caught sight of Graham's journal on the table and couldn't resist taking a quick peek at the first few pages to see if there was an obvious pattern to the encryption.

After an hour, Pixie appeared to demand a patting. Mabel set aside the journal, accepting that the code was more complicated than she'd expected. She was confident she could break it with enough time and a few tricks she'd learned over the years, but she was a bit rusty with this kind of puzzle, and she had more time-sensitive work to do first.

Mabel cuddled Pixie until the cat had had enough and then headed up to pack up the clutter in her aunt's room. By midnight, all of her aunt's clothes, shoes, and decorative items were in boxes in the hallway for donation to a local charity, along with two bags of trash. Mabel gave both Pixie and the newly named Billie Jean a snack before treating herself to one of the cheesecake bars Emily had left in the fridge, and then took Graham's journal with her to bed for another stab at decoding it. She tended to think best late at night, when it was quiet and there were no distractions.

By two in the morning, Mabel had to concede that either her brain had gotten out of the habit of late-night work or Graham had used a tougher code than a non-techie would be expected to use. Before abandoning the project, she'd sent out a call for help to some of her online friends with more decryption experience than she had. They were located all over the world, following wildly differing schedules, so it might take a day or two to get all the responses. Just in case there were any quick replies, she turned her phone off so pings wouldn't keep her up or wake her overnight. She couldn't afford to miss a night's sleep, not with a pregnant cat to care for, several hundred rhubarb seedlings to water and feed the next day, and murder suspects to identify.

She woke the next morning to find that Graham's neighbor, Lena Shaw, had texted to say she couldn't find a phone number for the brother-in-law, Rob Robinson, but had remembered that he worked for MassAssurance Company. Mabel also had some messages from her friends with what she assumed would be advice to crack Graham's encryption, but that could wait until after she talked to Robinson about who the likely heirs were, and, if possible, why he'd been so angry with Graham recently. She would have preferred to text or email Robinson, but she'd already had enough investigative experience to know that in-person interviews of suspects were much more effective than written ones. Real life didn't have an edit button for when self-incriminating information was inadvertently revealed.

A search of the town directory established that Rob Robinson no longer lived in West Slocum, but he couldn't have gone far if he still worked for MassAssurance. Their website showed the business in a tiny industrial park in an adjoining town, right on the border with West Slocum. She tried calling ahead to make an appointment, but the voicemail system was so slow, with so many levels, none of which were relevant to what Mabel was interested in, that she decided she could drive out there faster than she could get through all the phone options.

MassAssurance filled an entire, single-story, box-like building in the twelve-site industrial park, which she found surprising, since the website had described it as a niche insurance company covering certain business risks she'd never heard of before, so she'd assumed it couldn't possibly employ more than a handful of people. The parking lot must have held closer to two hundred cars than the single digits she'd expected.

Robinson didn't make her wait, but invited her into his spacious office as soon as his assistant buzzed him. He was a tall man with dark, thick curly hair that was cropped short, as if to deny anything about himself that might be seen as unruly. His suit was conservative and dark, with a traditional, boring red-and-navy striped tie, but when he sat, Mabel caught a glimpse of hand-knit socks with bright-yellow, orange, and purple stripes that didn't match either his tie or his overall image. Had all of his usual dull socks been in the laundry, leaving him with no other choices, or were the wild stripes a hint that he wasn't entirely what he seemed?

Once seated behind the antique, carved table that served as his desk, Robinson asked, "So what can we do for you today, Ms. Skinner? We can offer customized coverage for most business risks."

"I don't need insurance." Mabel wanted to ask about his socks, but she settled for saying, "I'm here about your brother-in-law, Graham."

Robinson leaned back in his leather executive chair with a sigh. "What's he done now?"

She didn't know how to answer. Maybe Lena had been telling the truth about being unable to contact Robinson. Mabel had assumed the police had found him, with or without Lena's help, and had already talked to him about the murder. Even if the police hadn't contacted him, he ought to have heard about his brother-in-law's death. It had been too big a story for the local paper to worry about whether next of kin had been notified before running it on the first page, complete with the identity of the victim. She'd checked the newspaper's website this morning, just in case the police had made any obvious headway in their investigation, but they hadn't. And now it appeared that she'd figured out who Graham's next of kin was before they had. That didn't bode well for a successful investigation, one that would clear her of any suspicion.

"It must be bad," Robinson said, "if you need to figure out how to break the news. I'm not bailing him out again. I told him just last week that I was done paying for his mistakes."

"He doesn't need bailing out." Mabel perched on the edge of one of the three leather chairs across the desk from him. "I'm sorry to be the one to tell you, but I thought the police would have contacted you already. Graham is dead."

"What kind of sick joke is this?" He got to his feet and glared down at her. "Who are you anyway?"

"I'm an innocent bystander. I just found Graham in his greenhouse on Monday. Dead." To forestall the assumption that it was natural causes, she added, "Stabbed in the back."

Robinson shook his head emphatically. "That's not possible. There must be some mistake."

"I'm afraid not."

He collapsed back into his chair. "But why would anyone kill him?"

"That's what the police want to know," Mabel said, as if she herself didn't also want to know the answer. "I barely met him before he died. I only stopped by his greenhouse to discuss our mutual interest in compost."

Robinson looked down at his hands for a long moment before speaking in a thoughtful tone. "I suppose it must have been one of his low-life clients who killed him then. He always managed to represent the very worst people. It was like there was a grapevine among the local criminals, or some sort of business listing that said, 'if you get caught doing something really stupid, and you earn just a little too much to qualify for a public defender, but not enough for a really good lawyer, then call Graham.' He also represented slumlords and some questionable small businesses. Hardly ever someone normal."

"Why would his clients want him dead if he was popular with them?" Mabel asked.

"You mean besides the fact that everyone hates lawyers?" Robinson said with the hint of a smile. "I don't know. And I suppose most of the clients did like him or they'd have taken their business elsewhere. Some of them probably did fire him, but Graham never discussed his work with me. I did hear about one unhappy client, not from Graham, but from the news. It was a guy named Sam Trent, who blamed Graham for his marriage failing. With difficult divorces, there's usually plenty of blame to go around before the lawyer gets involved, but Trent claimed that Graham revealed some confidential information during divorce negotiations that caused the wife to back out of reconciliation attempts."

The librarian, Josefina, had mentioned Sam Trent as a possible suspect too. Mabel decided she should add the name to a note-keeping app on her phone as soon as she left, but for now, she needed to keep the conversation casual. The last thing she needed right now was for Robinson to tell the detectives that she'd been interrogating him. Surely they'd get around to contacting him eventually.

"That sounds like good information to share with the police," Mabel said. "I'm just here to talk to you about the rhubarb plants."

"I wish I'd never heard of rhubarb," Robinson said irritably. "My sister would have been appalled to know that her casual interest in it had led her husband onto a self-destructive path. At first, it was just a way for Graham to spend his weekends, to distract himself from his loneliness. He would talk about his plants the way some people talk about players on sport teams, with all their game statistics and how likely the players were to perform well in the future. I even encouraged him in his hobby originally. It helped him to get through the grief of losing my sister. But then it turned into an unhealthy obsession. He was putting in hours and hours of work with the plants and his records every day, not just on weekends. Cut back his legal practice to have more time for his so-called breeding program."

"He did some really good work, from what I saw in the greenhouse," Mabel said. "There's even another breeder who might be interested in taking over his breeding efforts, and I'd like to buy some of the plants if you're interested in selling."

"Me?" Robinson frowned. "Oh, you think I'm Graham's heir?"

"You're the only person he had any connection with, from what I've heard."

"That much is true, but I'm not his heir. I may be the estate's executor unless he changed it recently. He didn't have any remaining family, and sad to say, I'm about the only person he ever talked to outside of his work in the last few years."

"So you are the most likely heir."

"The only thing I'm inheriting, if anything, is a hassle. Graham didn't own anything of value. The law practice itself is worthless, he didn't own the building it was in, and he didn't have any savings. He didn't even own his home. My sister insisted on putting that part of the real estate into a trust before she died, so Graham could live there as long as he wanted, but when he was gone, it would go to my kids. It used to belong to our grandparents, so she wanted to keep it in the family. At least, that's what she told me. In retrospect, I wonder if she knew he was going to fall apart after she died, and she did it to make sure he'd have a place to live during his lifetime. He couldn't sell it or even mortgage it as long as it was in trust."

"Do you know where the will is?" Mabel asked.

"In his office safe, if he bothered to keep it," Robinson said. "Sort of like the cobbler's kids having no shoes, he was the kind of lawyer who didn't follow his own advice. He had a will before my sister died, because she insisted on it. She even gave me a copy of it, since I was nominated as the executor for both estates. The terms were pretty basic. When one of them died, all the assets went to the other person, but when they'd both died, everything went to my kids. I wouldn't be surprised if Graham never got around to changing the old will after she died. It doesn't matter to me if he did, since there's really nothing to inherit. He put everything he had—time and money—into his plants."

Robinson didn't sound like he'd hated Graham, just felt sorry for him. Unless he was lying about not knowing Graham was dead, and had prepared a story about Graham not having any assets other than what was tied up in the trust. Graham had been a lawyer, after all, and that was generally a lucrative career. He obviously hadn't been spending any money on his house, so perhaps he'd accumulated a good bit of savings. Money was a common motive for murder, but killing so one's kids would inherit sooner than they would otherwise seemed less likely than killing to get one's own hands on the assets. Besides, Robinson seemed to be doing well enough for himself, judging by his executive role in the company he worked for and his luxurious office.

"Those plants are worth at least a little something," Mabel said. "Assuming you're the administrator of the estate, would you consider selling them to me? I can't pay a lot for them, but I was hoping you'd give me a discount in return for my taking care of them until the estate is ready to sell them."

"I'd just as soon see them burned to ashes because of what they did to Graham," Robinson said fiercely.

"That would be a waste," she said. "I spoke to another breeder, and she was impressed by what he'd created."

"I know," Robinson said more calmly. "It's just such a shock. I need time to absorb it all."

"I understand," Mabel said. "I don't need an answer right away. I just wanted to let you know I was interested in some of the plants, and that you didn't have to worry about them dying in the meantime."

"Thanks," he said. "Poor Graham. He just never got over my sister's death. I hope he's at peace now."

He wouldn't be though. Not until his killer was brought to justice.

Chapter 12

Mabel's phone rang while she was on her way to her car. Hoping it was finally Jeff Wright returning her calls, she checked the screen. It wasn't her attorney, but her boss, Phil Reed. "Listen, Mabel, I really need you for this project. I'll even give you a raise."

"I can't do any work for you right now," Mabel said. "I might be able to come back part-time ahead of schedule, but not for at least another month."

"By then, I might be out of business," Phil said. "Or I'll have hired someone else, and I won't need you any longer."

"You promised to keep my job open for six months."

"I didn't know this project was going to come along," Phil said, demonstrating the persistence that made him an outstanding salesman, but not necessarily a great boss. "I really need you, and I need this contract. It's not just your job on the line. It's everyone who works here who will be unemployed when I go bankrupt."

"You can't pin that on me," Mabel said. "If I could help, I would, but right now I have to make sure the farm is in the best possible condition to be sold. And that means planting next year's garlic crop before the end of this month. I'm going to be out straight dealing with that."

"So maybe you'd be able to do some work in November?"

"Maybe," she conceded. It all depended on whether she'd been arrested for Graham's murder in the meantime. If so, she might be unable to work for months. Years if she were convicted of the murder. But she couldn't tell Phil that, or he'd make good on his threat to hire someone to replace her. "I'll let you know."

"When?"

"As soon as I can." Mabel disconnected the call so Phil had to accept her answer without further arguing. He wasn't the type who'd call her back just to have the last word, but she'd only bought herself a day or two before Phil tried again. By then, she needed to have a better idea of when she could return to work. And that meant being confident that Graham's murder would be solved quickly.

She wasn't at all confident about that though. If the police hadn't even found Graham's brother-in-law yet, perhaps because they were satisfied with the one suspect they already had, it could be months before they found the real culprit. As long as Mabel didn't need to pack up the farmhouse for an imminent sale, the best use of her time would be to come up with some leads the police could follow to catch the real killer.

Mabel had already talked to three people with motives—the neighbor, the rival breeder, and the brother-in-law—but she didn't have any evidence that might convince the police to take them seriously as suspects. The only other possibility she knew of was Sam Trent, the unhappy client Robinson had mentioned.

Still in her car, Mabel searched the internet for information about Trent. There wasn't much on him, just a LinkedIn account that showed a history of working in sales for about twenty years, plus the legal notice that had been published when his wife filed for divorce a year ago.

Josefina at the library might know more than the internet did. Instead of going home, Mabel headed for the center of West Slocum.

She waited until Josefina was finished helping the only other patron in the lobby before asking, "What do you know about Sam Trent?"

"I know you should stay away from him," Josefina said without even the faintest pause to think. "He's a slick talker, good at selling himself and whatever he wants you to buy, but he never follows through on his promises. And if you question him about problems with the deal, he goes from your best friend to your worst enemy in a flash. He's got quite a temper."

"What does he sell?"

"Anything he can," Josefina said. "He worked for his wife's family's home siding business while they were married, but more recently he's been selling solar systems."

"Do you know why they got divorced? I heard Trent blamed Graham for not being able to reconcile with his wife."

"You heard that, did you?" Josefina's eyebrows raised. "Who from?"

"Rob Robinson." Just in case the name wasn't familiar, Mabel added, "Graham's brother-in-law."

"I know who he is. You wouldn't be investigating the murder, would you?"

"I'm interested in buying some of Graham's plants, and Robinson or his kids will likely inherit everything. I contacted him to make sure he knew I was interested in the rhubarb before anything happened to it."

Josefina smiled slyly. "And it's a convenient excuse for questioning him about who might have wanted his brother-in-law dead."

"I really do want the plants, especially now that the sale of the farm has fallen through." Mabel was fairly sure Josefina would have heard about both the proposed sale and its cancellation by now, and her lack of surprise at the news confirmed it. "Aunt Peggy had planned to add a field of rhubarb, so I'm going to plant it if I can. Having another crop already in place might make the farm more attractive to a buyer."

"Right," Josefina said, clearly not convinced. "That was all you cared about when you saw Rob. So when you go talk to Sam Trent, what's your excuse going to be then?"

"I don't know yet," Mabel said, not bothering to pretend any longer. "I just can't sit around and wait for the police to figure it out. My boss is pressuring me to come back to work. I can put him off for a few weeks, until after the garlic is planted, but not much longer than that or I probably won't have a job to go back to."

"Just promise me you won't talk to Trent alone." Josefina brightened. "You could take that nice Charlie Durbin with you. He's always been a good person. I've known him since he was a toddler and first started visiting the library. Not only would it be safer to have him watching your back, but he would have a more credible reason to talk to Sam. Charlie offers solar systems in some of his developments."

"I hate to bother Charlie. I'm sure he's busy."

Josefina folded her pink-clad arms across her chest. "Either you agree to take Charlie with you or I'm not telling you where you can find Trent. And I'll call Charlie to make sure you follow through, so don't think you can flimflam me. I may be old, but I'm not a fool."

"I wouldn't flimflam anyone," Mabel said. "Even if I wanted to, I wouldn't know how."

* * * *

Charlie was surprisingly easy to convince to drop whatever he was doing and invite Sam Trent to his office to talk with Mabel. She hadn't wanted to put Charlie in the awkward position of pretending he wanted to buy a solar system, so the cover story was that she was considering it for the farmhouse. Trent had taken the bait immediately, and agreed to a late-afternoon meeting.

Mabel filled the time before then by responding to some voicemails inquiring about the farmhand job she'd posted. Three applicants were new, so she arranged to interview them later in the week. She was relieved that the two students who'd helped with the summer harvest had left messages saying they wanted to return for the fall planting. She returned their calls to let them know when the work would start. She already knew they were reliable, and their return would also make it easier for Rory to convince her teen-aged daughter to work too, since Dawn had had a bit of a crush on the boy.

Mabel left a little early for the meeting and stopped by Graham's greenhouse to do a quick watering. Fortunately, there was no sign of the neighbor or the rival breeder, so she was able to do the necessary work without interruption. Then she headed across town to where Charlie had a construction trailer on one of his work sites. He was building a fifty-five-plus community on what had once been a small apple and pear orchard. Some of the trees had been left along the edges of the property and in a little area set aside as a park near the entrance, but she couldn't help wondering how the old farmer had felt about the leveling of the orchard.

She knocked on the trailer's door, and Charlie let her in while talking on his phone. The white, vinyl-clad exterior was unremarkable, except for the solar panels on the roof. The interior, however was more luxurious than she expected. The walls were paneled in real wood, and there were nice-looking light fixtures in the ceiling, and a pair of small, custom-upholstered chairs for visitors. A desk and filing cabinets were built into one end, with a storage closet and a tiny bathroom on the other end. Charlie had even installed Roman shades on the windows for privacy, although they were all raised at the moment to let in light. Plans for the subdivision were framed and hung on the walls.

Charlie ended his call and gestured for Mabel to have a seat in one of the upholstered chairs while he pulled the rolling office chair over next to them. "Before you ask, I bought this land fair and square. The farmer died, and no one in his family wanted to take over the orchard. I didn't lie to them about my plans for the land. And I kept as many of the trees as I could."

"I know you wouldn't lie to the sellers," Mabel said. "And I don't need to save every farm. I just need to save Aunt Peggy's."

A knock on the door was followed by the entry of a short man in a beige suit and a navy baseball cap with the distinctive B of the Boston Red Sox on the front. His tie was askew and the top button of his shirt undone.

Mabel imagined Trent standing next to Graham, and being dwarfed by the lawyer. Could he really have stabbed the larger man?

"I'm Sam Trent." He tugged off the baseball cap to reveal a completely bald head, despite his not being over forty. "You must be Mabel Skinner." He offered his hand for a shake, his grip firm to the point of discomfort. "Charlie and I go way back. He's a big believer in solar energy and how it improves property values. You probably saw the panels on top of this trailer, and he's installed them in several of his developments too."

Mabel noted that Trent hadn't actually said he'd sold those systems, just implied it. Josefina had warned her that he was slick. She glanced at Charlie for confirmation. He shrugged and indicated that Trent should take the other upholstered chair.

Trent threw himself into the chair, balancing a tablet on his lap. "So, what can I do for you?"

He'd addressed Charlie, but Mabel answered him.

"I'm having trouble selling my aunt's farm, and I thought adding solar panels might make the property more attractive to potential buyers."

"You're right about that." Trent said, tapping his tablet to bring up a chart to illustrate his words. "Solar systems can add thirty percent to the property value."

Out of the corner of her eye, Mabel could see Charlie's dubious expression, suggesting that Trent's figure was more of the slickness that Josefina had warned her about. It didn't matter whether it was true, though, since she wasn't actually planning to buy anything from Trent. At least not without getting another quote or two and running the contract past Jeff Wright. The thought reminded her that she still hadn't heard back from him and she'd forgotten to find out why. Right after this meeting, she was going to do whatever was necessary to talk to someone who knew what was going on with him.

But first she had to find out whether Trent might have killed Graham Winthrop.

"If the panels add that much value, they must be expensive. I don't have much in my budget. Maybe I should forget about the solar panels and just add a greenhouse," Mabel said. "It's simpler. And I could probably get a used one. Maybe even buy Graham Winthrop's. His heirs might even appreciate having someone willing to cart it away for them."

"I wouldn't recommend having anything to do with Graham Winthrop or his family," Trent said. "If they're as incompetent as he was, you could end up with a real mess on your hands."

"You could just be saying that so I'll buy your solar system instead."

"No, really," Trent said. "I hired Graham to represent me when my wife wanted a divorce. We were seeing a counselor, and we were making some real progress, getting close to a reconciliation, but then Graham went and told my wife's attorney about an affair I'd had that she didn't know about, and that was the end of our marriage. And my job, since I worked for her father."

"Why would a lawyer reveal confidential information like that?"

"Because he was crazy," Graham said. "He wasn't bad when I hired him, and I got a bunch of references from people he'd worked for. But he was losing his mind by the time I met him, forgetting things like what was covered by lawyer-client privilege. I found out too late that he'd messed up other cases too, and he covered them up somehow. I reported him to the Board of Bar Overseers, and their investigators talked to him, but he must have been having a good day or something when he was interviewed, because they couldn't tell that his brain didn't work right. They said he was fine, and the only thing I could do after that was to hire another lawyer and sue him for malpractice if I wanted."

"Did you?"

"No point," Trent said. "My marriage was over by then and there was no fixing that. Besides, I was also unemployed, so I had no money, and good lawyers don't work for free. Or even for cheap, like Graham did."

"Weren't you tempted to get some revenge on him outside the court system?" Mabel asked. "I would have."

"I was too busy looking for a new job," Trent said, but something in his eyes suggested that he had indeed gotten some revenge. The only thing Mabel couldn't figure out was whether it was something petty like keying Graham's truck or something serious like stabbing him to death.

"Fortunately," he went on, "solar is a booming business, so it didn't take long to find a new job and get on with my life. My company installs the best, most efficient products at the best price. If we can go over the specs you're interested in now, I can get you a quote in twenty-four hours."

"I'm not ready to talk details yet," Mabel said. "I'm just trying to figure out what my options are for improving the property value, and then I'll need to go over them with my broker before I even get to the point of figuring out the specifications."

"You mean Danny Avila?" Trent said, a note of irritation in his voice, although he tried to cover it up with a laugh. "He's got a sweet gig, doesn't he? No one hires him for his knowledge of real estate. They just do it out of respect for his daddy. Wish I'd had a parent like that. I'd be a millionaire by now. Like Charlie here."

"My parents weren't particularly well-known or financially successful," Charlie said. "The mayor's job is harder than it seems. I wouldn't want to be dealing with constant calls he must get from constituents."

A flash of anger crossed Trent's face and he clenched his hand more tightly around the tablet. He obviously didn't like being corrected. He looked away for a moment, probably to get his irritation under control. When he turned back, his face was all smiles again. He stood, saying, "You may be right. I love getting calls, but I guess not everyone does. And speaking of phone calls, I'd better get back to answering the messages I have from my customers. It was a pleasure to meet you, Ms. Skinner."

Mabel couldn't say that it had been all that pleasant for her. "Thank you for taking time to see me. I'll let you know if I'm ever ready to get a quote on solar panels." She owed him that much at least.

Charlie stood and walked Trent the few feet to the door, deftly rejecting the salesman's offers to submit quotes for solar panels for future developments.

Mabel was glad she'd followed Josefina's advice not to talk to Trent alone. If he'd come out the farmhouse and realized he'd been wasting his time, would he have become violent? After all, she suspected him of killing Graham, and despite Trent's short height, she thought he was more than strong enough to do it. Mabel would be an even easier target for him.

She wasn't about to find out how easily he could be provoked. If she had any more questions for him about his role in Graham's death, or anything else that might anger him, she was going to pass them along to the police to pursue.

Charlie shut the door behind Trent and leaned against it. "I don't like this."

"What?"

"If Trent is right about Graham making mistakes with other clients, there could be dozens of people out there who were looking for revenge. And if one of them was the killer and thinks you've figured it out, you could be in danger."

"Don't worry about me,' Mabel said. "I've got an early warning system for visitors at the farm. Pixie won't let anyone sneak up on me."

"What about when you're not at the farm? Who's going to warn you then?"

"No one's going to attack me at the library or the farmers' market."

"Perhaps not, but you must go other places than that."

"Not if I can help it." In the interest of complete disclosure, Mabel added, "Well, except for Graham's greenhouse. I've volunteered to keep his seedlings alive until the estate takes over."

"Alone?"

"I do everything alone."

"I'm hoping to change that," he said. "Call me next time you're heading there, and I'll go with you."

"Why?"

He shrugged. "Consider it payment of a debt to your aunt, making sure you're safe."

His words were casual, but something about his tone suggested his offer wasn't all about her aunt.

"Thanks." Until she got some help from Emily in translating Charlie's meaning, Mabel wasn't ready to commit to anything, especially not a promise to keep a bodyguard close at hand. "I'll call if I need help."

Chapter 13

On the way back to the farmhouse, Mabel mulled over what Charlie had said. She was convinced that he hadn't been telling her the whole truth when he'd explained his offer to protect her. But what could he want from her? She had come to completely accept that he wouldn't try to steal her aunt's land from her, but maybe he was playing a long game and thought she'd eventually give up on her plan to keep it as a working farm, and he'd be right there to swoop in and buy it.

Or maybe he liked her.

She hated the uncertainty. She was too old for the "does he or doesn't he" of relationship drama. Besides, now wasn't the time to start a personal relationship. She'd be leaving West Slocum before long, and until then, she had more important matters to deal with.

Like checking on the pregnant cat and moving the boxes of charitable donations down the stairs and out to the barn for delivery or pick up. And making another stab at decoding Graham Winthrop's journal.

Back at the farmhouse, Mabel fed and watered Billie Jean, Pixie, and herself, finishing the leftovers from Maison Becker and the last of the cheesecake bars. Then, hoping there might be some leads to Graham's murder in his journal, she tried some suggestions from her friends to break the code, but nothing worked. Graham must have been really paranoid about his information being stolen. She couldn't imagine that much espionage going on in the world of rhubarb breeding, but then again, she'd worked with clients who were obsessed with a particular field of interest, one so tiny and specialized she'd never heard of it before and only about a thousand people in the entire world were even remotely interested in.

And yet some of those clients had become convinced that the whole world was out to steal their secrets.

Mabel hadn't heard back yet from the one person she was sure would have the solution to breaking the journal's code, so she nudged him with a text and then switched to reading her aunt's journal in bed.

She didn't remember falling asleep over it, but a yowl from Pixie brought her out of dreams. They hadn't been pleasant, and the memory lingered. She'd been trailing Angela Lansbury in her Jessica Fletcher role, snooping around Stinkin' Stuff Farm with a magnifying glass in hand, her expressive eyes widening over assorted things that might or might not be a clue. Jessica been particularly fascinated by a mound of compost and a row of rhubarb plants that had somehow transported themselves, undisturbed, from Graham's back yard to the garlic farm, right where Aunt Peggy had indicated she would have put them.

Mabel was tempted to roll over and go back to sleep, but a repeat yowl—and the memory of Charlie's warning that she stay safe—got her to jump out of bed and run over to the window to see who was in the driveway. She couldn't see anyone, but the parking lot outside the barn wasn't visible from there. It was probably just Rory, making an impromptu visit, but Charlie's suggestion that Graham's killer might target Mabel had her on edge. She needed to be sure the visitor wasn't someone dangerous.

She quickly splashed some water on her face and grabbed her phone before running outside to deal with the visitor. The late-afternoon air had turned chilly, more typical of early November than mid-October, making her glad she'd already been wearing a sweatshirt before she left the farmhouse.

There was no sign of Emily, and neither Rory's pickup or any other vehicle was parked outside the barn. Pixie never yowled except when someone entered the property, and she was never wrong about there being a visitor. So where were they?

Mabel peered down the driveway, in case the intruder had stopped short of the buildings, but she didn't see anything out of the ordinary. A vehicle could have stopped on the far side of the bend in the driveway, but there wasn't any reason to do that, and in any event, she ought to be able to hear a running engine from that short distance, and the only sounds were a few birdcalls.

She had to consider the possibility that Pixie had gotten it wrong. Perhaps the presence of another cat in the house had caused Pixie to act out and demand more attention. She hadn't liked being kept out of Aunt Peggy's bedroom, so maybe she planned to yowl at random until she got the full run of the house again.

Mabel realized then that she hadn't actually seen Pixie, just heard the yowl, and hadn't stopped to check on the pregnant cat before racing outside to look for a visitor. What if Pixie had gotten inside the off-limits bedroom somehow, and the yowl wasn't a warning about visitors, but an aggressive challenge to Billie Jean? The poor pregnant cat didn't need any more stress than she was already experiencing by losing her caretaker and then being cooped up in an unfamiliar place with people she didn't know.

Mabel was halfway back to the farmhouse to check on Billie Jean when there was a commotion behind her. She turned to see all thirteen of the barn cats come streaming out in a panicked jumble and run off into the adjoining woods. Usually they were asleep at this time of day, saving up their energy for dusk when hunting time began. Something must have spooked them. Some sort of predator?

Mabel raced into the barn. She grabbed a hoe from where it hung immediately to the left of the entrance, so she'd have something to defend herself against the intruder. Most of the barn's interior was empty now that most of the harvest had been sold. There were few hiding spaces or even shadows except near the bins stacked along the far wall, which held a few butternut squashes for Mabel's personal use, plus the garlic heads that would soon be broken into cloves and planted for next year's crop. The cats wouldn't have been afraid of anything that might have hidden there—it was their job to hunt down the vermin attracted to the food, after all. So what could have scared the cats out of their naptime sanctuary?

And then she smelled the smoke. It was coming from her right, about ten feet from the entrance. Wisps of gray smoke rose from a rusty old wheelbarrow that held garlic that wasn't quite perfect enough to go to Jeanne's Country Diner or Maison Becker or any of the farm's other commercial customers. It hadn't gone bad, but some of the heads had a damaged section that would rot eventually. Rory had suggested taking it to the farmers' market with a heavily discounted price and a warning to discard any damaged cloves immediately and to use the rest as soon as possible. If no one bought them, they could be pickled, using Aunt Peggy's recipe. Emily said it was easy, but Mabel had been hoping not to have to do that, since she'd never been much of a cook, and she didn't have the patience for peeling all those cloves.

Now, it was too late to do anything with the garlic. The dried outer skins of the heads were smoldering. The least bit of breeze would ignite flame, so it was fortunate that the air, despite being chilly, was calm. If that changed though, and the smoke turned to fire, the whole barn could soon follow the contents of the wheelbarrow.

The hoe might have been useful against other types of intruders, but not a fire. Mabel needed something to smother it, a blanket or a tarp, but she couldn't see anything like that. Rather than wasting any more time, she tossed the hoe aside and pulled off her oversized hoodie to drop on top of the garlic. It seemed to have done the trick, but just in case, she pushed the wheelbarrow out into the gravel parking lot where fire couldn't do any damage, continuing until it was thirty feet from the barn.

She dropped the handles and raced back inside to grab a fire extinguisher that she'd belatedly remembered hung on the wall next to the doors. She carried it over to the wheelbarrow, but then realized she didn't know how to use it. Meanwhile, her hoodie, cotton and thin from years of use and repeated washings, had fed the fire instead of smothering it. The fabric was now smoldering and producing even more smoke than the garlic had.

Mabel was studying the instructions printed on the side when a boxy purple SUV screeched to a halt nearby and the faux farmer, Thomas Porter, jumped out, leaving the driver's side door open in his rush to join her. No longer hiding who he was, he wore a hoodie like the one she'd sacrificed to put out the fire, except it had the name of his company, PORTER DEVELOPMENT, embroidered on the left side of the chest.

"Here," he said, reaching for the extinguisher. "No time to waste. I know how to use it."

She didn't like Porter or his lies, but now wasn't the time to quibble over his rudeness. She silently handed over the extinguisher, and was relieved to see that he did indeed know what he was doing when it came to this bit of physical labor, even if his hands were soft and uncallused. He had the stream of fire retardant aimed at the contents of the wheelbarrow in mere seconds, and the smoke was quickly abating.

Eventually, Porter set the extinguisher on the ground at his feet and looked at her. "What happened there?"

"I don't know," Mabel said. "I went into the barn and found the wheelbarrow smoking. There's garlic underneath the sweatshirt." Her poor, beloved, comfy hoodie. It was going to take years to get another one that soft through repeated wearings and washings.

"Never heard of garlic spontaneously combusting before," he said. "But I've bought a number of farms at literal fire sales, and I remember one of them burned down after damp hay overheated when it began to break down. Maybe that's what happened here. Except with garlic."

"I suppose it's possible." She had her doubts though. Rory had taught her about the importance of drying of the garlic after harvest, not so much to prevent fires but to make sure it would store well. Dampness led to decomposition, which ruined the crop, and it did also lead to heat, as Porter said, which at least theoretically could lead to fire. But Mabel had followed the drying instructions carefully, and she was sure she'd have heard from Rory if it hadn't been done properly.

The timing of the fire was suspicious, too, happening right when the cats had been disturbed by something, or someone, causing them to race out of the barn. She didn't think they'd simply been reacting to the smoke, which had barely begun to waft out of the wheelbarrow when she noticed it, and that had been several minutes after they'd run away. If they'd been sleeping as they usually were at this time of day, she doubted they would even have noticed the earliest wisps of smoke that would have existed when they'd been spooked.

No, Mabel was convinced that someone had been inside the barn, disturbing the cats' naps, and starting the fire. He'd disappeared before she'd arrived, probably slipping out the small back door that faced Emily's property.

But why? To convince her to sell the farm? As Porter himself had admitted, it wouldn't be the first time he'd managed to buy property after a fire had reduced its value. Had he simply taken advantage of an accident, or had he created the damage himself?

She shivered and wasn't sure if it was from nerves or from the chilly air on her uncovered arms. She wished she could go inside, but she had to get rid of Porter first. She wasn't about to invite him inside, not when she suspected him of arson, to go along with his attempted fraud.

"I appreciate the help, but why are you here?" Mabel rubbed her arms for warmth.

"I wanted to talk to you about your decision not to sell the farm," Porter said. "Why don't we go inside, where I can explain everything."

"I don't think we should be discussing the deal without my broker here."

"That rule is just for parties to a lawsuit. They can't talk to each other without their lawyers present. But we're not in some kind of court battle. We're just trying to come up with a mutually beneficial deal. A nice little conversation among friends who can help each other out."

"I'm not looking for new friends," Mabel said through chattering teeth. "And I'm not going to sell the farm to a developer. Not now, not ever."

"You might not have a choice." Porter nodded in the direction of the barn. "Nothing's guaranteed in this world. That fire could have been a lot worse. Most barns go up in flames in moments, before anyone notices, and by the time the firefighters arrive, there's nothing they can do to stop it."

He turned to look in the other direction. "Not much distance between the barn and your home. If the barn burns, the house will too."

Mabel's shivering increased, and this time she was sure it wasn't from the cold air. "Fortunately, the fire was caught quickly."

"This time," he said. "Why not cut your losses and sell now before anything else can go wrong?"

"I'll take my chances. I'm not in that much of a hurry to sell, and the property's fully insured." At least, she hoped it was. Her aunt had been cutting some financial corners before she died, and Mabel hadn't paid much attention to the insurance, just paying the renewal invoice when it came due without looking at the extent of coverage. "Even if everything burned down and I lost everything, I still wouldn't sell to you. Nothing personal, but I want the land to remain agricultural."

"I could—"

"No." Mabel held up her hand. "I'm not listening. I'm going inside, and you're leaving."

Porter gave her a long look before nodding. "I'll go, but you're going to regret this."

She let him have the last word, turning her back on him and forcing herself to walk slowly and deliberately to the kitchen door without breaking into a run like her instincts insisted.

Chapter 14

Inside, Mabel found Pixie sitting on the kitchen windowsill, glaring at where Porter's SUV was turning around.

"You're going to get fat from all the treats you earned today." Mabel opened a cabinet to retrieve the bag of pricey kibble that the local vet said most cats found addictive and then dropped three pieces in front of Pixie. "I just wish you could tell me who was in the barn when you yowled."

Pixie silently gobbled up her treats before turning pleading eyes on Mabel. "Okay, three more pieces, but that's it for now. There will be more though if Thomas Porter gets anywhere near the farm again and you warn me about it."

Mabel put away the bag of treats and called the mayor. He didn't answer, so she left him a message that he needed to do more to get Porter to accept that the deal was off. She considered sharing her suspicion that Porter had started the fire in order to show up in the nick of time to be her savior, with respect to both the flames and taking the farm off her hands. She didn't have any real evidence against him, at least not related to the fire, so she hung up without mentioning it.

Emily might have seen something to confirm Mabel's suspicions, so she tried calling her. There was no answer, which meant she was probably outside working with the goats. She usually turned the phone off so the animals could have her full attention.

After a quick trip upstairs to check on Billie Jean—still eating and glaring—and to get her second most favorite hoodie, which had just graduated to first favorite, Mabel headed next door. She found Emily coming through the gate from the back field.

"What's up?" Emily asked.

"I was wondering if you'd seen anything strange on my property in the last hour or so."

"Sorry." Emily shook the gate to make sure it was latched securely behind her. "I've been out back with the goats all morning. I can't see or hear anything from your property from there."

"What about smell?"

"When I'm working with the goats, all I can smell is *parfum de chevre*. Actually, the does don't have much odor. It's just the bucks that do, but they stink enough for everyone." Emily frowned. "Why? What should I have smelled?"

"Nothing, I guess. But there was a little fire in the barn. Some garlic heads in a wheelbarrow caught fire."

Emily gasped. "A fire? What happened? How did I miss the fire engines? I should have been able to hear the sirens even if I were in the farthest corner of the field and all the goats were bleating."

"There weren't any sirens. The situation wasn't that bad. I was able to get the wheelbarrow out of the barn and put out the fire myself."

"What did the police say?"

"They don't know about it."

"You need to tell them," Emily said. "It could be related to Graham's death."

"More likely it was just a natural bit of combustion," Mabel said, although she was relieved that someone else thought it was suspicious. "It's just that the cats were acting weird, running out of the barn when they should have been napping. That's why I found the smoking garlic so quickly. I went into the barn to check on what had spooked them and instead found the fire."

"Did you ever figure out why the cats ran?"

"No. That's why I wondered if you'd noticed anything out of the ordinary," Mabel said. "You'll probably think I'm crazy, and I'm sure the police would laugh if I told them, but Thomas Porter, the guy who wants to buy the farm, arrived right as I was putting out the fire, and I can't help wondering if he might have set it."

"Why would he do that?" Emily asked.

"I turned down his offer to buy the farm, and he's not taking no for an answer. At least not graciously. It felt like he was threatening to burn everything down if I wouldn't sell to him."

"What if the fire wasn't a threat but a warning?"

"A warning about what?" Mabel said. "That I shouldn't leave imperfect garlic in a wheelbarrow where people can set it on fire?"

"No," Emily said. "That you shouldn't be poking around in the circumstances of Graham's death."

"If the fire was intended to convince me to leave the murder investigation to the police, it wasn't a very effective message," Mabel said. "Someone needs to learn to use his words instead of acting out."

"Not everyone can do that." Emily reached out and would have pulled Mabel into a hug if she hadn't stepped back. Emily settled for taking Mabel's hand and patting it for emphasis. "Just promise me you'll be careful. A fire, even if it's quickly put out—*especially* if it's quickly put out—can be a sign that a person is facing other dangers and needs to take extra precautions."

"I've never been a risk-taker," Mabel said. "I'm not doing anything crazy, just trying to figure out who, besides me, might have a motive for killing Graham. It's not like I'm planning to hang out in a haunted house or go anywhere isolated. I've just been to Graham's brother-in-law's place of business where there are at least a hundred employees, and Graham's greenhouse, where the next-door neighbor is probably taking detailed notes about my every move."

"She didn't see whoever killed Graham," Emily reminded her. "Otherwise the killer would have been arrested already."

Mabel hadn't thought about what that implied. "That's suspicious in itself, isn't it? She should have noticed if anyone visited Graham the morning he died. She confronted me about the subdivision's parking rules within a very few minutes of my arrival, and she called a tow truck even faster when Sandy Faitakis parked on the street."

"If you go back there, you should take someone with you, just to be on the safe side," Emily said. "The omens right now are better for joint endeavors than for solo ones."

Mabel didn't believe in omens, but she did believe in personal responsibility. "It's my job, not anyone else's. I'm the one who committed to caring for Graham's rhubarb. I'm even thinking about buying some of the plants. Did Aunt Peggy ever tell you she wanted to plant a field of rhubarb? I found it in her journal. She even mapped it out. I thought adding that field might make the property more appealing to a buyer. What do you think?"

"I think that would be perfect."

"You're not just saying that, because it was Aunt Peggy's idea, and she was your friend so you want to be loyal to her?"

"Why would you think that?"

"I'm just not sure what the market is for rhubarb, and I haven't had time to research it. I've never even eaten it, and when I met Sandy Faitakis, she admitted it's not very popular. That's why she's trying to breed a different variety that people would like better."

"Lots of good plants aren't terribly popular here in the US," Emily said. "That's starting to change though as more people get interested in foods that grow well locally so they don't have to be shipped long distances. Rhubarb can thrive in climates and environments where other edible plants are harder to grow."

"I remember Aunt Peggy used to make stewed rhubarb a lot, but I never tried it. I found the recipe in her journal along with one for rhubarb crisp that sounded more appealing. Anything covered with a streusel topping can't be all bad. Maybe I should make it before I commit to growing a whole field of rhubarb."

"It's too late in the year to find any fresh rhubarb for cooking, and I can't think of anywhere you could get it frozen. And don't get me started on canned rhubarb in sugar syrup." Emily shuddered. "But one of the farmers' market vendors makes amazing rhubarb jams. Next time I see her, I'll ask if she has any for sale, so you can try it."

"Thanks."

"But in return, you have to promise me you won't go to Graham's greenhouse alone. Not until the killer is caught."

"It isn't fair for me to drag people away from their own work to help me."

"You wouldn't have to drag them," Emily said. "I bet Charlie Durbin would love to spend more time with you."

Everyone's a matchmaker, Mabel thought, surprising herself with how little it annoyed her. "He already offered."

Emily's face lit up. "Really? That's wonderful. He's a really good person, and he's got such a crush on you, but I didn't think he'd ever make a move. You two would make a great couple. Your aunt would have been so thrilled for her niece and her friend to be together, and you could both settle down here on her farm."

So Charlie *had* been flirting with her, Mabel thought. "I'm not going to date anyone just because my aunt would have liked it, and I'm certainly not settling down with someone for that reason."

"I suppose marriage is a bigger commitment than protecting your aunt's farm," Emily said. "But you should at least consider getting to know Charlie better. And definitely take him up on his offer to be your bodyguard until Graham's killer is arrested."

"That may take weeks or even months, and Charlie's got to be busy, getting his construction projects done before winter. Besides, I don't want to give him the wrong idea about our having a future together. I'm still planning to go back to Maine as soon as the farm sells."

"If you don't want to take Charlie with you to the greenhouse, at least take someone else," Emily said. "I'll even do it if you want."

"Thanks, but you've got your own work to do. I'm sure I can come up with someone else."

On her way back to the farm, Mabel considered who that might be. She didn't know that many people in West Slocum, even fewer who might be willing and able to visit Graham's greenhouse with her. Then she remembered Terry Earley, the college student who'd been part of the crew harvesting the garlic in July, and had signed up to do the fall planting too. Maybe he would accompany her to the greenhouse. She could pay him for his time, and he might actually know something about rhubarb, since he was majoring in agriculture. Terry would have a useful role, helping with the watering, instead of wasting his time standing around looking fierce when the worst thing that might actually happen was harassment by the next-door neighbor for breaking obscure homeowners' association rules.

* * * *

Mabel texted Terry to see if he had some time available to help her at the greenhouse. While she was waiting for his response, she fed Pixie and Billie Jean, and then settled down to study Graham's journal again, hoping she could break the encryption and find some new leads to his murder there.

A few minutes later, she finally got a message from the friend she was counting on to break the code. She settled in the kitchen with a glass of iced tea and her laptop to see if his suggestion would do the trick. She quickly found the pattern and was able to make sense of a whole sentence. Translating the rest would be time-consuming work. It would have been so much easier if Graham had typed his journal into a computer document and she could apply an algorithm to translate it. Then she could have had the entire book decoded in just seconds. But Graham had been old school, handwriting his journal, so she would have to do the decoding manually. She could try scanning it and applying an optical character reader to it, but that would probably just introduce errors.

The first page of the journal was dated January of the current year, but Mabel was more interested in recent entries. She turned to the last one, near the back of the book. It was dated the day before Graham had died. She started painstakingly translating the entry's two pages of coded letters into words. After just a few lines, it was apparent that, like Aunt Peggy, he hadn't limited his notes to information about his breeding program but had included tidbits about his personal life and the people he interacted with. Unfortunately, even after translating the words, Mabel couldn't make much sense of them. They were rambling, more word salad than coherent observations. On top of that, there was yet another layer of obfuscation. Graham mentioned people he interacted with, including those he was angry with and presumably were angry with him, but he always used nicknames instead of their real names, like a code within a code. Perhaps it was a way of accommodating his legal training, since he couldn't be sued for libel if no one knew for sure who, for example, "the Enforcer" was when he made derogatory comments about the person. Mabel assumed it was the next-door neighbor, Lena, but she wouldn't be able to prove it in a court of law.

Maybe Graham had included context earlier on in the journal that would make it obvious who the Enforcer was. Mabel flipped back toward the beginning of the volume until she found a date that translated to March, and began decrypting the entries. The first one was considerably more coherent than the later entry, with fewer word salads. Graham still used nicknames for the people in his life, but there was at least one she thought she understood: Bad Brother. Since Graham was an only child, it probably referred to his wife's brother, Rob Robinson.

Apparently Robinson had loaned Graham some money, and then became unreasonable—according to Graham, at least—in demanding repayment right when he was on the cusp of finally achieving his goal of establishing a rhubarb hybrid that would revolutionize the industry and be named after his wife. Graham had grown frustrated with having to explain that he needed just a little more time, and then they would both profit from the Carolina variety of rhubarb becoming the new standard.

Robinson hadn't mentioned any loans when Mabel had talked to him. Assuming the money was still outstanding, it gave him a motive for murder, separate from any inheritance he or his children might get. He could file a claim against the estate and get paid when the farmhouse was sold. As long as Graham had been alive, it seemed unlikely that the loan would ever have been paid, given the deteriorating state of both the farmhouse and Graham's mental capacity. Could Robinson have been desperate enough for repayment that he'd have killed his brother-in-law?

Mabel would have to go back to his office and ask him. First, though, she wanted to see if the journal had more information about the loan and also about the Enforcer, and whether she might have been inclined to kill someone who wouldn't follow her rules.

She resumed the slow process of decoding the pages until Pixie warned her of the arrival of a visitor. Mabel had lost track of time while hunched over the journal, and it was almost six o'clock. It was just as well someone had come to interrupt her, or she'd still be hunched over the journal at midnight, having forgotten to eat.

She stretched on the way to the kitchen window to see who'd arrived. Rory was just getting out of her truck and would soon see the wheelbarrow that hadn't yet been emptied of its charred contents. Perhaps Rory would know if it was possible for the garlic to have spontaneously combusted or if it would have needed a little help—from Porter or someone else—to catch fire.

Rory was peering at the contents of the wheelbarrow, her confusion obvious even from a distance as Mabel hurried over to join her. "Have you been experimenting with new ways to roast garlic without using an oven?"

"No," Mabel said. "Although now I wish it wasn't covered with fire retardant. If I hadn't been in such a panic to put out the fire, I'd have transferred the garlic to a pot to roast it."

"Then how'd it catch on fire?"

"I was hoping you'd know," Mabel said. "Thomas Porter said it might have been spontaneous, like damp hay that heats up when it composts."

"I suppose it's possible, in theory, since organic materials need to be damp in order to break down, and it's that breakdown that releases enough heat to potentially cause a fire," Rory said. "I'm not buying it though. It certainly never happened in all the years that Peggy grew garlic. She was pretty inexperienced in the beginning, so she might not have dried the crop as well as she should have, and she lost some garlic to decomposition, but there weren't any fires. I know you dried everything properly this year, so there's no way it could have spontaneously combusted."

"I was afraid of that," Mabel said. "Someone must have started it on purpose. But who?"

"Someone who wants you to sell the farm," Rory said without hesitation. "I heard you canceled the deal with Porter, because he was going to turn it into ugly houses. My money's on him having a motive for arson."

"Mine too," Mabel said. "But I can't prove it."

"Did the fire change your mind about selling? To Porter or anyone else? I tried calling your attorney in Maine to make sure he was keeping an eye on the situation, but I got a message that his voicemail box was full."

"I'll ask him to call you when I get in touch with him," Mabel said. "But don't worry. I wouldn't sell to Porter even if the farm burned to the ground, and I told him as much."

"I hope he believed you and doesn't try to test you," Rory said. "You should double-check the smoke detectors in the farmhouse. If whoever started the first fire tries again and the barn burns down, the house isn't very far away. I hate that you're all alone out here. I'd offer to come stay with you, but my husband's been filling in on night shifts recently, and I can't leave my daughter alone overnight."

"I'll be fine on my own." Mabel hadn't lived with anyone since her grandparents had died shortly after she'd finished her master's degree. Even sharing her space with Pixie and Billie Jean was something of an adjustment for her. Having another human being around all the time, forcing her to be quiet during her peak work hours after midnight, and then waking her up in the morning, wasn't something she wanted to experience. Especially not right now, when she was already dealing with the fallout from Graham's death, plus making plans for the garlic planting and starting a rhubarb field.

"Are you sure you don't want someone to stay with you?" Rory asked. "Maybe Emily could come over until her husband gets home. She could probably use the companionship herself. He's been gone longer than usual and won't be home for another week yet."

"I'm not a very good housemate with my late hours," Mabel said. "Besides, Emily knows about the fire and my suspicions, so I'm sure she'll be keeping an extra eye on me."

"I guess that will have to do," Rory conceded. "But I'll mention it to my husband, too, before he goes to work tonight. Perhaps he can arrange for a patrol car to drive by occasionally."

"Thanks." Mabel liked her privacy, but she also believed in reasonable precautions. "So what are you here for?"

"Just wanted to see how you were doing with hiring help for the garlic planting. My daughter isn't terribly enthusiastic about the prospect, and I was hoping you'd heard from her friends from the summer harvest."

"I did. Terry Earley and Anna Johnson have both signed up to help with the planting. And a few other students have expressed interest."

"That's a relief. I was planning to tell Dawn she had to work it if she wanted to stay out late for a Halloween party she's been invited to, but now I won't have to face all the moaning and groaning about my being the mean mom. She'll want to see Terry and Anna again."

"There may be some more work too. I'm definitely going to try to buy some of Graham's plants to start a rhubarb field. I just need to look at my aunt's journal notes on where they would do well."

Rory nodded. "I remember your aunt talking about it a year or two ago."

"Graham's brother-in-law, Rob Robinson, seems willing to sell them, assuming he's Graham's heir, but Sandy Faitakis might try to steal them out from under me. She showed up at the greenhouse when I was there, and I couldn't tell if she wanted the plants or the breeding program data."

"I've seen Graham's greenhouse," Rory said. "Even if Sandy wants the plants, she doesn't have enough space for all of them. I don't even know what Graham thought he was going to do with all those seedlings once they outgrew their starter cells. He'd need ten times the size of his yard to plant all of them."

"I can say for sure that he wasn't thinking very logically in the last few weeks," Mabel said. "I found his journals in the greenhouse, and I was hoping the most recent one would tell me what needed to be done to keep his seedlings healthy. I haven't found any useful information yet, but I've barely started to read it. He encrypted it and it's slow going to translate it. The latest entry was a whole bunch of gibberish that almost sounded like dreams with surreal elements. He talked about going to a party with his wife, who was somehow alive again, and she was yelling at the Enforcer, who I think is his neighbor, Lena Shaw, when the Broker, who's probably the mayor, interrupted to say he and the Enforcer were getting married. Does any of that make sense to you?"

"Sounds like a nightmare to me," Rory said. "And nothing that would happen in real life. Graham's wife never even knew Lena. She came to West Slocum from somewhere in New York, I think, when someone she knew through her real estate brokerage company bought the property to develop the subdivision and she decided to retire. And Graham's wife wouldn't have yelled at anyone. Carolina was a strong woman, but she got things done through her quiet competence, not by shouting at anyone."

"What about Danny and Lena as a couple?"

Rory laughed. "Seriously? Everyone's pretty sure that Danny is gay, or perhaps just not interested in sex. He might be in Lena's pocket, based on some substantial campaign contributions she's given him, but I can't imagine any sort of personal relationship between them."

"I couldn't imagine it either, but I'm not very good at noticing that sort of thing."

"You know," Rory said, "the dream makes a little sense if you look at it metaphorically."

"I never look at anything metaphorically."

"What I mean is, Graham could have seen Lena and Danny as being 'married' in the sense of being united against him. I know from my husband that Lena liked to call the station to complain about Graham, and if they wouldn't do anything, then she'd call the mayor, and he'd arrange for the police to send someone out. Joe made a few of those visits himself."

"Looking at it that way makes a lot more sense to me than a personal relationship between Danny and Lena."

"Definitely." Rory nodded. "Did Graham mention anyone else in his journal who might have had a reason to kill him? The police may want to take a look at it now that you've decoded it."

"I've just done a few pages," Mabel said. "The only people he's mentioned there besides the Enforcer and the Broker were the Brother, who's probably Rob Robinson, and the Professor, who I think is Sandy Faitakis."

"That's probably everyone Graham interacted with, other than his clients," Rory said. "Ever since his wife died, he pretty much kept to himself outside of work."

"I'm not entirely sure the journal is going to be helpful. The most recent entries didn't make much sense. I wonder if it's because he was eating the rhubarb leaves and it affected his ability to think straight. Do you remember when he first started talking about edible leaves?"

"Less than a year ago, but I'm not sure exactly when. Best guess is about six months ago."

"So around April?"

"That sounds right," Rory said. "I know it was before the CSA started up with its deliveries again in May. He didn't want to participate this year, claiming he didn't have time. He mentioned then that he'd been experimenting with eating the leaves, but other than the craziness of the statement itself, he didn't seem particularly unbalanced. Not like he was when you met him on Sunday night."

"I haven't gotten to the April entries in the journal yet," Mabel said. "I'm still in March."

"My husband would say you should hand the journal over to O'Connor and let him finish translating it."

"I'm afraid he won't bother," Mabel said. "But I suppose you're right. I'll take it to him first thing tomorrow."

But not before she made a digital copy for herself in case O'Connor didn't consider it worth reading. She couldn't trust him to do it, not when her freedom was at stake.

Chapter 15

After Rory left, Mabel had dinner and took care of the cats. Billie Jean was still wolfing down more than what the instructions on the kibble bag said was a regular daily intake for a cat of her size. Of course, she was eating for five or six, so maybe her appetite was normal in the circumstances.

Mabel spent the evening alternately scanning the journal and decoding a few pages. The copying was monotonous work, so there was still a handful of pages left to scan when she went to bed. She finished them the next morning right after feeding the cats.

As soon as those chores were done, she called Jeff Wright's assistant at her direct office number, but the line was busy. Mabel kept trying every few minutes while she made and ate breakfast, but continued to get the busy tone. She tried the main office number, too, but no one picked up and the voicemail box was full, so she couldn't leave a message.

She couldn't delay going to the police station any longer, so she drove into town to deliver Graham's journal. According to the young male officer at the front desk, O'Connor was at Graham's office, searching it with the detective from the state police.

"What do you think of her?" Mabel asked. "The visiting detective, I mean."

"Deanna Cross?" The young officer chuckled. "The name's easy to remember. She's definitely not anyone you'd ever want to cross."

"Have they found anything useful?"

"All I can say is that the department is following all leads and they expect to have an arrest in due course."

It had already been four days since the murder with no arrest, so Mabel had to wonder about their definition of "in due course." Jeff Wright had frequently told her that the legal system, including law enforcement, had a more leisurely view of time than most people did, but surely in the context of a murder, there would be pressure to move quickly. The delay in making an arrest suggested to Mabel that the investigation wasn't going well.

"I understand," Mabel said. "I'm not here to get you into any trouble. I've got something O'Connor and Cross might be interested in."

She showed the young man the journal and explained that it had belonged to Graham, that it was encrypted, but that she'd left the key to translating it inside the book, and O'Connor had her contact info if he had any questions. The officer politely insisted on taking her phone number and address again, and then promised to pass the book along to the detectives as soon as they returned.

On the way back to the car, Mabel's phone pinged with a text from the agriculture student, Terry Earley. He had classes until one o'clock, but he could help at the greenhouse after that if she could pick him up at the university. The only other commitment she had that day was a meeting at three o'clock at the farm that Emily had arranged with Betty Comstock, the woman who made jam for the farmers' market. It shouldn't take more than two hours to get Terry, take care of the rhubarb, and then get back to the farm, so she texted back that she'd pick him up as soon as his classes ended.

She had about ninety minutes before she needed to leave to get Terry. It was too little time to make it worth her while to go back to the farm and dispose of the fire-retardant-covered garlic that had been left to cool overnight, but she could squeeze in a visit to Rob Robinson if he was in his office. This time, she was able to call ahead and confirm with his assistant that he was there and had a few minutes to talk to her.

The assistant let her into the private office where Rob Robinson was on the phone, but he gestured for her to take a seat across the desk from him.

He hung up a moment later. "I've been making the final arrangements for Graham all morning. The aftermath of a death is more complicated than I ever realized. Graham took care of everything when my sister died, and my parents had pre-arranged everything for themselves, so I never had to deal with funeral homes before. Or all the other details. I was just talking to a tow company to pick up Graham's vehicles and put them in storage so there will be one less thing for his neighbor to complain about."

Robinson seemed truly overwhelmed, and a bit irritated by how much work he had to do for Graham, not like someone who was benefiting from the death of his brother-in-law.

"I'm sorry," Mabel said.

"I don't have time for this. I'm up for a promotion, and it's like Graham is once again sabotaging my life, even from the grave." Robinson wiped his hand over his face and emerged with a half-hearted smile. "Anyway. That's not your problem. So what can I do for you today?"

"Before I spend too much time on the rhubarb plants, I want to be sure you'll be able to sell them to me eventually. The police won't tell me anything, but I was wondering if you'd heard about whether they've found a will."

"They called about half an hour ago to say they had what seemed to be the most recent will, although it's more than ten years old," Robinson said. "They read the relevant sections to me, and it's the same one I have a copy of, naming me the estate's personal representative, but leaving everything to my kids. So you can rest easy about the plants. I'll make sure you get whatever you want from the greenhouse. I thought about it after you left, and I realized the only thing worse than the mess Graham made of his life because of his obsession with his breeding program would be if the fruits of his work were wasted, so it was all for nothing."

"You still may not have any say in who gets the plants if there are creditors who claim all of the assets."

"I'm probably his biggest creditor," Robinson said. "I paid for the greenhouses, and Graham signed a promissory note and mortgage to me, with my kids' assent as the beneficiaries of the trust. He hadn't paid much on it in years, so the balance is probably more than his assets are worth by now."

If there was a mortgage, Rob Robinson could have foreclosed and forced a sale of the property during Graham's lifetime. At least, Mabel thought he could have. Normally, she'd have asked Jeff Wright, but that wasn't an option right now.

"Why didn't you foreclose when he stopped paying?" Mabel asked. "Then you wouldn't have had to deal with him any longer."

"I threatened to foreclose plenty of times, and he'd make one payment, but that was all for the next year or two until I pressured him again." Robinson smiled ruefully. "I've got a business reputation for being tough, but it's different with family, even an in-law. He knew I wouldn't foreclose on him, because it would feel too much like betraying my sister. I didn't really need the money, just wanted to use the leverage to make him see reality. When the threats of foreclosure didn't work, I even considered having him hospitalized for observation of his mental status. Now I wish I'd done it. I could have been appointed his guardian and made sure he was taken care of."

If everything Robinson said was true, and he seemed sincere, he really didn't have a motive for killing his brother-in-law. At least not a financial one. He wouldn't have needed to commit murder in order to control or inherit the assets. If Robinson had killed his brother-in-law, it had to have been for more personal reasons.

"If you had become his guardian, he might still be alive."

"Trust me, I know," he said. "I realized it in the middle of last night and didn't sleep much after that. My only consolation is that he'd have hated me for it and wouldn't have considered his life worth living if he couldn't pursue his breeding program. It would have been like losing his wife all over again for him."

"So who do you think killed him?"

"That's the other thing that kept me awake last night," he said. "Usually I sleep like a baby, but I couldn't stop thinking about who could have hated him that much. I mean, he could be annoying, but enough to make someone kill him? I don't think so. Even in his most delusional moments, he usually knew when he was pushing too hard and he'd back down. And I can't see who would benefit from his death. My kids don't need the house, assuming it isn't sold to pay his debts. They're in college, and I don't expect them to come back to live in West Slocum after they graduate. So despite what my sister was hoping, I expect the property will be sold now and not kept in the family for future generations."

"The police seem to be focused on Graham's clients as potential suspects."

"That's as likely as any other theory," Robinson said. "The only other person I could think of last night was Sandy Faitakis. She's an academic with an interest in rhubarb. And an even greater interest in vodka. Graham told me she'd been making a nuisance of herself, trying to get him to sell her the hybrids he was developing, so who knows what she might have done while under the influence."

"How bad is her drinking problem?"

"I don't know her personally, but I remember Graham showing me a newspaper article about her being arrested for driving drunk six or seven years ago. It was quite a scandal, what with her being a professor and all. She's expected to be a good role model for her students or she could lose her job. The university apparently decided to give her a second chance. She was ordered to undergo counseling, and she must have done it since she's still employed, but alcoholics frequently relapse."

Maybe Robinson was onto something. If Sandy had a serious drinking problem, and she was as obsessed with her breeding program as Graham had been, she might well have gone on an all-night bender, culminating with an alcohol-fueled plan to make a final offer for the plants while Graham did his early-morning chores in the greenhouse. Then they'd argued, and with her inhibitions suppressed by the alcohol, she'd become enraged and killed him with his own knife. He'd been stabbed from behind, with no obvious signs of a struggle, so being female and smaller than her victim wouldn't be as limiting as if it had been a frontal attack.

The scenario even explained the rhubarb leaves in Graham's mouth. Initially Mabel had thought that Graham had eaten them voluntarily as part of his theory that they were healthy, but if he'd been killed because of the rhubarb, and the killer hadn't been thinking too clearly, then it made sense that the killer might have angrily thrown them at him after Graham died. A warped kind of sense, at least, the kind that would appeal to a person whose mind was clouded by alcohol.

* * * *

Mabel left Robinson's office thinking she needed to find out more about Sandy Faitakis and her possible drinking problem. Maybe Terry Earley would know something about it from university gossip.

Terry brought up the subject of Sandy Faitakis without any nudging as soon as he'd lowered his tall, skinny self and his laptop backpack into the Mini Cooper and clicked the seatbelt into place. "I stopped in to see Professor Faitakis after class," he said in his British accent. "I'd heard she was trying to breed the perfect rhubarb variety, and I thought she could give me a few pointers on rhubarb cultivation."

"I met her the other day, but she wasn't particularly helpful," Mabel said. "How well do you know her?"

"Not at all really," Terry admitted. "Just what's in her bio on the university's website. It mentions her work with rhubarb. I've never actually taken a class with her and I don't know anyone who has."

"What did she tell you?"

He shrugged. "She kinda brushed me off. I explained that I'd be helping out at Graham's greenhouse and didn't know much about rhubarb so I could use some advice. She said she was too busy to give me a comprehensive lecture, and she'd never been inside Graham's greenhouse, so she really didn't know enough about what he was working on to pinpoint what I needed to know."

Mabel had gotten the impression from Rob Robinson that Sandy had been to Graham's property several times to try to get him to sell to her, but perhaps those conversations had happened somewhere else, possibly his law office, rather than at his home.

"I appreciate your trying to help," Mabel said. "I'm sure we can muddle along on our own with some help from Google." "It's strange though." Terry fidgeted with the zipper of his backpack. "Students talk about professors all the time, and everyone knows who on the faculty is too busy with their research to care about their students and spend time with them, even on extracurricular matters. I'd never heard that she was one of the unavailable ones."

"She may have just been having a bad day."

"I suppose," Terry said. "I still think it's weird how she wouldn't help at all. I mean, most of the faculty like to talk about their research, at least in general terms, not the confidential stuff. And they hardly ever get the chance to talk about it to an eager audience instead of a student who's kind of required to listen even when they're not interested, so I figured if I asked for the basics of rhubarb cultivation, she'd be happy to share her passion for it."

"She could just have been busy and you caught her at a bad time."

"I don't think that was it," Terry said, giving the backpack's poor zipper a strenuous tug for emphasis. "I don't care how busy I am, if you ask me about my interest in diversification as the key to small farm prosperity, I'm going to drop everything else I need to do and tell you far, far more than you ever wanted to know about it. Worst-case scenario, if I really don't have time, I'm going to give you a list of at least ten resources you absolutely, positively have to read right away and then I'd make sure I had your contact info so I could follow up with you later and grill you on your reading."

Mabel would do the same thing, she thought, except about app development, not agriculture. "Did Sandy give you any advice at all?"

"She just told me I shouldn't get too attached to Graham's plants, because I wouldn't be able to keep them." Terry gave the zipper another irritated tug. "Like she was my mother, telling me I couldn't adopt a puppy or something."

"I'd let you adopt some of the plants if you do get attached to them," Mabel assured him. "Graham's brother-in-law will decide who gets them, and he's promised I can have whatever I want from the greenhouse. And unlike Sandy, I'm willing to share."

"She doesn't think you'll be able to buy any of them from the estate," Terry said. "She told me there was some sort of agreement already in place between her and Graham, but she shut the door in my face before I could get any details."

"I don't think she really wants the plants all that much, or at least not the bulk of them," Mabel said as she turned onto Graham's street. "She might be interested in a few specific seedlings, but for the most part, I got the impression she was mostly interested in Graham's journals. He kept really detailed records on his work."

Terry nodded. "That sounds about right. For a breeder, data can be worth more than gold or even compost."

That reminded Mabel she needed to figure out what to do about replacing the yard waste they'd planned to use to mulch the garlic, but had abandoned because of Graham. Rory might have some ideas. She'd probably want to go to some other pesticide-free neighborhoods to collect their lawn clippings and leaves, now that they didn't have to worry about Graham's interference, but Mabel didn't think that was wise. There was too much risk that the late-night activity would bring them to the police's attention, and they'd think Mabel—or, even worse, Rory—had committed murder in order to have free access to the best composting mulch materials.

Mabel parked in front of Graham's house, out of sight of the neighbor, where there was no risk of being towed. Terry left his backpack in the car and followed her along the sidewalk.

"I really appreciate your coming out here with me," Mabel said. "If you've got some time available over the next few weeks, I'd like to hire you to stop by here and check on things for me."

"I can always use the cash, and I'd love to learn more about an amateur breeder's work. My mornings are taken up with classes, starting early, but my afternoon commitments can be moved around pretty easily."

"Perfect." Mabel paused at the foot of the driveway that was still completely filled with Graham's vehicles. Robinson probably hadn't been in as much of a rush to have them towed away as Lena would have been if she'd had the chance. "If you come here without me, make sure to park where I did, not inside the subdivision or the homeowners' association will tow your truck."

"Good luck with that," Terry said with a laugh. "My truck is so old, none of the tow companies will touch it for fear of it crumbling into bits and them getting blamed for it. Some of the reason I need the extra work is to get the brakes looked at."

"As long as I own the farm, you've got part-time work whenever you want it," Mabel said. "That may be longer than I'd like, but at least I can help you out a bit in the meantime. I thought I had a buyer, but he turned out to be a developer, and I'm not going to let anyone dig up my aunt's legacy."

"It's hard to come up with the money to buy a farm these days, especially a small one, since so few of them actually turn a profit," Terry said. "It's why I'm so interested in diversification on farms. Your aunt did some of that, but there's more that could be done with the property."

"Aunt Peggy talked about the importance of diversification in her journal," Mabel said. "Did you inspire her?"

"I wish I could claim responsibility, but I never met her."

"I'll show you her journal sometime, and we can talk about what you think would improve the farm's value if you wouldn't mind." Mabel led the way up the driveway to the greenhouse. She unlocked the door and propped it open, pushing aside a length of sidewall support that had tumbled down from the pile of rusty and bent metal pieces. "I'm thinking about adding a field of rhubarb with Graham's seedlings."

"That would be great," Terry said eagerly. "I'd have to research the rhubarb market, but that would probably be a good next step. The only thing I know for starters is that it's harvested earlier than either the garlic or the squash you've already got in place, so that would make it a good fit."

Mabel knew that spreading out the peak work was good for diversification, but until she sold the farm, it also meant more weeks when she'd be completely absorbed in agricultural chores, with no time left for her real job, the one she was as passionate about as Terry was about farming. "My boss is going to fire me if I can't get back to work fairly soon."

"You could always hire a manager," Terry said. "There are people who'd love to own a farm but can't scrape together the money or financing for the land. Managing someone else's property is the next best thing to owning the place, especially if there's an option to buy down the road."

"I'll think about it," Mabel said. "After I know for sure that I'll be able to buy Graham's plants." And not be locked up in jail.

Chapter 16

It took about an hour to get the greenhouse plants watered, and then Mabel forced herself to walk past where Graham's body had lain, to go out that door with Terry and wander through the beds in the back yard to see if there were any obvious problems there. The plants looked sickly to Mabel, but Terry said they were sending all their energy into the roots for overwintering. That meant she'd have to wait until the spring to transplant the seedlings in the greenhouse to her farm. Rhubarb transplanted in the fall would waste too much energy on adjusting to the new location and not survive the winter.

On their way back through the greenhouses to leave, they passed the metal file cabinet holding Graham's notebooks. Given what Terry had said about how valuable his records might be to a breeder, and Sandy's obvious covetousness of the data in them, Mabel decided to pack them up and bring them to someone for safekeeping. Terry offered her the use of his backpack and ran back to the car to get it.

After it was filled with Graham's notebooks and they were heading back to the car, they found Lena Shaw waiting for them on the sidewalk at the edge of the driveway with her arms crossed over her chest and one foot tapping the concrete impatiently. Mabel sent Terry on ahead to the car. Bosses were supposed to cushion their employees from having to deal with annoying people like Lena, after all. That kind of protection was one of the main reasons why Mabel continued to work for Phil Reed instead of going freelance, and she owed the same consideration to her own employee.

"Who is he?" Lena demanded with a glare at the departing young man.

"His name is Terry Earley," Mabel said. "He works for me, and he'll be helping take care of the rhubarb. Just until everything gets settled with the estate, as we discussed."

"You didn't tell me about strangers coming onto the property and taking things out of the greenhouse," Lena said. "I can't do my job if I don't know all the details. You'd been in there for long enough today that I thought something might have happened to you. Especially in light of Graham's death."

"I'm fine." Mabel wanted to ask Lena if she didn't have anything better to do with her life than to spy on her neighbors. Or perhaps to ask how it was, given how much Lena apparently knew about Graham's daily routine, she hadn't caught a glimpse of his killer either arriving or leaving. Pointed questions would only upset the woman though, and Mabel needed her goodwill or the police would rescind their permission for her to visit the greenhouses to take care of the plants. She settled for saying, "It's good to know someone's keeping a close eye on the property while it's unoccupied." She truly was grateful for that, especially after the incident with the fire in her wheelbarrow. If anyone tried to damage Graham's property, Lena would notice before everything was destroyed.

"Someone has to do it," Lena said primly.

"Did you happen to see the woman who was here with me yesterday?"

"The professor, you mean?"

Mabel nodded.

"Oh, yes. She used to come here all the time, and I almost had to call the police on her more than once."

Mabel might have been more impressed with Sandy's apparent bad behavior if it weren't for Lena's obvious intolerance for even small infractions like brief on-street parking when there was no significant traffic to be hindered. "Why would the police need to be called?"

Lena glanced around, as if her neighbors were as nosy as she was and might be eavesdropping. Confident no one could hear her, she said, "Sandy is a drunk, and not a happy one, from what I saw. I thought she might get violent."

"It's hard to imagine Sandy being much of a threat." She had a motive for murder, but she was so tiny, and Graham had been such a large man. If his size alone hadn't been enough to ward off an attack, he'd kept a deadly knife within easy reach. The whole idea seemed like the desperate imaginations of someone who wanted to throw suspicion on someone other than herself.

Lena sniffed. "It's not up to me to decide things like that. I just report incidents to the police and let them settle it."

"What did you report Sandy for, exactly?"

"Most of the time Sandy's and Graham's fights ended after the first heated words, so I never actually called the police," Lena said. "The closest I came was about a month ago when Sandy was drunker than I'd ever seen her before. She was furious about something, and I heard her shouting that Graham would be sorry."

Mabel wondered where Lena had been that she'd been able to hear the exact words. And whether it had been as bad as Lena claimed, given her tendency to see minor infractions as major crimes. Without any police report, it was hard to judge whether Lena was making the incident up or not. "If it was that bad, why didn't you call the police?"

"I should have, but Graham saw me, and he managed to calm her down." Lena frowned. "I really should have called it in anyway. Maybe Graham would still be alive if I had made the police aware of just how dangerous Sandy could be."

Lena didn't sound terribly regretful, but maybe she was just hiding it well. Mabel always had trouble reading people. She wished she hadn't sent Terry away. He might have been able to interpret the woman's facial expression for her.

"It's hard to believe someone as responsible as you are would let it drop completely." Mabel remembered what she'd read in Graham's journal, where he'd described Lena and the mayor as a couple. "I'm sure you did your duty and let someone know. The mayor perhaps? Did you tell him about how dangerous Sandy was? He might have been able to do something about it. I understand you two are good friends."

Lena snorted genteelly, and Mabel had no problem reading her disdain. "The mayor is useless. I'm sorry I ever backed his candidacy. I had such high hopes for him in the beginning. He hates the blighted spots in his town as much as I do." She glanced pointedly at Graham's run-down property and the vehicles crammed into the driveway. "But he wouldn't actually do anything about it. Just about anyone else would have been more proactive."

"Are you planning to run against him in the next election?"

"Me?" Lena assumed a startled expression that seemed obviously fake even to Mabel. "I never even thought of such a thing. Although, now that you mention it …" She stopped and looked away for a moment before her head gave an emphatic shake. "No, no, I couldn't. I have far too much to do already."

Mabel needed to keep Lena from interfering with the visits to maintain the rhubarb plants, so now was not the time to comment on the woman's obvious insincerity. And Emily had been giving Mabel hints on how to find something positive to say about almost anyone. "You're very detail-oriented. I think you'd do a good job as mayor."

"That's the problem—anyone who's got the skills to do a good job as mayor knows better than to take it on. Done right, it's too much work for too little reward." Lena sighed. "It's terribly frustrating, but Danny's probably the best of the folks who are actually willing to do the job. I just wish he cared more about the actual work than the title and prestige."

Lena looked like she could go on at length about the mayor's shortcomings, so Mabel was relieved when Terry called from the corner that he really needed to get back to school to do some studying.

Mabel excused herself, and hurried toward her Mini Cooper, only then realizing she was going to be at least a few minutes late for her meeting with Betty Comstock, the jam-maker. Mabel's inability to keep track of time was another reason why she really needed to get back to her day job. She'd always been better working in a virtual world than one that involved interacting with people face-to-face.

* * * *

Mabel was fifteen minutes late by the time she dropped off Terry and then returned to the farm, but Betty had waited. An old but well-maintained, bright-yellow hatchback was parked in front of the barn, and a woman was sitting at the outdoor table on the patio outside the farmhouse's back door. Mabel was a little surprised her visitor hadn't simply gone inside. According to Emily, Betty had been a friend of Aunt Peggy, and it seemed as if all her friends had routinely made themselves at home when she'd been alive. Some, like Rory and Emily, still did.

Mabel hurried over, apologizing as she went. "I'm so sorry. I hope you haven't been waiting long."

"Not a problem at all." Betty stood up. She was short and round, and in her fifties. She wore a red jersey dress with a ruffled gingham apron the same sunny color as her car, and she held a canvas bag with yellow handles, and SWEET BETTY JAMS printed on it in bright red. "It's so peaceful here, and I just love Peggy's fountain. I'm sorry I couldn't be here for the memorial event."

"Thank you." Mabel had had the pineapple-shaped fountain installed in her aunt's memory, along with a small herb garden at its base. "My cat likes watching the birds who drink from it."

"That's right," Betty said with a laugh. "I heard you'd adopted a cat from the shelter. And that you've taken in a pregnant barn cat."

"I have."

"I wish I could take some of the babies, but my house is full up. I'll let you know if I hear of anyone else who needs a kitten though." Betty handed over the bag, which on inspection held three small jelly jars.

"Thanks," Mabel said. "What do I owe you for this?"

Betty waved her hand dismissively. "It's the least I can do for Peggy's niece. Although I would love to see the pregnant cat."

"She is upstairs." Mabel led the way to the kitchen door. "Come on inside."

"Have you ever dealt with a pregnant queen before?"

"Not even a pregnant peasant." Mabel left the jam bag on the kitchen table and showed Betty up the stairs with Pixie following, presumably hoping to slip inside the bedroom to check out the new member of the household.

"I used to breed Maine coon cats, so feel free to call me if you have any questions."

Mabel opened the door to her aunt's bedroom and stepped aside to let her guest through while also blocking Pixie from joining them. She followed Betty inside and closed the door just a whisker's breadth away from Pixie's disappointed face.

"I thought pregnant cats knew what to do on their own." That was what the animal shelter guy had told her.

"Most of the time they do." Betty tiptoed into the room and sidled up to the crate. "Oh, my. She looks like she's going to pop any day now."

Mabel followed her gaze. Billie Jean didn't look much different than she had the day she'd arrived. Having made major inroads into the kibble bowl again, she was curled in a ball in the far corner, glaring and occasionally hissing.

"How can you tell?"

"It's just instinct, after all the kittens I've seen born," Betty said. "You'll know the queen's getting ready for labor when she stops eating and acts restless. She's not quite there yet, judging by how still she's sitting. We should probably leave her alone now. She doesn't need any stress and she needs all the rest she can get. She's not going to get much sleep after the kittens arrive, and it looks like she won't sleep while we're here."

Mabel quickly topped off the kibble bowl again and then followed Betty downstairs with Pixie trailing behind.

Once they were back in the kitchen, Betty pointed at the canvas bag on the table. "You've got to try the jam and tell me what you think. Rory said you'd never had rhubarb before, and I love seeing how people react to their first taste."

Mabel emptied the bag, laying out the three tiny half-cup glass jars and a small box of animal crackers.

"They're for dipping into the jam," Betty explained.

The jars had custom-printed red-and-yellow labels. One jam was all rhubarb, and the other two combined rhubarb with berries.

"Rhubarb-strawberry is traditional, and I'm partial to the blueberry one," Betty said. "But you should try the plain one first, if you want to get a real taste of rhubarb."

Mabel hesitated. The stewed rhubarb she remembered from her visits to her aunt really hadn't been appetizing at all. What if she hated the jam and gagged or couldn't hide her expression of distaste? People sometimes took unimportant things like food preferences too personally, and Betty seemed almost as obsessed with her jams as Graham had been with his rhubarb.

"Why don't I get us some iced tea to cleanse the palate first?" Mabel said, not waiting for a response before claiming the pitcher from the refrigerator. She poured two glasses and handed one to Betty. Maybe she'd be too busy drinking to see Mabel's reaction to the jam.

Mabel dipped an animal cracker—a giraffe—into the plain rhubarb jam and cautiously raised it to her tongue. It was tart, but not face-twistingly so, and had a nice hint of lemon. She knew rhubarb was sour, so the jam had obviously been sweetened, but the sugar didn't dominate the fruity flavor.

Mabel swallowed and dug in the box of animal crackers for another one. "This is good."

"You don't have to worry about hurting my feelings," Betty said. "Rhubarb isn't to everyone's taste."

"No, I mean it." Mabel opened the jar with the strawberry mix and sacrificed a tiger to it. "Mmm, this is good too." She tried the blueberry one next. "I don't know which one I like best."

"That's how I feel about all my jams," Betty said, blushing happily.

"Where do you get your fruit? Do you grow it yourself?"

"I have deals with local berry growers to buy some of their crops, but I grow my own rhubarb. At least I have until now. Demand is rising, and I may not be able to keep up with it. I don't have a farm, just a small yard." Betty took a sip of her iced tea. "This is really good."

"Thanks. It's my only claim to fame in the kitchen." Mabel stuck a bear-shaped cracker into the plain rhubarb jar. "Did you ever consider buying some of Graham's rhubarb?"

She wrinkled her nose. "I asked him once if he had any for sale, but he was a difficult person, as I'm sure you know. I thought he'd appreciate having another market, and since I live near him and wouldn't mind picking it up, we'd both benefit by not having to pay for shipping."

"Relying on local food sources is good for everyone," Mabel said, parroting Rory's pitch for joining the CSA.

"Exactly," Betty said. "But you'd have thought I was asking Graham to sell me his children or something. He chased me off the property—literally! The woman who lives next door to him told me later that she'd been so worried for me, she almost called the police."

"Lena does like chatting with cops," Mabel said. "But why was Graham so upset about the prospect of selling his crop? Did he tell you?"

"He did, although it didn't make any sense. He said I was a mole, and at first I thought he was hallucinating and thought I was a giant, talking version of a garden pest. But then he went on to rant about how Sandy Faitakis at the university was desperate to get samples of his plants so she could clone them and take all the credit for his breakthrough work. He seemed to think I was there to get some stalks for her to analyze by pretending to want them for my jam."

"What was the breakthrough he was so worried about protecting?"

"That's the thing that really doesn't make sense. I don't know what he was so worried about protecting. And it's not like someone couldn't have broken into his greenhouse and stolen a few tissue samples if they'd wanted to. No need to come up with an elaborate story."

Mabel wondered if there was something in Graham's journal about his supposed breakthroughs. And if the information was in there, would she even recognize it or dismiss it as gibberish like most of the other entries?

"I'm thinking about starting a rhubarb field if I can buy some of Graham's seedlings," Mabel said. "Let me know if you're still looking for a supplier next year."

"It'll take more than a year before you'll have a harvest," Betty said. "More like two years from next spring when you plant them. But I'd definitely be interested in buying locally, so let me know what you decide."

That was encouraging. Mabel still hoped she wouldn't still be in West Slocum in two years or whenever the rhubarb was ready for harvest, but surely having an additional field planted, along with a local buyer lined up for some of the crop, would appeal to anyone interested in buying a small farm.

Mabel took two more tastes of the jam—one each of the strawberry and blueberry versions, so she could compare them all again—and decided to redouble her efforts to get Rob Robinson to sell some of the rhubarb plants to her. Even if he sold the most valuable, newly developed plants to Sandy, the greenhouse would still have a large number of more standard varieties of no particular interest for research, and they would be adequate for the farm.

Mabel licked the last bit of jam from her lips and decided she wasn't just going to plant a field here on Stinkin' Stuff Farm; she was going to bring some plants back to Maine with her and Pixie.

Chapter 17

After Betty left, Pixie yowled to announce yet another visitor. Mabel tossed her a treat before going outside to see who it was.

Sandy Faitakis was getting out of her black sedan, and without any introductory pleasantries, shouted, "You're messing with things you don't understand."

"I don't know what you're talking about."

"Graham's greenhouse." Sandy stomped across the driveway. "I was just there to check on my plants, and that nosy neighbor woman made me leave. She said you were the designated caretaker, and she was going to call the cops if I didn't leave."

"She's a bit trigger-happy with her phone."

"Well, you've got to tell her to let me inside the greenhouse."

"Why?" Mabel asked. "I talked to Graham's brother-in-law, who's apparently in charge of the estate, and he gave me permission to keep the plants alive. That's what you want, isn't it?"

"Of course I want to keep them alive," Sandy said. "But I should be the one doing it."

For a scientist, Sandy wasn't being very logical. Mabel wondered if the woman was drunk. It fit with the aggression and irrationality. Of course, it could also be explained by desperation to get her hands on Graham's journals. Sandy couldn't say that was what she wanted, so she was making nonsensical excuses.

"Why would you want to take on extra work?" Mabel asked. "Don't you have a full-time job? Plus your breeding work? It's quiet here at the farm right now, so I have some free time."

"You don't understand," Sandy said. "The plants are mine. Graham owed me that much."

Sandy was right about one thing—Mabel didn't understand why the woman was so upset. "If you're worried that I'm not doing the right things for the plants, I'd be glad to hear any advice you might have."

"Growing rhubarb is not that difficult," Sandy said in exasperation. "Water the seedlings that are dry and drain the soggy ones. And make sure the greenhouse doesn't overheat on sunny days."

"That's pretty much what I'm already doing. You don't have to worry about the plants' well-being, and I'm not going to charge for my time. Once Rob Robinson's position as the estate's representative is made official, you can make your case to him about the plants you think you're owed."

"And the rest of the contents of the greenhouse?" Sandy asked. "How are you protecting that?"

She couldn't mean the dirt and the trays and benches, Mabel thought. They could take care of themselves and no one—not even Sandy—would have any interest in them. She had to mean Graham's breeding records.

"If you're wondering about Graham's journals getting stolen or damaged, you don't have to." Mabel forced herself not to look at the Mini Cooper where the journals had been transferred from Terry's backpack into a canvas bag that now sat on the passenger seat. The doors were locked, but in Sandy's current state, that might not be enough to stop her from trying to get at them. Mabel didn't want to have to physically restrain Sandy from breaking into the car. The professor might be tiny, but she was fueled with righteous indignation at the moment. "They've been put in storage for safekeeping."

"You could give them to me," Sandy said, her tone softening. "They'd be more secure at the university than here on the farm."

"They're fine where they are." That wasn't entirely true, but as soon as Sandy left, Mabel was driving them to the office of her local lawyer, Quon Liang. "Once it's decided who they belong to, they'll be released to that person."

"But that could take months," Sandy whined like a teenager. "So much wasted time when I could be moving forward with Graham's research. It's what he would have wanted."

Mabel didn't believe Sandy's supposed concern for Graham's wishes. It was far more likely that she wanted to get her hands on the journals for her own selfish reasons. If Graham really had made some breakthrough in his breeding program, Sandy could use that information to advance her career at the university. But only if she knew which plants were part of that new development, and how it had been accomplished.

"I thought his research wasn't rigorous enough to be of any use to you."

"Considering how little work has been done on rhubarb, any little bit of information is like water to a desert," Sandy said. "There might be some small nugget of useful information. But only a trained professional like me would be able to spot it."

That didn't sound terribly urgent, Mabel thought. If that was true, Sandy wouldn't be in such a rush to get the journals. After all, what were the odds that another breeder would announce a breakthrough in the next couple of weeks before ownership of the journals could be determined? No, Mabel thought the only reason for urgency was that Sandy was less interested in the breeding notes and more interested in the more personal comments that Graham mixed in with his agricultural information. Sandy might be worried that there was something in them that implicated her in Graham's death.

"Reading the journals is going to have to wait, no matter what," Mabel said. "They're encrypted."

Sandy barely paused before saying, "There must be someone in the math department at the university who can decode it for me."

"I'm sure they could," Mabel said. "As soon as the estate decides what to do with them."

Sandy sighed in apparent defeat. For the moment, at least. "If you change your mind, let me know. I'd be glad to pick them up if you decide they'll be safer at the university. Or you could stop by my trial field with them. While you're there, you could see what a real breeding program looks like."

"I'd enjoy that," Mabel said. Not that she'd ever hand the journals over to Sandy without proper authorization. But she would like to see a larger field of rhubarb than what was in Graham's back yard, now that she'd decided she was definitely adding the crop to the farm.

But first she had to get the older journals safely into the hands of her lawyer.

* * * *

Mabel walked Sandy out to her car, not so much to be polite, but to make sure the professor didn't notice the canvas bag filled with journals in the passenger seat of the Mini Cooper. As soon as the woman was out of sight around a curve in the driveway, Mabel opened the driver's-side car door to go to her lawyer's office. Pixie's muffled screech from inside the house warned that either Sandy had turned around and was coming back or some other visitor was on the way.

Mabel shut the door with a sigh. She never had any visitors in Maine, and that was how she liked it. Once they moved back there, Pixie would never have any reason to yowl again.

Charlie's truck appeared a moment later. Some visitors were acceptable, she decided.

Mabel waited for Charlie to park beside her car. He climbed out and said, "I've got some more information on Graham's client, Sam Trent."

"Why didn't you just text me?"

"It's too impersonal," he said. "I like visiting the farm. And you."

"Me?" Mabel still wasn't entirely sure Emily was right that he was interested in her.

"Yes, you," Charlie said. "Apparently I crave being taken down a peg occasionally, and you're good at it."

"I never mean to insult you."

"Could have fooled me," he said lightly. "I'm reasonably sure you intended to make me feel guilty about being a developer when we first met."

"Okay, I did mean that," Mabel said. "But I didn't realize you were a good-guy developer back then. I thought you were like one I'd run into back in Maine, and you wanted to destroy all the work Aunt Peggy had put into her farm."

"I'll chalk your insults up to the grief over your aunt then."

"It wasn't grief exactly," Mabel said. "I loved her, but didn't know her that well, so it was mostly guilt I was feeling. I should have spent more time with her."

"True," he said. "But you're doing the right thing now, taking care of her farm. I heard about the fire in the barn. That could have been bad if you weren't here."

"Some other owner could oversee the farm just as well as I could." Mabel shrugged. "Better actually. I didn't even know how to use the fire extinguisher."

"You bring other good qualities to the farm. You care about it more than almost anyone else would."

"A real farmer would care *and* know what to do with the place."

"All right, all right." Charlie raised his hands in surrender. "I give up. I told Rory it wouldn't work, trying to appeal to your emotions to get you to stay in West Slocum."

"So you'll help me find a buyer who's not a developer?"

"I'm not willing to go quite that far, but I won't interfere with a sale."

"That's fair," Mabel said. "So what did you find out about Trent?"

"If I tell you," he said, "you have to promise to stay away from him. Leave investigating him to the police. Trent's dangerous."

"I know," Mabel said. "He definitely has a temper, even if he tries to hide it."

"He lies too. He said he wasn't all that upset any more about the divorce," Charlie said. "And he may have learned to say the right words, but it's unlikely he's really over it. I talked to his ex-wife, and she had to get a restraining order against him before the divorce was final. He kept harassing her, claiming they'd still be together if it weren't for Graham. When they first separated, he was just depressed, but toward the end, he got violent every time there was a setback in his attempts to get Graham punished. He never hit her, but she thought it was just a matter of time."

"He might have come to accept the end of the marriage later," Mabel said. "Especially after he got a new job. He said it was better than the one he'd had working for his ex's family business."

"That's not the impression the ex had," Charlie said. "Apparently Trent has visitation rights with their dog, so she still sees him a couple of times a month. The last time he was at her place was a week ago, and as she was bringing the dog to the door, she heard him talking on his cell phone. She didn't know who was on the other end, but Trent was complaining bitterly about what Graham had cost him. His marriage, his job, and even most of the time with his dog."

"He's definitely a solid suspect in Graham's murder," Mabel said. "But it's all just speculation. Not enough to get the detectives to do anything."

"There's more," Charlie said. "His ex confirmed that Graham really did make a big mistake in handling Trent's case. She'd had no idea about her husband's infidelity, and she'd been close to reconciling when her lawyer told her what Graham had revealed. She never understood why Graham had made such a stupid mistake, but I think it might have been an early indicator that he was having some mental glitches. Back then, the issues might have been occasional, so he could hide them, but it got a lot worse before he died."

"So he could have ruined another client's case more recently, and that's what got him killed."

Charlie nodded.

"If you're right, then I've got no chance of figuring out who killed Graham. Not without his client files, and I'll never get them."

He nodded again, and didn't look particularly unhappy about it.

"Unless the killer isn't one of Graham's clients," Mabel said. "I can still look into that possibility. I'll also let the detectives know what the ex told you, in case they think Trent had gotten over the anger. I was just on my way to deliver some of Graham's journals to my lawyer for safekeeping. I can stop by the police station while I'm in town."

"You're not just texting the information? Should I be jealous that there's someone you want to see in person at the police station?"

"No," Mabel said. "I'd text if I could, but I don't have a mobile number for O'Connor, and even if I did, I'm pretty sure he'd just ignore the message. I need to be there in person to make sure he doesn't dismiss the information out of hand."

"Ah, so even a hermit like you believes that sometimes an in-person interaction is better than a virtual one."

"You make *hermit* sound like an insult."

"No more so than *developer*."

He had a point. "I don't hold your career against you any longer."

"Then I can accept that you're not a people person," he said. "As long as you make an exception for me."

"I will," she promised. "For as long as I live here in West Slocum, at least. Just don't expect me to stay forever."

"I don't expect it," Charlie said. "But I can hope."

Chapter 18

Quon Liang worked out of a small Victorian house that must have been converted into office space some forty years earlier—a decade before he was even born—and as far as Mabel could tell, it had never been redecorated since then. Quon might not have been able to afford to make any purely cosmetic changes, between paying law school loans and whatever debt he'd incurred to purchase the practice from an older attorney who'd been forced into early retirement due to a debilitating stroke. Quon's investment was likely to pay off now that he was the only lawyer left in West Slocum after the death of Graham Winthrop.

The parking lot behind the building was empty except for the boring white sedan in the far corner, which Mabel recognized as belonging to Quon. It might not look like a typical lawyer's vehicle, but it suited Quon. He and his car were both reliable and reasonably priced. She knew, because while Jeff Wright hadn't rendered a verdict specifically on the car, he had checked out and approved the young attorney when Mabel had needed someone to probate her aunt's estate.

Mabel opened the passenger door of her Mini Cooper to get the canvas bag full of journals. Before she could retrieve them, Thomas Porter's distinctive purple SUV came to a screeching halt beside her.

He jumped out, saying, "We need to talk."

"No, we don't." She turned her back on him and bent to grab the bag on the seat.

"Hey," he said. "You can't just ignore me."

"I can ignore anything if I'm focusing on something else." Mabel straightened and pushed the door shut. "It's my superpower."

Porter grabbed her shoulder, and Mabel lost her own grip on the bag. His touch had been light, so she was able to jerk away from him. She'd never liked being touched casually, not even by friends, and he definitely wasn't a friend. His touch was an assault.

She spun to face him, placing her back against her car. She felt trapped, but at least he couldn't sneak up on her again. "Don't touch me. Ever."

He raised his hands in false surrender. "I just wanted to get your attention."

"You've got as much of it as you're ever going to have," she said, getting her phone out of the barn jacket's roomy pocket. "Now go away."

"Look," Porter said. "We got off on the wrong foot. I just wanted to apologize."

"What is it with people who don't know how to send a text?" she muttered irritably.

He blinked. "So if I texted you an apology, we could talk?"

"No," Mabel said, preparing to dial 911. The police station was just a block away, so it wouldn't take long for them to arrive. "There's no point in talking. I'm not selling the farm to you or any other developer. Not today, not tomorrow, not ever."

"You're being unreasonable."

"Yes, I am," Mabel said. "I'm allowed. My lawyer told me so."

Porter flicked a glance at the sign on the building, which gave away Mabel's destination. "Whoever you're getting advice from, he can't be anything but a country bumpkin. You should talk to a real lawyer."

"I did," Mabel said, stretching the truth. Years ago, Jeff Wright had told her she could be unreasonable with anyone except him, and he'd back her up. "Quon Liang is only one of my lawyers."

"They're all just in it for themselves anyway," Porter said, changing tactics. "I'm trying to make your life better. I saw you visiting that dead guy's property. Is that what you want? A place with a greenhouse? I could help you get it if you sell the bigger farm to me. Those greenhouses are solid, and I could fix up the residence if you want. All part of the deal."

"You've been stalking me." He'd done more than just follow her, Mabel realized. He couldn't have known there was a second greenhouse unless he'd been inside the first one. The smaller one wasn't visible from the street or even from the entrance to the first greenhouse. "And you've been trespassing on Graham's property."

"Just doing what had to be done," Porter said. "Persistence is part of being a businessman."

"Not taking no for an answer is also what gets successful businessmen subjected to restraining orders." Without looking away from Porter, Mabel bent her knees and reached behind her to grab the handles of the canvas bag filled with Graham's journals. She straightened and said, "I'm going inside to see my lawyer right now, and I'm absolutely sure, country bumpkin or not, he'll know how to get a restraining order against you. And then I'm heading down the street to the police station to report both your stalking and your trespassing."

"Don't be ridiculous—" Porter began, but she cut him off.

"I already told you I'm allowed to be ridiculous if I want to," Mabel said. "And when it comes to you and anything related to my aunt's farm, ridiculous is just the start. If you don't leave me alone, I'm prepared to become as crazy as Graham Winthrop was. And I won't have to eat rhubarb leaves to get there."

Mabel turned her back on him, but not before she caught a glimpse of how confused he looked. Good. Confusing people was another of her superpowers.

* * * *

Quon Liang hadn't been in his office, having walked over to a client's office for a meeting, but his personal assistant had accepted the bag full of journals and promised to put it in their safe, pending instructions from a duly authorized estate representative.

Porter's purple SUV wasn't in the parking lot any longer, so Mabel collected her Mini Cooper and drove to the police station. O'Connor seemed considerably more pleased to see Mabel than she'd expected. That couldn't be good. He might try to hug her.

Mabel kept her distance.

"Can I get you some coffee?" O'Connor asked.

"No, thanks."

"I know police stations have a reputation for bad coffee, but ours is really good." His nervous laughter undermined his claim.

"I don't drink coffee," Mabel said. "And I don't expect to be here that long."

"I could get you tea instead," he said as he led her down a hallway to where he'd said they could have a nice quiet chat.

She didn't want either a nice, quiet chat or a beverage. She just wanted to alert him to Thomas Porter's behavior and also what she'd heard from Charlie about Sam Trent's motive for killing Graham.

"No, thanks."

"What about a soda?"

She shook her head.

"Water then. Everyone drinks water."

Deciding she wasn't going to be able to get this conversation over with until she had something to drink, Mabel said, "Fine. Some water would be nice."

He opened a door marked "Interrogation Room B," and gestured for her to go inside. "Have a seat, and I'll be back in a sec."

It was actually more than seven minutes later according to her phone's stopwatch app when he returned with two bottles of water and a large notepad, along with an extra-large, uniformed officer. The last seemed too big to fit in the tiny room that was furnished with nothing but a small table and four straight-backed chairs. The officer stationed himself in front of the door while O'Connor squeezed around him to the far side of the table.

O'Connor handed her one of the bottles. "So, what can we do for you today? You weren't thinking of leaving town, were you?"

"I can't leave until the farm is sold," Mabel said. "And that could take some time. Which is why I wanted to talk to you. As long as I'm stuck here, I need to feel safe. A real estate developer named Thomas Porter has been stalking me. And trespassing at Graham's property. My lawyer can do what's needed to get a restraining order against him, but I also wanted to file an official complaint."

O'Connor dutifully wrote down the name. "Spelled P-O-R-T-E-R?"

"Yes."

"And why would he be stalking you?"

"He wants to buy Aunt Peggy's farm, and I won't sell it to him, and he keeps trying to change my mind. He accosted me outside my lawyer's office just a few minutes ago."

"Were there any witnesses?"

"Besides me and him? No. Unless Lena Shaw saw him on Graham's property."

O'Connor set down his pen. "Is that all you've got?"

"That's all I know for sure," Mabel said. "But it seemed suspicious when he showed up at the farm right after a fire started in the barn, and he made a point of telling me he'd still be interested in the property even if all the buildings burned to the ground."

That seemed to get his attention. "There was a fire in your barn? I hadn't heard about that. Did the fire department tell you what caused it?"

"It wasn't that big," Mabel said. "Porter and I were able to put it out."

"So he helped you put out the fire you think he started?"

This was why she usually left things to Jeff Wright to handle. He knew the right things to say. "I think it was just intended to scare me, not necessarily to do any damage."

"I see." But his giggles contradicted his words. "Would you like some more water?"

Mabel glanced at her bottle, which had exactly one sip missing from it. O'Connor was stalling her. Why?

"I'm sufficiently hydrated now, thank you," Mabel said, suddenly anxious to leave. If they still considered her a suspect, they either hadn't read Graham's journal or hadn't found anything useful in it. "I need to get back to the farm. Lots to do. Just one last thing before I go. I heard from a reliable source that one of Graham's clients, Sam Trent was more upset with his lawyer than he might let on in public. I'm sure you're looking into him as a possible suspect in the murder, so I thought you should know."

"We always appreciate information from the public," O'Connor said without writing anything on his notepad. He giggled before adding, "But I'd like to hear more about Porter and his stalking of you."

O'Connor wasn't a good liar. And he was definitely stalling. His nervous laughter was becoming more pronounced. Mabel was convinced he'd already decided she was imagining the problem with Porter and he certainly wasn't going to do anything about it. She wasn't entirely sure he even could do anything beyond what her attorney would do in seeking a restraining order. So why did O'Connor want her to talk about it and waste more of his time?

The answer came to her suddenly: she wasn't just one of several suspects, along with Sam Trent or Graham's other unhappy clients. She was the prime suspect. O'Connor had probably been told to keep her here until the state detective could come to do an informal interview. *Oh, you don't need a lawyer present,* they'd say. *It's just a formality, nothing to worry about.*

Jeff Wright had warned her about that sort of thing back when she was just a kid, with updated warnings every year when he took her out to lunch for her birthday. The advice hadn't been for dealing with police detectives specifically, since even Jeff, with his tendency to always imagine the worst that might ever happen to his clients, hadn't anticipated her involvement with not just one but now two murders, but it was the same advice for dealing with anyone who was snooping around in her private life. When she'd been a newly orphaned kid, it had been reporters trying to interview her without her grandparents or her lawyer present, and later it had been headhunters looking to hire her away from Phil or grifters looking for a share of her inheritance.

If the detectives were focusing on her as the prime suspect, she needed to leave right this minute and talk to Jeff Wright. No more waiting for someone to call her back from his office. And then she would finish decoding Graham's most recent journal, no matter how boring and time-consuming it was. She was reasonably sure there would be useful information there about the real killer if she could just separate out what was part of Graham's delusions and what was real. She couldn't do that if she was stuck in the police station being not-really-interrogated.

Mabel stood up. "If you need me to sign a complaint against Porter, you can contact Quon Liang, and he'll make the arrangements." She turned toward the door, realizing belatedly that the uniformed officer was blocking her exit. He was looking at O'Connor, clearly waiting for instructions about whether to let Mabel pass.

She turned back to the table and said, "Tell him I'm leaving now. Unless, of course, you want me to call my lawyer about being held here against my will."

"No, no, of course not," O'Connor said with a chuckle. "We'd never do anything like that."

At a not-too-subtle nod of O'Connor's head, the uniformed officer opened the door and held it open for her to leave.

Mabel swiped her water bottle off the table before heading to the door. "Thanks for the hospitality."

* * * *

Even if Quon Liang had been in his office, Mabel didn't entirely trust him to advise her on something as critical as dealing with the homicide detectives. Losing some money if her aunt's estate wasn't handled efficiently was one thing. Going to jail was quite another. With that possibility hanging over her head, she had to talk to Jeff Wright.

But first she had to get out of easy reach of O'Connor.

She drove over to the library on the theory that no one would try to arrest her there, for fear of upsetting everyone's favorite librarian, and parked to call Jeff Wright. Once again, there was no answer on either the public line or the private one, and when she tried to leave a voice mail, she got a message that the inboxes were still full.

Something was definitely wrong, and if Mabel hadn't been so distracted by her own problems, she'd have done more to find out what was going on back in Maine before now. She started down her list of contacts, dialing everyone who might know what was going on with Jeff, one after the other. His paralegal, the housekeeper who took care of his office as well as Mabel's home, and a lawyer with a part-time practice based in her house, who sometimes rented Jeff's conference room for depositions. No one answered until she finally thought to call Jeff's nephew, who'd been her frequent babysitter the summer she'd turned twelve. She dialed his number.

"Hey, Mabes."

Joey was the only person who'd ever called her that. There'd been a few instances when people had misheard it as "babes," and they'd gotten some disapproving looks at the inappropriateness of a college-aged guy dating a twelve-year-old girl. She hadn't understood the implication at the time, and Joey had always set the record straight before anyone called the cops. She'd only tolerated the nickname at the time because he'd bribed her by letting her use his cell phone when her Luddite grandparents wouldn't let her have her own.

"Thank goodness you picked up," she said. "I've been trying to contact your uncle all week, and he hasn't called back. He never ignores me. I'm starting to get worried."

"Ah." The teasing note in his voice was completely gone. "I guess no one thought to tell you."

"Tell me what?"

"I'm sorry, but Uncle Jeff died."

"No," Mabel said automatically. "That's not possible."

"It is possible." His tone was gentle. Despite Joey's insistence on calling everyone by an annoying nickname, he'd always been kind to people in every other way. "He was close to eighty, you know. And people that age tend to die. He had a massive heart attack."

"I didn't know," Mabel said faintly, feeling the sudden sting of tears. Fortunately, she was already sitting down and the small size of her car meant that she and her tears were somewhat hidden from public view. "I should have been there."

"There was nothing you could have done," Joey said. "I'm told it was quick and relatively painless. He was in the lobby of the courthouse with a client he liked almost as much as he liked you, so he wasn't alone. It was all over before the ambulance even arrived. It's what he would have wanted."

He was right about that. Jeff had lived—and now died—for his work. He would have been miserable as a retiree. It was something they had in common. Mabel never wanted to stop developing apps.

"When you get a chance," she said, "text me the details for the memorial service."

"You can count on me, Mabes." Joey disconnected the call.

She had always counted on Joey, and he, like his uncle, had never let her down.

What was she going to do now? For more than twenty years, she'd relied on Jeff to take care of all the annoying aspects of life, and now he was gone. It was like losing her grandparents all over again.

She had to go pay her respects, once she knew when the memorial service would be. Assuming O'Connor didn't stop her from leaving town.

He could try, she thought, but he wouldn't keep her from saying her final farewell. For Jeff, Mabel was willing to go on the lam and dare the police to arrest her for it. Of course, Jeff would have told her not to take any chances by irritating the police, either by ignoring a request to stay in West Slocum or by meddling in their murder investigation to prove someone else was a better suspect than she was.

She considered his likely advice for a moment, and then started the car to head back to the farm and Graham's journal. It wouldn't decrypt itself, and it was the only lead she had to find the real killer.

Jeff would have understood that this was one situation where Mabel couldn't follow his advice.

Chapter 19

The mayor was parked outside the barn waiting for Mabel, when she returned to the farm. She'd been crying for the entire short trip home from the library, so she had to take a moment to wipe her face. The rearview mirror told her that while she'd successfully mopped up all the tears, there was nothing she could do about the puffiness of her eyes or the red blotches on her cheeks.

The mayor got out of one side of the car while a stocky woman in jeans and a denim jacket who appeared to be in her thirties got out of the other. Her weather-worn face, long braids, bandana scarf, and clean but worn jeans and navy t-shirt could have earned her a spot in a Norman Rockwell painting as the very ideal of female farmer. A potential buyer for the property, presumably, or else Mabel would have told the mayor to come back another time, because she'd just lost a member of her family.

Mabel took one last swipe at some renewed tears and left the safety of her Mini Cooper. She strove for a natural tone, but her voice wavered slightly. "Hello, Danny. I hope you haven't been waiting too long."

"No, no," he said. "Jill here was just so anxious to see the property that we took a chance on your being here if the viewing went well."

"Did it go well?" Nothing else had today. Mabel looked at Jill for her reaction.

"Oh, yes," she said in a child-like, high-pitched voice that seemed at odds with her no-nonsense image. "It's perfect."

It seemed too good to be true, so Mabel forced herself to look into the woman's eyes. Jill looked away guiltily before their gazes locked.

Mabel gave the mayor a closer look. He too avoided eye contact. She tried to remember if he'd been more at ease in prior dealings with him.

She couldn't fault anyone for avoiding eye contact, since she found it difficult herself. She was certain though that she'd been the one looking away before, not him. She'd been told often enough that her avoiding eye contact made people anxious and caused them to distrust her. That was definitely not the kind of reaction a politician or a broker would want, given both professions' reputation for dishonesty. He'd want to come across as the exception to the rule.

She was in no mood for games right now. She needed time to process Jeff's death before she made any major decisions. And she needed to get the rest of Graham's journal decoded in the hope of clearing herself of suspicion.

Mabel was pretty sure Jill didn't know the first thing about farming despite her costume, and if that was true, this meeting could be ended quickly. "Did the mayor show you the fallow fields?" Mabel didn't know a lot about farming, but she knew about the immutability of planting times. A real farmer would know if she got them wrong. "One field needs to stay fallow for rotation, but I'm thinking about planting the other one with rhubarb. Is that something you'd be interested in growing? I need to decide soon, since the plants need to go into the ground by the end of this month. And then, of course, the garlic gets planted in the spring. There's never an end to work on a farm."

"Whatever you think best is fine with me," Jill said in her child-like tone. "I just want to be a farmer, and you've obviously been successful, I'd be a fool not to take your advice."

"I see." Mabel turned to the mayor. "Could I speak with you for a moment? In private?"

"Sure," the mayor said, still avoiding eye contact. "Jill can wait in the car until you're ready to sign the contract."

Jill hurried over to get into the passenger seat and slammed the door behind her. Once inside, she slumped, as if aware that she'd failed to put on a convincing show of agricultural expertise.

Mabel led the mayor over to the barn entrance. "She's lying. She's no farmer. Garlic is planted in the fall and rhubarb in the spring."

"Anyone could make that mistake," Danny said.

"Not if they were a farmer," Mabel said. "She's a friend of Thomas Porter, isn't she? He finally accepted that I'll never sell to him so he got someone to act as a straw buyer for him."

"I wouldn't know," Danny said. "I can only go by what the buyers tell me. I can't vet them all, get references and everything. My job is just to make the introductions and then see that everything goes smoothly until the papers pass."

"That woman is not a farmer," Mabel repeated. "You don't have to get references to figure it out. And the only reason I can imagine for her to lie about it is because she's a developer herself or she's working for one. And I'm not selling to a developer. Tell her I'm not interested in her offer."

"But she's willing to pay more than the asking price."

"And that didn't make you suspicious?" Mabel waved her hand. "Never mind. I don't care. It's not about the money. It's about Aunt Peggy's legacy. She poured her life's blood into this farm. Literally."

"If it's about her legacy, what if the buyer promises to name the subdivision after her? Skinner Acres perhaps. I could have that written into the contract."

"No. That's not the legacy my aunt would have wanted. She didn't care about fame. She cared about keeping small farms alive."

"You don't understand how hard it is to sell farmland these days," Danny whined. "Especially here in New England where real estate is worth far more as housing."

"I never said it would be easy."

"I might have to increase my commission …"

"I might have to fire you for disregarding my instructions for eligible buyers."

He sighed. "All right, all right. I'll keep looking for a rich farmer."

"And I'm going to look into some other options." Mabel had wanted to use her internet skills originally, advertising in discussion platforms where small farmers gathered online. But Jeff had advised against it. She'd done it his way, and it hadn't worked. Now she was going to do it her way. It felt a little bit like a betrayal of his memory, but with the mayor not following her instructions, she thought Jeff would agree with her looking into other ways to sell the property.

"You'll still owe me a commission if you find the buyer yourself," Danny warned.

She didn't know if that was true, and she started to think she'd ask Jeff, only to be brought up short with the realization she couldn't ever ask him anything ever again. Before the tears prickling her eyes could multiply, she reminded herself that now wasn't a good time to break down in grief. Besides, she wasn't entirely without a source of legal advice. She could ask Quon Liang.

"I'll discuss it with my lawyer," she said. "But for now, take Jill back to wherever you found her. I've got work to do."

* * * *

Mabel fed Pixie and Billie Jean and then threw together a dinner of some canned tomato soup and a corn bread muffin from the freezer. She wasn't hungry, but she had to eat something. It reminded her of how, after her grandparents had no longer been around to keep an eye on her, Jeff had frequently arranged for delivery of a week's worth of prepared foods whenever he'd thought she'd been working too hard and forgetting to eat regularly.

She had a feeling everything she did for a while was going to remind her of Jeff and just how much she'd relied on him. He'd been one of the very few people who'd been invited to her birthday celebrations when she'd been living with her grandparents. And he'd been the person who'd encouraged her to pursue a work-from-home career as best suited to her personality, and he'd been the person who'd taken care of all the details of buying her house in Maine. She'd expected him to also be the person who took care of the sale of the garlic farm and the person who welcomed her back to her house in Maine, but that wasn't going to happen now.

Mabel flopped down at the kitchen table and stared at the tomato soup, corn bread, and iced tea. Jeff had even been the person who, after tasting her first attempt at brewing her own iced tea had explained that its lackluster flavor wasn't her fault, but had been due to the cheap tea bags she'd used, so he'd introduced her to better varieties.

Jeff had been like another grandfather in some ways. She'd been fortunate to have him in her life for so long, but the flip side of that was how much it hurt to lose him now. And there was nothing she could do about the pain she was experiencing now or would experience in the future when she lost other friends. She could stop caring about people, becoming even more of a hermit, she supposed, but she'd already gone and messed that up by getting close to Emily and Rory. They hadn't let her keep a distance from them. And they would all die someday too.

She was tired of losing people she cared about. Her parents, her grandparents, her aunt, and now Jeff. She couldn't stop any of them from dying, but there was one thing she could keep alive—the farm. It had practically been Aunt Peggy's child, the closest thing Mabel had to a cousin. She was not going to let it die too.

Mabel abandoned her dinner and took her iced tea and her laptop with the scanned copy of Graham's journal into the home office. The monotonous work of decoding the book had the virtue of both distracting her from her grief and also potentially enabling her to protect the farm. If she was locked up for a murder she hadn't committed, she wouldn't be able to manage the farm, and she'd have to sell it to the first legitimate bidder, regardless of what they wanted to do with the land.

Mabel started to feel sleepy around midnight, with only about two more months' worth of the journal decoded and another five months to go. In the past, she'd have been wide awake at this hour, but while she'd never become the kind of person who could cheerfully—or even grouchily—get up at dawn like a real farmer to feed the chickens and plow the fields, she had managed to get in the habit of going to bed around midnight and getting up at eight o'clock since moving to West Slocum. It was going to be hard getting back into her later-night routine once she returned to her regular work.

She considered going to bed then and resuming her decoding work first thing in the morning, but as soon as she closed the journal, she remembered what she'd been using it as a distraction from: thinking about Jeff Wright's death. She wasn't going to be able to sleep until she was completely exhausted, so she took a quick break to feed Billie Jean, looking for—and not finding—any signs of either fasting or restlessness that might indicate the beginning of labor, and then settled back in to work on the decryption again.

A couple of hours later, her eyes felt too gritty to keep peering at Graham's handwriting, so she gave in and went to bed. The next morning, she was awake at eight, too early to get up. When she turned over to go back to sleep, it wasn't the noisy birds keeping her awake, but memories of Jeff bringing tears to her eyes. She might as well get out of bed, she decided. She could cry while she checked on the cats.

Billie Jean hadn't done more than nibble a bit at the bowl of food that had been refilled at midnight. Had she stopped eating in anticipation of going into labor? She could just have finally been sated and come to understand that there would always be food available, not just at certain times as Graham must have done. Or maybe she wasn't feeling well. Cats were known to have fussy digestive systems. Mabel decided she'd better check back in a couple of hours to see if anything had changed.

Pixie announced the arrival of a visitor, and a quick peek out the bedroom window revealed Rory's truck outside the barn. Mabel hurried downstairs, stopping to change the water in Pixie's bowl and top off her kibble before going outside to see what Rory was up to. She'd backed her truck up to the barn doors and was unloading some bins she'd borrowed for the CSA, but that would be needed for the garlic planting in another week or two. She stopped as Mabel reached the back of the truck.

"How are—" Rory stopped suddenly and peered at Mabel's face. "What's wrong?"

"I didn't get much sleep last night."

Rory shook her head. "You've been crying. Is it about losing the buyer for the farm? It's for the best, really."

"It's not that," Mabel said. "It's my lawyer. The one in Maine. He died."

"Oh, honey, I'm so sorry." Rory pulled her into a hug. "I know he was more than just your lawyer."

Mabel gingerly pulled away. "He was old though. I never really noticed, but he was almost eighty."

"And he was still working? You were lucky to have him so long then." Rory took her hand and tugged her back toward the farmhouse. "Come on. Let's do something about your puffy face, and you can tell me all about Jeff, since I never had a chance to meet him and see for myself what a great guy he was."

"I'll start crying again if I talk about him."

"That's okay."

"No, it's not." Mabel dug in her heels, refusing to go any farther.

"Then what can I do to help?"

She considered asking if Rory would keep an eye on the farm while Mabel left town for Jeff's funeral. She might have to ignore police requests to stay in town though, and that would unfairly put Rory in a difficult position, torn between loyalty to her friend and loyalty to her police-officer husband. She'd probably end up telling Joe, and he'd be obliged to keep Mabel from leaving.

"There isn't anything you can do," Mabel said. "They say loss gets easier with time, and it's sort of true. In any event, I'll feel better as soon as Graham's killer is arrested and then I can concentrate on selling the farm so I can go back to my old life."

Rory peered at her. "Are you really sure that's what you want? Or is it just habit?"

"It's what I want," Mabel insisted, although even as she said it, she realized Rory might have a point, that it was mostly a knee-jerk reaction, not a conscious choice. With Jeff gone, the only thing she had left in Maine was her house. And the ability to work in peace without stupid birds chattering at her or people wandering onto the farm and into her kitchen. She did miss the privacy. "Maine is where I belong."

"Just promise me you won't make any big decision for a few days," Rory said. "Wait until you've recovered a little bit from the shock of Jeff's death."

Mabel didn't need to wait. She never let her emotions get in the way of her decisions. But she owed Rory for all her help since Aunt Peggy had died. "There's nothing for you to worry about. I don't have any offers for the farm right now, and I don't expect to for a while. I'm going to place some ads online though. I'm done with waiting for Danny to do his job. He brought me another buyer today. She claimed to be a farmer, but she wasn't. I'm pretty sure she was just a shill for Porter. She didn't seem tough enough to be a developer herself."

"And if you get an offer from someone online?"

"Then I'll consider it," Mabel said. "And make sure it's a real farmer, not a developer. But don't worry. I won't rush into a deal. Even if I do find the right buyer, I can't go anywhere until the police stop thinking I killed Graham."

"Joe knows you didn't do it."

"Your husband might believe in me, but he's not a homicide detective. O'Connor tried to hold me at the station yesterday so the state police's detective could interrogate me without actually arresting me. I left before she arrived, but it was obvious that they both think I'm the prime—possibly the only—suspect. I'm not sure how much longer they'll hold off on arresting me. I tried to give O'Connor some information to follow up on, but he wasn't terribly interested. Like he thought he already knew who'd done it, and they were just gathering the last bits of evidence against that person, so it would be a waste of time to follow any other leads."

"I'm sorry," Rory sad. "Joe can't intervene officially, but perhaps he could have a word with the state police detective, just to offer a character reference for you."

"It would be better if I could figure out who killed Graham," Mabel said. "I've been decoding his journals in case there are clues in it, but it's slow work. I've gotten to early August, and the entries are becoming less and less coherent. Even after I decode the sentences, they don't make much sense."

"Did you find anything useful at all?"

"Nothing concrete," Mabel said. "There are some references to escalating tension with someone. But most of them are in the incoherent sections, so I can't tell if he's describing reality or some kind of hallucination. He was convinced Sandy Faitakis—assuming she was *the Professor*—was trying to steal his work."

"That's not entirely crazy," Rory said. "If he really had made some sort of breakthrough and she could claim it for her own or even just build on the work to make it better, it might help her to regain some of the academic reputation that she lost with her drinking binges. And with him dead, there's no one to say she didn't do all the work."

"It's risky though," Mabel said. "If anyone found out she'd stolen her breakthrough from Graham, that would have to be the end of her academic career."

"Sandy has a long history of risky behavior," Rory said. "She attributed it to her drinking, and she's supposed to be sober now, but who knows?"

"Graham's neighbor thinks she's still drinking heavily," Mabel said. "And Graham did say in his journal that he was on the verge of a breakthrough in his breeding. He just needed a little more data, which he expected to have soon. Assuming that was true, and not a hallucination, it certainly gives Sandy a motive for killing him."

"It's worth investigating," Rory agreed. "Preferably by the professionals."

Mabel ignored the caveat. She couldn't make the detectives do their job, not without some solid evidence. "Sandy invited me out to visit her test field. I could take her up on the offer, but I wouldn't know a rhubarb breakthrough if it bit me."

"I could go with you."

"It's better that you stay out of it," Mabel said. "If Sandy realizes we're there to gather evidence against her as a murder suspect, she won't be happy, whether she did it or not. And she seems like the kind of person who wouldn't let it go quietly."

Rory shrugged. "I'm not afraid of her."

"I know, but ..." Mabel would have liked the help, but not at the price of creating problems for Rory or her husband. "The thing is, the whole reason I got dragged into this mess in the first place is because I went to Graham's house to try to convince him not to get criminal charges filed against you like he threatened to do. I didn't want you to get in trouble on my behalf then, and I still don't now. You've got a reputation to uphold as an officer's wife."

"That's so sweet," Rory said. "But you didn't need to protect me from Graham. Joe can handle a little teasing, and that's all that would have come of it. No one would have taken Graham seriously."

"Are you sure?"

"Absolutely," Rory said. "And now I'm even more convinced that you should stay here in West Slocum instead of going back to Maine. You're more like your aunt than you know. She was always going out of her way to protect her friends."

"But I'm not like her in the way that matters, when it comes to where I live," Mabel said. "I'm not cut out to be a farmer."

"We'll see," Rory said, turning to drop the truck's tailgate.

Rory was right about one thing: Mabel did feel the need to protect her friends, perhaps now more than ever, as she coped with her helplessness over Jeff's death. She had to save Rory from herself.

As soon as they'd put the bins away in the barn, Mabel would follow up with Sandy on Graham's allegations against her. Without involving Rory.

Chapter 20

Sandy Faitakis's rhubarb field couldn't have been more different from Graham's tiny back yard. The professor had about five acres of land that held nothing but a single small greenhouse near the road, and then rows and rows of plants that were, like Graham's, not looking great, since they were putting most of their energy into the roots for overwintering.

Right after Rory left, Mabel had called Sandy and arranged to meet her at the field. Mabel had tried to get Terry Earley to go with her to point out anything that might suggest Sandy's breeding program wasn't doing well so she'd be desperate for a breakthrough, even if she had to steal it. Unfortunately, Terry must have been in a class, and didn't respond to her call. She could have waited, but she was afraid she was running out of time.

Mabel parked next to the professor's black sedan. There was no sign of the professor in the field, and while she was petite, she would have been visible if she were anywhere out among the plantings that were only a couple of feet tall at most, so she had to be inside the greenhouse. As Mabel got out of the Mini Cooper, she felt a wave of foreboding deja vu. The last time she'd entered a greenhouse to meet someone, she'd found a dead body.

She tugged her barn jacket closer around her, as if it could protect her from more than the chilly afternoon breeze. She knew she was being silly, and had nothing to worry about. She couldn't let her friends' unnecessary worry about her safety get to her.

Mabel forced herself to walk over to the greenhouse. It was about half the size of Graham's main building, with seedling-covered benches only on one long side. What it lacked in size and contents, it made up for in other ways. It looked newer, and it was definitely tidier on the outside, without any broken pots and discarded sidewall supports strewn out front.

Mabel stopped in the open doorway, hesitant to cross the threshold, even though she could see Sandy, vertical, alive, and free of any bloody wounds, about halfway down the center aisle. She had traded in her professorial clothes for beige camouflage-printed scrubs and a matching brown sweatshirt with rubber boots. She'd even been singing quietly, something about growing things row by row, until she'd looked up and seen Mabel.

Sandy hurried over to the doorway. "Don't make the mistake of thinking Graham was a better breeder than I am just because his greenhouse was bigger and fuller than mine is. It's just that I'm further along in the work, so my most promising plants are growing outdoors already and I don't have as many in here." She brushed her hands on her camouflage-print pants to remove some dirt. "Come, let me show you the really impressive work product outside."

While they walked, Mabel paid only minimal attention to what Sandy was saying about the various plants, all of which looked essentially the same to an untrained eye. Maybe Terry would have appreciated the differences, but Mabel couldn't see the supposedly vast improvement in color or size that Sandy described when comparing new plants with their parental stock.

Instead, Mabel tried to figure out how she could ask Sandy if she had killed Graham. There had to be some subtle way to bring it up, but subtlety had never been one of Mabel's strong points. She'd never needed it for her job, since her clients understood that her sometimes-pointed questions were for their own benefit. She couldn't develop their app if she didn't understand exactly what they wanted. She asked, and they answered. No social niceties, no beating around the bush. That was all she knew how to do.

When Sandy paused in her description of the fields, Mabel asked, gesturing at their surroundings, "If you've got all this, why do you care about getting Graham's plants?"

"It's mostly just intellectual curiosity. I've got some great hybrids, but who knows what else might be possible? Sometimes, it's luck and a spontaneous somatic mutation, that's responsible for a breakthrough. That seemed to be what Graham was counting on. His plan involved sprouting as many seeds as possible, aiming for quantity over quality, in the hope of stumbling across a winner. And maybe he did. In any event, it would really be a shame for that work to be lost."

That explained her wanting the plants, but not the data that Sandy seemed to covet even more. "If he wasn't being scientific, then why do you want his journals?"

"More curiosity," Sandy said. "If he did come up with a good new variety, the journals will tell me which crosses created that seedling."

It all sounded reasonable and not like the desperate person described by Graham. "Is anyone else doing the work you and he were doing? Someone who might have wanted to get the plants and data even more than you do?"

"Not really," Sandy said. "Most varieties of rhubarb came about by accident, with plants cross-pollinating and the seeds producing a new plant that caught someone's attention. I'm trying to be more scientific about it. And efficient, which you need to be in order to be profitable. I've got access to technology that would let me clone the best of Graham's plants to produce them faster than the traditional root divisions. He never could have made them commercially viable without my help."

Mabel wondered if Graham had ever realized that. His comments about Sandy in the journal, at least as of three months before his death, had been much more combative than collaborative. "Did you ever discuss the possibility of working together?"

"All the time," Sandy said easily. "We worked out an informal agreement years ago. But he got a bit delusional the last few months. He thought I was trying to steal his work, when I was just trying to make sure he would let me know about any breakthroughs so they could get the publicity they deserved."

"And you could get some of the credit."

"Okay, sure, I wanted my name associated with anything that came out of the research," Sandy said. "But why shouldn't I? Graham wasn't in a position to write academic papers on his work, and he didn't have the contacts to sell any discovery to a wholesaler. I do."

That made sense. It still didn't completely exonerate Sandy. After all, she'd admitted that Graham had become difficult in the end. Maybe she'd lost patience with him, or they'd had one last argument like the ones Lena had overheard, and he'd reneged on their earlier agreement, so Sandy had killed him in frustration.

Mabel didn't know what to believe, and subtlety wasn't getting her anywhere. Time to go with her strengths and be blunt. "Look, I'm pretty sure the detective thinks I killed Graham, and it's not a good idea to leave the state to go to a friend's funeral until the killer is caught, so I need to know who really did it, and I don't have time to play games. Where were you the morning Graham died?"

Sandy laughed. "I thought you weren't as interested in my fields as you claimed to be."

"They're really nice fields." Even to Mabel, it sounded lame, but she didn't know what else to say. How would she have described her aunt's fields in positive terms? "They look all … fertile and … um, weed-free."

"Thanks," Sandy said, still clearly amused. "And you can cross me off your suspect list. I wasn't anywhere near Graham's greenhouse that morning. I was doing some last-minute prep for a lecture until about eight thirty, and then I was giving that lecture between nine and ten."

If that was true, she couldn't possibly have killed Graham. She'd have to ask Terry if he could confirm whether there really had been a class then. "I suppose your students will confirm that you were there then."

Sandy shrugged. "Who knows what students remember. Every time I grade exams, I'm reminded of their wandering attention. But you know who can tell you I definitely wasn't at Graham's place the morning he died?"

"Who?"

"His nosy neighbor. She gave me the evil eye every time I visited. She must have some sort of sensor that tells her the minute I set foot on Graham's property."

"I already asked her," Mabel said. "She told me she didn't see anyone that morning."

"Then maybe she killed him," Sandy said, her amusement waning. "Or the cat did. But it definitely wasn't me. And I don't know why anyone would think it was."

Mabel hesitated. She didn't particularly want to name any names, not when she couldn't be absolutely sure Sandy hadn't killed Graham and wouldn't go after anyone who'd incriminated her.

Sandy snorted. "I get it. The nosy neighbor told you Graham and I argued a few times and I raised my voice in frustration. She might even have claimed my words were slurred, but it's just because I get tongue-tied when I'm angry. I haven't had a drink in seven years. That woman creates drama out of every little thing. I swear, if you inadvertently drop a scrap of paper on a sidewalk, she tells the cops you dumped toxic waste."

Sandy seemed legitimately upset that anyone would consider her a murder suspect. But, Mabel didn't trust her judgment at the moment. Not when Thomas Porter had seemed so genuine to her, and she'd believed his lies. Her only consolation was that he was apparently a professional liar, since he'd duped other people, too, so it wasn't entirely her fault that she'd bought his story.

Mabel decided to give Sandy the benefit of the doubt. Unless something new came along to incriminate her. "I'm sorry I upset you. I'm just worried that the police aren't doing as much as they could to find Graham's killer."

"We can agree on that much, at least," Sandy said. "I want to dig into Graham's data, but I can't while the murder is actively being investigated. Until there's an arrest, his heirs won't be able to dispose of his assets, in case they turn out to have killed him. There are rules against letting killers benefit from murder."

Mabel hadn't thought of that before, but Sandy was right, and the rules would also apply to anyone overseeing the estate, like Rob Robinson, if he was a suspect. If the investigation dragged on long enough, no one would get the plants in time to do anything with them, and all of Graham's work would be wasted.

* * * *

Back at the farmhouse, Mabel went to check on Billie Jean. The food bowl didn't seem to have been touched at all, which was worrisome given her previous constant appetite. Was it a sign of imminent labor or could it be some sort of illness?

Mabel tried calling the animal shelter, but got a message that no one could take the call, because they were busy with the animals, so she should leave a message to be returned when someone was available.

She decided she was probably panicking unnecessarily and hung up. Billie Jean was huddled in the rag-filled box in the far corner, but she'd done that every time Mabel came into the room before, so it didn't mean anything. If she was still not eating in the morning and hadn't gone into labor by then, she'd call the animal shelter again and leave a message.

She'd just closed her aunt's bedroom door behind her when Pixie announced a visitor to the farm. Mabel went downstairs to see who it was. Parked outside the barn was a little truck—even Mabel wouldn't have been afraid to drive something that size—that had once been white but now had so much rust, it looked like it had a polka-dotted paint job.

There was a magnetic sign on the tailgate, presumably covering even more rust, that advertised the solar panel company that Sam Trent worked for. The truck's bed was so small, she doubted it would actually be useful for installation jobs. The most it could carry was a few toolboxes, not the panels themselves.

As she watched, Trent climbed out of the truck and was either talking to himself or using a Bluetooth connection with his phone. He paced the short length of the truck and back several times as he talked.

Mabel would have liked to just ignore the situation and hope Trent would give up and go away. It had worked back in Maine, but it never seemed to work on the farm. Just another reason why Rory and Emily were wrong, and she didn't belong here.

Mabel gave Pixie a quick pat as a promise for a treat later on. "Thanks for letting me know about Trent. I wish you could scare off the unwanted visitors instead of just warning me of their arrival."

Pixie rubbed her head against Mabel's hand, asking for more attention.

"Sorry," Mabel said. "I've got to go chase the unwanted visitor off. Unless you'd like to take on that job from now on?"

Pixie jumped down from the windowsill and headed out of the kitchen for the front of the house, probably to resume her napping.

"I guess you're not interested in becoming a bouncer." Mabel took a deep breath, preparing herself for the confrontation to come and then left the security and comfort of the farmhouse.

The closing of the kitchen door caught Trent's attention. He immediately stopped talking and trotted toward the patio. Mabel hurried forward, preferring not to let him get close enough to wangle an invitation to talk indoors.

When they met at the edge of the driveway, he said, "I was starting to think you might not be home."

"I'm here." It figured, Mabel thought. She'd reluctantly come to accept that ignoring people wouldn't work around here, and now she finally found someone who might actually go away if she didn't acknowledge him. She should have waited longer. "What do you want with me?"

"Oh, I'm not here to ask you for anything," he said, with the cheerfulness of a natural salesperson, or perhaps just one who truly believed in his product. "I'm here to give you something."

"That's not necessary," Mabel said. "I don't need anything from you, and I don't like to be indebted to anyone."

"You just say that because you don't know what you're missing." Trent urged her over to the truck, where he opened the tailgate to reveal a sample solar panel.

So she'd been wrong about the tiny truck's functionality. It could transport panels. One of them anyway. "I've seen solar panels before."

"Not like this one," Trent said. "It's state-of-the-art. Just a few of them could provide all of the farm's energy needs."

"It doesn't have many energy needs. It's a low-tech farm." And that was a significant understatement. She could probably run the place on a handful of batteries. Plus the diesel to run the tractor, of course, but solar panels wouldn't help there.

"What about the future though?" Trent asked. "Don't you want the farm to grow and be more than it is already?"

She did, but not in ways that would require more electricity. "No. And even if I did, I told you I'm not ready to make any decisions about solar panels."

"But—"

"Look," she said. "I'm not the best at dealing with people in the best of circumstances, and right now the only energy I need is the kind that would help me to be polite to you while still making you leave. And I don't think you can supply that. It's really best if you go away right now."

"Or what? You'll kill me like you did Graham?" Trent laughed, making it clear he was just joking. "I know it's ridiculous to think you did it, but I've got to say it's worked out well for me. It's gotten the cops off my case."

"Did they tell you I'm a suspect?" The situation was worse than she'd realized if the police were going public with their suspicion of her. She might need to get out of town right away so they couldn't arrest her before Jeff's funeral.

"They didn't say it in so many words," Trent said. "But I'm not stupid. The detective spent a lot of time asking me questions about where I was on Monday and just how mad I was with Graham for ruining my marriage. I guess they finally believed me when I said I'd put it all behind me."

"But I know you haven't." Mabel refrained from adding that, thanks to her, the police also now knew he wasn't as laid-back as he claimed. "You still think you'd have gotten back with your wife it hadn't been for Graham."

"It was a mutual decision." He shrugged, but he also looked away as he spoke, unlike how he'd been so eager to make eye contact while he was trying to sell her a solar system. "We weren't meant to be together for the long term. If we'd really been soul mates, we'd have worked everything out, despite Graham. He just sped up the end a little."

"So you didn't harass her so much that she got a restraining order? Or lose your temper and get violently angry every time you had a setback in your efforts to punish Graham?"

Trent looked at her again, muscles tightening in his jaw. "Of course not. I'm a good guy."

Lots of people thought they were heroes, when they were actually villains. And generally only a bad guy had to go around telling people he was a good guy. Everyone else let their actions speak for themselves.

"Prove it," Mabel said. "Tell me where you were when Graham was killed."

"I don't even know when that was."

"Early morning. Before nine."

"Then I was asleep. Or having breakfast at home. One of the reasons I like my current job better than working for my ex's family is that I can choose my own hours. And that means not leaving the house before noon most of the time." Trent patted the solar panel. "So now can we talk business? I really think you'd benefit from a solar system. The house is even oriented in the right direction for easy installation and maximum energy collection."

"Now isn't the right time to discuss it," Mabel said.

"But—"

She cut him off, tired of being ignored when she expressed her wishes. "It's time for you to leave. I promise to call you if I do decide to install solar panels. But if you come back without me inviting you, I'll report you for harassment. I'm already working on getting a restraining order against one person. It wouldn't be all that hard to add you to the process."

"All right, all right." Trent's tone was light, but he lifted the tailgate and slammed it shut with more force than necessary. "I can take a hint. Call me when you change your mind."

"I will."

She almost hoped he did come back without an invitation, so she'd have a reason to take out a restraining order against him. The detectives might look at him more closely for Graham's murder if they found out he was stalking her. But she couldn't go back to Detective O'Connor until she found some solid evidence implicating Trent or whoever had actually killed Graham. She'd been hoping to find that evidence in the journal, but it hadn't helped at all so far.

Still, the journal seemed to be her only hope of identifying Graham's killer and freeing herself of suspicion so she could go to Jeff Wright's funeral.

Chapter 21

Mabel turned off her phone so she could concentrate on the journal pages. After two hours, with nothing useful turning up, she needed a break.

She checked on Billie Jean first, who had curled up in the rag-filled box near the crate's door until Mabel approached, and then jumped out to huddle in the far corner again. The cat seemed fine, although she still wasn't eating. Mabel refreshed the water bowl and then went to get herself some iced tea, checking her phone on the way. There was a message from someone who'd seen her online ad for the farm.

Mabel returned the call and listened while the man, who gave his name as Kyle Tellman, told her at length, and without giving her a chance to respond, about his family farm, Tellman Fields, at the other end of Massachusetts, and how he was getting on in age, and the property wasn't big enough to support two adult sons, and he couldn't divide it between them, so that meant the younger one would be left without an inheritance, so he was looking for another small farm he could buy for the second son, and her farm sounded perfect for that.

When Tellman finally ran out of words and gave her an opening to speak, she said, "If you're serious about it, you'll have to put the offer in writing so my lawyer can review it." Only after the words were out did she realize she no longer had a lawyer she really trusted with big decisions like this. Still, the buyer didn't need to know that.

He promised to send her a written offer immediately and ended the call.

Mabel knew she ought to be excited about the possible buyer, but she just felt uncomfortable. She recognized that Tellman was trying to play on her heartstrings with his family saga, but all he'd done was to confuse her. She understood numbers, like the lying developer had relied on, trying to sway her by raising the purchase price. She could test those numbers and then decide whether they worked for her or not. She couldn't do that with Tellman's story about his desire to set up both of his sons with their own farms. Was his emotion heartfelt or manufactured? She couldn't tell, and she no longer had Jeff to do the vetting.

She could check out the underlying facts at least. She texted Rory and Emily to see if they'd ever heard of Tellman or his farm. Within five minutes, they'd both responded in the negative. Rory had added that the library had an off-line database of small farms in Massachusetts, and she could look him up there.

Josefina was at the front desk, standing behind a younger woman who looked to be still in high school or perhaps just graduated, who was apparently a new employee or volunteer learning to use the library's computer.

Mabel waited until the patron had been helped and then told Josefina what she was looking for.

"That database is on a different computer and we can't access it from here." Josefina turned to the younger woman. "I'm going to the computer room to help Mabel. It's quiet enough that you should be fine without me, but I won't be gone long."

Josefina walked with surprising speed to the computer room and logged in. Mabel looked over her shoulder, resisting the urge to ask if they could switch places, since she could type so much faster and less painfully. But she knew Josefina wouldn't appreciate the offer.

"What was the name again?" Josefina asked.

Mabel told her, spelling it out, and the librarian slowly keyed it into the search box. The database immediately indicated there were no results.

"Try Tellman Fields," Mabel said.

Again, no results.

Mabel sighed, and Josefina said, "Wait. There's a forum for Massachusetts farmers. Maybe someone there knows who he is."

"Thanks, but you're needed at the front desk, and I can do that search at home," Mabel said.

Josefina had already finished typing in the URL, and the forum landing page was loading. "It will only take a minute."

Mabel watched as the farmer's name was keyed into the forum's search box, and this time there was a long list of results.

"Uh-oh," Josefina said. "It's never good when the subject line for the thread includes the word *beware*. In all caps."

"No, it's not," Mabel agreed, skimming the thread that Josefina had opened. Apparently Tellman was a well-known conman preying on farmers.

He wasn't a developer, but a grifter abusing the legal system to get money. He would enter into a contract, then play legal games, delaying the sale while recording the purchase and sale agreement at the Registry of Deeds to make it harder to sell the property to someone else, until the seller finally paid him to go away.

After checking three additional threads along the same lines, Mabel sighed. One person complaining about him might have been a fluke, someone unfairly blaming a buyer for legitimate delays, but there had been at least a dozen people commenting with very similar experiences.

Mabel didn't need Jeff Wright to tell her that it would be foolish to believe, like so many fraud victims did, that she was the exception to the pattern, that Tellman really truly wanted her farm because it was so amazing, and he wouldn't do anything to jeopardize the acquisition. It still would have been nice to talk to Jeff about it, and know that she had him in her corner. It would have been nice to talk to him, period, about anything, even the social chitchat she normally avoided at all costs. She just wanted to hear his voice again. But that wasn't going to happen.

Mabel dropped into the chair beside Josefina's, fighting the moisture gathering in her eyes. "I really miss my lawyer."

"You mean the one in Maine?" Josefina said. "I heard about his death. I'm sorry for your loss."

"Thanks," Mabel said. "I never had to worry about anything financial, because I always knew he was there for me, and he'd keep me from making any really huge mistakes. He'd have known this Tellman was a con right away. I don't know how Jeff did it, but he'd always been able to tell instantly when someone was lying or was trying to take advantage of me. I was never any good at figuring out who I could trust, other than Jeff. And now there's no one left."

"You can trust your friends," Josefina assured her. "Like me and Rory and Emily." After a brief pause, she added slyly, "And Charlie."

Mabel ignored the matchmaking. She didn't have time for that right now. "I do trust them, but they don't want to buy my farm. No one does." She couldn't help the whiney tone that infected her words.

"I know," Josefina said gently. "You're going through a lot, and you're still mourning your aunt, and now you've experienced another loss. I'm sorry for teasing you."

"It's okay." Mabel had gotten better at telling when someone was teasing, but even when she got it wrong, she'd found that there was often a lot to be learned from something said in jest. Frequently, it showed her who the person really was. Like in this case, it meant that Josefina cared about Mabel and wanted her to be happy. And presumably Josefina cared about Charlie too, and wanted him to be happy.

"Maybe you should think about your ownership of the farm differently," Josefina said. "One of the things I love about being a librarian is watching how books can suggest options that the reader hadn't thought of initially, and it changes their lives. I get to be part of making that happen by recommending things to read."

"So what should I be reading to get a new perspective?"

"Hmm." Josefina stared at her monitor, her arthritic hands hovering over the keyboard while she thought. "I suppose this is a bit like deciding on a career."

"I already have a career," Mabel said. "I'm an app developer."

"Yes, but you're assuming it's the only thing you can do. And that you can only do one thing at a time instead of multi-tasking or compartmentalizing. What if you were meant to be *both* an app developer *and* a farmer?" Josefina started tapping on the keyboard without actually applying enough pressure to activate the keys, as if it helped her to think.

Finally Josefina's fingers stopped and she said, "Have you ever considered being just a farm owner, not the person who's doing the actual growing and harvesting? Get someone else to do that for you, so you can do your app work?"

The college student, Terry Earley, had said something similar about separating the ownership from the agricultural work. Perhaps she should learn more about how it would work. "What have you got for me on farm managers?"

"Let me see." Josefina entered a few slow, painful-looking key strokes. "Mostly games, and I don't think they'll be helpful." Another minute of laborious typing. "This is better. There's a lot of resources on farm management generally. They should give you an idea of how much work you could do yourself and how much you'd want to hire someone else to do."

"Okay," Mabel said. "I'll take whatever you recommend."

"I can send you one digital resource now, but the rest will take a few days. They're not in this library, so I'll have to get them through the inter-library loan program."

"Thanks."

After a handful of additional slow jabs at the keyboard, Josefina looked up. "Done. Now will you do something for me?"

"If I can," Mabel said warily.

"I hate losing my favorite patrons, so promise me you'll keep an open mind about staying here in West Slocum. At least until the books come in and you've read them."

"I will." She didn't add that, regardless of what she wanted, she might not have a choice about staying here, not when leaving would only make Detective O'Connor more convinced that she was the best suspect in Graham's murder.

* * * *

Mabel checked on Billie Jean as soon as she got home. The water and kibble bowls still looked untouched. She called the animal shelter, and found that it was closed until the next afternoon. She still had the business card of the jam-maker who'd said she had experience with cats giving birth, so Mabel texted her to ask if she should be worried about Billie Jean's lack of appetite.

While she waited for a response, Mabel went downstairs and settled at the kitchen table with some iced tea and the book Josefina had checked out for her. The information quickly overwhelmed her. She'd never imagined how much management a farm needed. It had always seemed sort of quaint and straightforward. Get up at dawn, work with nature, feed the community. But it was a business, and a complicated one at that. Especially since she didn't know anything about either the growing aspects or the business aspects of farming.

She'd probably already irrevocably damaged the next year's profits. Any experienced farmer who might otherwise be interested in buying the farm would figure out pretty quickly that she'd made a mess of things, and wouldn't make an offer. In her ignorance, she was practically asking to be taken advantage of by buyers who were liars or scammers.

She decided she needed more time to straighten things out. And to find someone who could give her the kind of business and legal advice Jeff had always given her.

Mabel had just finished her tea when she got a text from the jam-maker: *Don't worry. But expect kittens soon.*

She wanted to ask for a more definite time frame than "soon," but then her phone rang with a call from her boss, Phil Reed. She considered ignoring him, but experience told her he'd just keep calling, and she might as well get the conversation over with as quickly as possible so she could go make sure Billie Jean hadn't produced any kittens in the last half hour.

She took the call, saying, "There's been a delay in the sale of the farm. I can't give you a definite answer right now on when I can come back to work."

"I can't hold your job open forever."

"I'm not asking for forever. Just a few months." When he didn't immediately respond, she added reluctantly, "But if you've got to replace me, go ahead."

"No, no," he said. "I don't want to lose you. But I really need you on this project, and it can't wait weeks, let alone months. It's right up your alley, and everyone else is overworked already."

Phil went on to explain the specs, and they did sound interesting.

"When's it due?"

"In a month," he said. "You could do it in half that time."

She could. Or in the same number of weeks, but working on it only part-time. She could spend her days finding a farm manager and still have the evenings to work on the coding. But not quite yet. First she had to focus on more imminent crises. Like kittens and killers.

"I'm not coming back full-time right now," she said, "but I can do this one emergency project, starting in about a week."

"I knew I could count on you." Phil's voice exuded even more relief than she'd expected. He was probably getting paid top dollar to do it in such a short time frame, or he wouldn't have been so desperate to get her back to work. Jeff Wright had always handled her salary negotiations for her, but now she was responsible for herself. What would Jeff have done in these circumstances?

"In return," she said, "You'll pay me overtime rates for the entire project."

"That's crazy," Phil said, sounding surprised she'd even brought up the issue of money. Had he heard of her lawyer's death and thought he could walk all over her now that she didn't have Jeff watching out for her?

If so, Phil was wrong. She'd grown accustomed to leaning on Jeff, but she'd also learned a lot from him over the years. She could take care of herself now, even if she wished she didn't have to.

"I guess you'll have to find someone else to do this project then."

Phil didn't answer right away, apparently trying to decide whether she was serious. She needed to get this conversation over with so she could go check on Billie Jean.

"Look"—Mabel put him on speaker and set her phone's timer for sixty seconds—"I'm going to hang up in exactly one minute. I've got plenty of other things to do here on the farm this month instead of working on your app. Hiring field hands, planting garlic, and midwifing kittens." To say nothing of finding a killer. "So, do you agree to my terms or not?"

With eight seconds left, Phil said, "All right, all right. But you don't get the overtime until the project is done. Regular rates up front, plus the rest as a bonus at the end."

"Fine," Mabel said "Send me the specs. I'll start in a few days, just as soon as I deal with some other crises here."

Like figuring out how to hire a farm manager. Fortunately, one of the books Josefina had ordered for her was about the hiring process. All she had to do was to follow the steps in the book. She had one addition to the checklist: The successful candidate would have to like cats. Even though she was taking Pixie back to Maine with her eventually, there were the barn cats to look after and now Billie Jean too.

Before she could even think about hiring the manager, though, she needed to get herself out from under police suspicion of murder. That couldn't wait weeks or months. Not if she was going to attend Jeff's funeral. And she was. Whether O'Connor liked it or not.

Chapter 22

Mabel was on her way to the stairs to check on Billie Jean, when Emily knocked and entered the kitchen. "I was wondering how your pregnant cat is doing, so I thought I'd stop by."

"I'm not sure." Mabel said. "Apparently not eating is a sign of imminent labor, and I don't think she's eaten anything since sometime in the middle of the night. Definitely not since early this morning."

"Labor should start soon then," Emily said.

There was that word again—soon. "Could you be a little more specific than that?"

Emily laughed. "Afraid not. I've only dealt with one set of kittens. I make sure all my barn cats are fixed, but I had a pregnant stray show up once a few days before she was due. I read up on what to do, but apparently each cat's experience is a little different. Just like with humans, I guess."

Mabel nodded toward the stairs. "Do you want to come with me to check on Billie Jean? It's been a while since I looked in on her, and I was on my way there when you arrived."

"Sure. But first you need to tell me why you look so miserable."

"I just feel so helpless," Mabel said on the way to the stairs. "I want to do something useful, but I don't know what. For Billie Jean and also to help find Graham's killer."

"For Billie Jean, the best thing is to just leave her alone except for occasional checks to make sure she's not having a difficult labor," Emily said. "Humans hovering around will only stress her."

"I'll keep my distance from her after we check on her, but I can't stay away from Graham's murder."

"It might be better if you did," Emily said. "You're not responsible for him the way you are for Billie Jean."

"No, but I have to leave town soon for a friend's funeral back in Maine, and I can't do that without bringing the wrath of Detective O'Connor down on me. As best I can tell, there are only four likely suspects, but I can't figure out how to narrow down the options."

"Four?" Emily said. "The only person I've thought of is his next-door neighbor. I've heard about what a nuisance she is. According to Rory's husband, she called the cops on every little thing Graham did. Are there really three other people who disliked him as much as she did?"

"There could be more than that," Mabel said. "The ones I know about are a client who was angry with him and another rhubarb breeder who had a rocky relationship with Graham. And then there's his brother-in-law, Rob Robinson. He isn't an heir, but he's a creditor and his kids will get whatever's left after the bills are paid. That's a motive, even if it's indirect."

"Rob Robinson? The name sounds familiar." Emily frowned in concentration as they made their way up the stairs to the second floor. "Oh, I know why. He works in insurance, doesn't he?"

Mabel nodded.

"I didn't know he was related to Graham," she said. "But if he's got any financial interest in the estate, no matter how distant, he'd be my prime suspect."

"You've dealt with him before?"

"Not me, but my husband," Emily said, pausing outside the bedroom where Billie Jean was. "He did a training program for Rob's company, and Ed's pretty used to normal cut-throat business behavior, but he said Rob was different. Like he wanted to hurt the competition, not just win a particular contract. My husband had the chance to do more work with the company, but he turned it down."

Mabel needed to have another chat with Rob, perhaps under the pretext of letting him know that she might be out of town for a few days, and she'd hired someone else to take care of the rhubarb seedlings. His office would be closed by now, so it would have to wait until morning.

She opened the bedroom door to show Emily that even if the investigation into Graham's murder was stalled, at least Billie Jean was doing just fine.

Except she wasn't. She was moaning and writhing.

"She's in labor," Emily said. "And look, the first kitten is born already and Billie Jean cleaned her up, just like she's supposed to."

Mabel peered at the little, rat-like creature lying on its back a few inches away from the momcat. It didn't seem to be breathing, and it definitely wasn't moving. "Are you sure it's okay?"

Emily nodded. "Childbirth comes naturally to most animals. Cats usually don't have problems."

"But what if Billie Jean does?" Mabel asked. "That kitten doesn't look good."

"Give it some time to adjust to being in the world. It may be waiting for some siblings to join it before it starts looking for food," Emily said. "I can stay with you for a while if you want to keep an eye on things, but mostly the momcat probably just wants to be left alone."

Mabel had found the same advice online. "If all we can do is leave her alone, I can do that on my own. I'll call you if I do need help, if that's okay."

"Of course," Emily said. "Don't worry if it's late. That's one good thing about my husband being gone at the moment. You won't wake him up."

"Thanks." She shut the door behind them to keep Pixie out and walked Emily to the back door. Mabel knew she'd be too worried about Billie Jean to sleep, so she grabbed her laptop from the kitchen table and went back upstairs, not to her aunt's bedroom but to her own, where she could work on decoding Graham's journal. The need to check on the cat would keep her awake, and as long as she was pulling an all-nighter, she could finally finish decoding the journal. She was running out of time to clear her name, and if there weren't any clues in the journal, she needed to know as soon as possible so she could come up with a new plan.

* * * *

After about an hour of intense work on the journal and a quick check on Billie Jean who had two kittens in the crate with her by then, Mabel was up to August in Graham's journals. The work had gone faster after she'd decided not to bother to decode the paragraphs that started with the word *data*, which she could recognize at a glance after having translated it so often, and generally just summarized some aspect of his breeding work. Instead, she focused on anything without that flag, and those sections were almost always something personal that, unlike the scientific information, might offer some insights into his murder.

No new leads presented themselves though. Graham continued to accuse the Enforcer of pressuring him to sell his property, and the Professor of wanting to steal his work. He seemed increasingly worried about them, but the only mentions of violence were his own fantasies of killing them if they ever became a real threat to his seedlings, rather than any fear of someone killing or even assaulting him.

Another few hours passed with regular visits to check on Billie Jean to break up the back-straining monotony of hunching over the scanned copy of the journal on her laptop. At last check, there were four kittens, all latched onto their mother, drinking ravenously, their tiny round ears twitching adorably.

As Mabel hit the September entries, she ran into a new nickname—the Salesman, who presumably was Sam Trent. For the first time, Graham had sounded legitimately afraid, rather than paranoid and angry. The fear wasn't of physical violence, but of being sued and forced to quit practicing law. He didn't seem to mind the prospect of losing his career per se, since it would give him more time for his breeding program, but he was terrified of losing his only source of financial support for his rhubarb.

She still had a month left to decode, but it was three in the morning, and she wasn't used to such a late hour any longer. Her attention kept wavering, and the work slowed exponentially. If she was going to finish it before falling asleep sitting up, she needed to narrow down the pages that needed to be decoded. She decided to look just for references to Trent, to see if there was something specific she could bring to the police.

Graham seemed to be getting more and more afraid of the Salesman as the days went on, but the comments remained cryptic, and while Mabel was reasonably sure the nickname referred to Trent, the connection wasn't spelled out anywhere. She'd pieced it together from what she knew about Trent and from Graham's description of the client's allegation against him about revealing confidential information during a divorce proceeding. It was possible, she supposed, that Graham had done the same thing to more than one client, but surely if that serious a breach had happened more than once, he would have been disciplined by the state entity that enforced professional ethics rules.

Graham eventually admitted in his journal that he'd been having blackouts, and it was perhaps possible he'd revealed confidential information when he wasn't in his right mind. And while his writing sometimes reverted to delusional detours where he suggested that Trent was part of a conspiracy by the Enforcer to force the sale of the farmhouse, at other times Graham was fully aware that Trent's accusations were enough, if people believed them, to force the closure of his law practice. No one would hire a lawyer who couldn't keep a secret.

Mabel continued looking for references to Trent, until she found something dated three days before the murder. It was a lengthy entry that described a physical confrontation with the Salesman in the greenhouse. It had just involved some shoving, not punching or the use of a weapon, but it had ended with Trent's threatening to kill Graham if he didn't contact his malpractice insurer and admit what he'd done. There was even a deadline of the following Monday, the date Graham was killed.

Unfortunately, even in the depths of Graham's fear, or perhaps because of that fear, he'd continued to use a nickname for Sam Trent, never mentioning his real name. It seemed obvious to her that Trent and the Salesman were the same person, but the police might be skeptical. Especially when the person bringing the information to them was herself a possible suspect.

There had to be a way to prove that Trent was the Salesman, not just to her own satisfaction, but beyond a jury's reasonable doubt. Mabel went over the section describing the shoving match again. Graham had gone into considerable detail, including the fact that Trent had been standing near the wall of tools and had grabbed a pair of clippers to wave menacingly, only to cut his finger on one of the blades and throw it away from him in frustration. Fortunately, the greenhouse was made out of some sort of heavy plastic, not glass that the impact could have cracked, so there hadn't been any damage. The clippers had fallen between the greenhouse wall and the planting bench, where they were difficult to retrieve, so Graham had decided to leave them there until the spring, when the seedlings would be moved outdoors, making it easier to push the benches out of the way. Graham had seemed almost as annoyed by the temporary loss of his favorite clippers as by the physical threat they'd offered in Trent's hands.

Graham might not have had an incentive to retrieve the clippers immediately, but Mabel did. Or at least to confirm that they were still where they'd fallen. If she could find them, and the police could verify that the blood on the blade belonged to Trent, it would be proof that he was the Salesman. Maybe not enough to prove beyond a reasonable doubt that Trent was also the killer, but enough to get the police to put him at the top of the suspect list and take their attention off Mabel.

She had to get to the greenhouse to see if the clippers were still there. She couldn't go right away, not at—she checked the clock on her laptop— four in the morning. If she went to the greenhouse now, Lena Shaw would undoubtedly call the cops on her, and they might actually take her seriously for once.

Now that Mabel wasn't totally immersed in the decoding, she realized the earliest of the early birds had already started their racket outside her windows. She really needed to soundproof her bedroom more thoroughly if she had to stick around long enough to hire a farm manager and make sure he was settled in before she returned to Maine.

Mabel checked on Billie Jean to find that there were now five kittens, all drinking from the dozing momcat. Mabel wished she could sleep too, but she was too wired in anticipation of finally finding some useful evidence to take suspicion off her. She might as well stay up and finish decoding the journal in case there was anything useful in the remaining pages.

* * * *

Mabel decided that seven o'clock was a reasonable time to go to the greenhouse, and then shook her head at the idea that she would ever, under any circumstances, consider anything before noon to be a sensible time to be awake. West Slocum had definitely made its mark on her.

She tucked her laptop with the scanned copy of the journal into its bag. She'd marked the relevant pages to share with the detectives after she got the clippers. While she'd been waiting for dawn, she'd gone back to look at the journal entries that weren't specific to Sam Trent, and she'd found that Graham's friction with both the Enforcer and the Brother had been escalating in the last four weeks before he'd been killed. One entry described how the Enforcer had visited early one morning to threaten having the property condemned if he didn't make some basic repairs to the exterior of the farmhouse by a specific date, the Friday before Graham was killed. Other times when Graham had mentioned the Enforcer's threats, he'd done so in the context of how foolish they were and how he didn't have time to deal with them. That was consistent with Lena's obvious irritation with having been ignored whenever she complained to Graham. This time seemed different though. Graham had even made a list of the work he thought would satisfy the Enforcer, although Mabel couldn't find any evidence that he'd taken any steps to get the projects done.

Another entry, just a couple of days later, mentioned the Brother stopping by with similar demands for repair, but with the added threat of foreclosure on the mortgage. Like the Enforcer, the Brother had given Graham a month to start work on a dozen repairs. That deadline for both sets of demands had come and gone the Friday before he'd been killed. Graham had even noted in his journal that the deadlines had passed without any of the work done, but that he was confident that both the Enforcer and the Brother would understand he was on the verge of a breakthrough in his breeding program. Once he had the perfect cultivar, Graham had written, then he'd have both the time and money to take care of the repairs.

Mabel wasn't as convinced that his critics would have been so understanding. Still, it seemed more likely that they'd take the threatened legal action, not attack him physically to force him to get the property cleaned up. Sam Trent, who'd shown his proclivity for both losing his temper and getting physical, was a much more credible suspect.

She checked on Billie Jean again—the crate still held five hungry kittens in a variety of colors and one exhausted momcat—and fed both her and Pixie before heading out to her car.

She was halfway to Graham's house before she remembered how her friends had insisted she shouldn't go there alone. She called Charlie, since construction work had a reputation for starting at dawn, so he should be awake. He must have been in a meeting though, because he didn't pick up. Mabel left a message to let him know where she was going and that she thought she had some new evidence. Or would by the time she left the greenhouse.

She considered calling Terry Earley to go with her instead, since she knew he was a morning person, but he had classes, and even if *he* didn't mind missing one, *she* didn't want to be responsible for his truancy. She couldn't ask him to jeopardize his education, not when she was certain the greenhouse would be perfectly safe. All she had to do was confirm that the clippers were still where the Salesman had thrown them, and then contact Detective O'Connor to send his forensic team to get them and look for fingerprints and blood. No reason anyone other than perhaps Lena Shaw would even notice she was there. Certainly not Trent.

Mabel continued to Graham's house and parked out front where the car would be safe from Lena's tow trucks. In the early-morning haze, the property seemed even more run-down than she remembered. Was that a normal effect of dawn light? She couldn't remember the last time she'd been outside at such an early hour. For all she knew, everything looked abandoned at this hour of the day. She hadn't paid much attention to what Stinkin' Stuff Farm looked like on the way down the driveway, concentrating instead on glugging down the iced tea from the travel cup she'd filled and brought with her in the hope of waking up more fully.

What if it wasn't just a morning thing or her sleep-deprived brain playing tricks on her, and her subconscious was trying to tell her to stay away? Perhaps she should wait until she talked to Charlie and he could meet her at the greenhouse. In the meantime, she could keep an eye on the property from the safety of her car to make sure no one sneaked into the greenhouse to steal the incriminating clippers.

She was still undecided five minutes later when a man jogged past her car and into the subdivision with a large dog. It wasn't on a leash, which was bound to be a violation of the homeowners' association rules. If Lena was awake, she'd be sure to come out and give the man a lecture.

Sure enough, less than a minute later, Lena appeared on the sidewalk in a terry cloth robe and teal-colored flannel pajamas, video camera in hand. Just another day in Robinson Woods, Mabel thought. No need to worry about safety, not with Lena Shaw on the job, watching and documenting everything that went on in the neighborhood.

Mabel finally left the Mini Cooper and headed for the greenhouse, telling herself she could still change her mind and go back to the car to wait for Charlie to return her call if the sinister feeling worsened. She paused at the foot of the driveway, noting that the truck, car, and tractor were all gone. Rob's tow company must have taken them. The view into the greenhouse was no longer obscured as it had been when Graham was killed. No one would be foolish enough to attack her when they'd be in easy view of the street at a time that probably constituted a rush hour for the subdivision, as commuters headed out to work.

It wouldn't take long to confirm that the clippers were still where they'd been thrown, and then she'd be gone before anyone could follow her inside. Besides, Lena was already up and chasing down rule breakers. She would notice if anyone who didn't belong on Graham's property showed up. It was a bit odd actually that Lena had noticed the dog-walker, given her claim to not being a morning person, but perhaps she'd been upset that she'd missed the biggest crime ever to happen in the subdivision and had redoubled her surveillance. If anything happened on Graham's property, Lena would be on her phone, calling the police, at the first sign of trouble.

Mabel spared a moment to consider whether Lena's presence was itself a risk. What if the Salesman wasn't actually Sam Trent? It couldn't be Lena though, since the nickname referred to a client who'd been getting a divorce. Lena was emphatically single, never married, so she couldn't be that client. And even if Mabel was wrong about the Salesman, and Lena was indeed Graham's killer, there was still nothing to fear. Unlike Graham, Mabel knew to stay alert and not let anyone get too close to her in the greenhouse.

Mabel was bent over the greenhouse doorknob, inserting the key, when she heard a shouted "Hey!" behind her. She turned to see Lena at the end of the driveway, shaking her video camera at Mabel.

"What are you doing here?" Lena demanded, stalking up the driveway toward Mabel.

Chapter 23

Lena looked even worse than Mabel felt. It wasn't just that Lena was wearing ragged flannel pajamas instead of her usual meticulously put-together outfit that was more appropriate to an office than a rural subdivision. There were dark circles under her unfocused eyes, and she wobbled once as she came up the driveway.

Had Lena been drinking? Or using some other recreational substance? If Lena were thinking clearly, she would know why Mabel was at the greenhouse.

"I'm just checking on something," Mabel said warily.

"That's not what you're supposed to be doing when you're here." Lena's words were irrationally angry, but not slurred with either inebriation or fatigue. "You've got permission to take care of the plants, not have parties in the greenhouse."

Mabel blinked. "I'm not having a party."

"That's what everyone says." Lena tapped her video camera. "I've got proof. There were a dozen people here an hour ago, way too early and making a ruckus, blaring their horrible music, and clearing out the vehicles to make room for who knows what."

Understanding dawned. "That wasn't a party. That was the towing company putting the vehicles in storage. I thought you'd be happy they were gone. You said they were an eyesore."

"They were," Lena said. "But that's no excuse for replacing them with a different kind of nuisance. All that noise, waking people up. It's not right."

"Of course not." Mabel hated early-morning noise at least as much as the next person, probably more. She felt a tiny bit of sympathy for the annoying woman. "I'll make sure it doesn't happen again." Easy enough to promise, since all the vehicles were gone now.

"That's not good enough." Lena stomped up the driveway until she was less than an arm's length away. She held out her hand imperiously. "Give me the key to the greenhouse. I'll return it to the police when I tell them you're not welcome here any longer."

Mabel took a step back, bumping against the greenhouse door. "If I don't visit, the rhubarb seedlings will die."

"I don't care." Lena shook her hand imperiously. "Give me the key."

Mabel hated confrontation, but she couldn't do what the woman wanted. Perhaps it would be best to just leave and come back another time. She took a step to her right to go around Lena, but the woman moved to block her again.

"The key. Now."

Mabel considered her next move. She was fairly confident that Lena didn't have a weapon on her. The outstretched hand was empty, and the other one held a video camera that might be a metaphorical weapon of sorts, but not one that Mabel feared. If Lena was still taping, the recording would show Mabel hadn't done anything wrong.

Of course, the lack of a weapon didn't mean Mabel was completely safe. Graham's killer hadn't been armed originally either, but had grabbed something close at hand. Then she remembered that while the unsightly vehicles were gone from the driveway, the pile of discarded materials was still nearby, to Mabel's left, including the broken pieces of metal sidewall supports that were about the same length as a baseball bat and potentially just as lethal if swung at a human head.

Mabel sidled to her right, away from the pile of debris that was a too-convenient source of makeshift weapons. "I'm willing to leave for now, but I'm not giving you the key. I'm not authorized to do that."

"You have to do what I say," Lena insisted. "I'm in charge here."

"No, you're not," Mabel said. "You told me yourself that Graham's property isn't part of the subdivision."

"It will be soon," she said. "Now give me the key, or I'll take it from you."

There was no room left for Mabel to back up any farther, and there was an overgrown bush to her right, limiting how far away she could get from the pile of potential weapons. What would Lena do if Mabel tried to push past her? Mabel had never been comfortable with physical contact, not even the friendly type like hugs, and an assault would be even worse.

Mabel leaned forward and without actually taking a step forward, twisted as if she were preparing to push her left shoulder into Lena's arm and brush past her. Anyone who wasn't intent on starting a scuffle would have read the body language and stepped back.

Lena didn't. She braced herself for impact, and her face took on a triumphant expression. She wanted Mabel to be the one to escalate from threats of contact to actual battery. Then she could tell the police that Mabel had started the scuffle. Lena had probably done the same thing with her neighbors when they'd violated some silly rule and wouldn't accept responsibility. She probably knew the police wouldn't back her up unless the other person had done something worse than break a homeowners' association rule, something that could be labeled a criminal assault.

Mabel sighed. It was too early in the morning for her in the best of circumstances, and after an all-nighter, she definitely didn't have the energy to play games. Her head hurt, her eyes were itchy, and she just wanted to find the clippers, tell the police what she'd found, and go back to bed.

Rather than do what Lena wanted, Mabel leaned back against the greenhouse's front wall. She was fairly sure that Sam Trent was the most likely suspect, but he hadn't actually done anything worse than wave the clippers around, as far as she could prove. It was a good lead for the police, but not definitive. So, what if she were wrong? After all, it still seemed odd that Lena hadn't seen the killer, even more so now that Mabel had witnessed how quickly the woman had responded to the jogger at what must have been essentially the same time of day as when Graham had been killed.

What if Lena had been this confrontational with Graham, intending to provoke him into assaulting her, but instead she'd accidentally killed him? Mabel had a hard time figuring out how anyone could have *accidentally* stuck a knife into a person's heart from the back, but perhaps there had been a struggle, and Graham had turned away, thinking he'd defeated Lena or in a show of not taking her seriously. Then with adrenaline racing through Lena, she'd lashed out, maybe even forgetting she had the knife in her hand.

It was possible, especially now that Mabel had seen just how unreasonable Lena could be in what she obviously considered her righteous upholding of the subdivision's standards. As long as they were stuck in a standoff—and Lena didn't have anything more dangerous than a compact video camera in her immediate reach—it wouldn't hurt to ask more about Lena's failure to see anything useful at the time of the murder.

"How was it that you didn't happen to see the killer the morning Graham died? You were incredibly fast at noticing the jogger and his unleashed dog just now, and it's about the same time of day as the murder."

"I don't have to justify myself to you."

That sounded like Lena really had seen something. She wasn't generally shy about explaining herself when she felt she was in the right.

"Did you tell the police what you saw then?"

"I always cooperate with the police."

"Even when it would implicate yourself? One possible explanation for why you didn't see anyone else here that morning is if it was you in the greenhouse with him. Confronting him like you're doing with me."

"What are you talking about?" Lena looked honestly confused. "I'm never confrontational. I'm just doing my job, protecting the neighborhood."

"I see." Mabel crossed her arms over her chest. "So the morning he died, were you just doing your job? Goading him into assaulting you, so you could claim self-defense?"

"I overslept that morning," she snapped. "I'd been so worried about the state of Graham's property that I developed insomnia. The kind where you can't fall asleep for hours and hours. I didn't want him dead, but I have to say, at least now I can sleep at night."

She sounded legitimately irritated, and Mabel was almost inclined to believe her, especially since she knew what it was like to stay up too late while obsessed with a problem, until Lena added, "And I'll sue you for slander if you repeat the insinuation that I was ever anything less than professional with Graham. Now give me the key and go."

Mabel was too tired to play any more games, so she leaned back against the greenhouse door. "I'm not giving you the key."

Lena set down her video camera and grabbed Mabel's hand containing the key.

Seriously? Now they were going to play keep-away? Mabel couldn't give up the key. She'd promised to care for Graham's seedlings, and the police wouldn't give her a replacement key if Lena complained to them.

Mabel tucked her hand behind her, between her back and the greenhouse door. Even as tired as she was, she should be able to win this game. She'd gotten stronger from her work on the farm, and she had the advantage of being some twenty years younger than Lena.

On the other hand, Lena was highly motivated. She wasn't going to give up easily. They might be stuck here for hours. Or until Charlie got her message and she didn't answer his return call, so he came looking for her.

Mabel wanted to slide down the door to sit on the ground, but that would leave her too vulnerable if Lena had completely lost her grip on reality, as she seemed to have. Mabel needed to be able to run if necessary.

It felt like an hour had passed in their standoff, but it was probably only a couple of minutes before a car pulled into Graham's newly emptied driveway. Mabel recognized it as belonging to the mayor. Lena wouldn't do anything violent in front of a witness, least of all a witness who, for all intents and purposes, was in charge of the police department. Mabel tucked the disputed key into one of her barn coat's big pockets.

Lena stepped back and turned to look at the mayor. "Well. It's about time someone got here. It's been at least fifteen minutes since I called the police dispatcher. Where's the patrol car?"

"They're not coming," Danny said. "The police chief asked me to come take care of it."

She snorted. "Like you could take care of anything."

Mabel slipped past Lena who didn't try to stop her now that there was a witness. Mabel kept the mayor between her and Lena before saying, "I'm glad you're here. And grateful you got here so quickly."

Danny shrugged. "No problem. I live just around the corner. In fact, I sometimes take my morning walk through the subdivision. It really is a lovely place."

"No thanks to you or the zoning department or the police," Lena said. "The neighborhood would have become a blighted mess if it weren't for me insisting that the laws be enforced."

"Of course," Danny said. "We all appreciate your work. But I think you can take a break now. From what I understand, Mabel is working to keep the greenhouse from becoming more of a problem than it already is. You two should be working together."

Lena peered at Mabel suspiciously. "I don't think she's here for legitimate reasons. She's never been here this early before."

Danny turned a questioning look on Mabel.

"I might have a lead for the police to investigate relating to Graham's death," she said, keeping her answer vague, just in case she was wrong. "I need to check something in the greenhouse before I give them the information."

"Really?" Danny said. "That's wonderful news. Can I help?"

Mabel glanced at Lena. "You can keep her from interfering."

"Of course." Danny wrapped his arm around Lena's elbow as if he were escorting her at a formal function and gently led her down the driveway. "I appreciate your letting us know about the situation," he told Lena, "but I can take it from here."

"But—"

"No, really," Danny said. "You've done enough today. You deserve a break."

"Well…" Lena let herself be led down the driveway.

Danny released her arm when they reached the sidewalk and watched for a moment as if to make sure she kept heading for her house. Apparently satisfied, he hurried back to the greenhouse.

"It's safe now. You can do whatever you need to." He frowned. "Why are you here so early anyway? You told me you weren't a morning person, so all appointments to view the farmhouse needed to be in the afternoon."

"I couldn't sleep." Mabel turned to unlock the greenhouse door. "I finally decoded Graham's journal for the last few weeks before he died, and apparently Sam Trent confronted him in the greenhouse and even threatened him with a pair of clippers. They should still be where they were tossed, complete with fingerprints and maybe even some blood, since Trent cut himself on them. I just want to make sure they're still there, and then I'll let the police know."

"Where do you think they are?" Graham followed Mabel inside. "I can help search for them."

"I'm not sure exactly. They were arguing over near where the tools are hanging next to the back door of the house, and then Trent threw them, and they fell between the planting benches and the wall of the greenhouse." Mabel nodded to the right side of the greenhouse. "If you look under the benches over there, I'll take the other side."

Mabel dropped to her hands and knees, not caring whether her jeans got dirty, while the mayor stayed on his feet and bent to peer under the tables. About halfway up the aisle, Mabel caught a reflection of light on metal blades.

"Found them!" Mabel shouted.

The mayor, who'd been proceeding more slowly, trotted over to peer under the table. "Shall we move the table and get them?"

"I think it's better if we leave them for the police to retrieve," Mabel said. "I don't want them to think we planted the evidence. I'll take some pictures, so they know where to look."

While she used her phone's camera, the mayor straightened. "Everyone will be so relieved to have this case closed."

Mabel got to her feet. "There's no guarantee that Trent did it, but this should at least get the detectives to take him seriously as a suspect."

"Don't be so modest," Danny said. "You solved the case. It has to have been Trent. The only reason anyone thought it might not be is that he kept saying he'd gotten over his anger and was moving on. This proves he was lying."

"It's still circumstantial," Mabel said on the way out of the greenhouse. "I don't know if simply having a motive will be enough to convince a jury, even with evidence of an earlier violent incident."

"Maybe not, but now that the police know where to focus their attention, I'm sure they'll find additional evidence to convict him." Danny waited while Mabel locked the greenhouse door behind her, and then gave the handle a tug to make sure it was secure. "I bet Lena knows more than she's saying. I just don't know why she keeps denying it. Unless someone's paying her to keep quiet. I'll go talk to the police chief now about having someone question her a little more closely."

"Thanks for your help," Mabel said while the mayor got into his car. She waved and headed down the sidewalk to her Mini Cooper. She hoped the mayor was right, and the clippers led to more evidence and then an arrest.

As she reached her car, it dawned on her that she hadn't heard the mayor's car start or pull out of the driveway. What was he waiting for? Could Lena have come back to complain some more?

She listened but didn't hear any voices, and if Lena were confronting the mayor, the conversation would be easily audible. The woman seldom bothered to keep her voice down, even when complaining about other people's noisy behavior. If she was being quiet, something was wrong.

Chapter 24

Mabel turned off her phone's ringer so it wouldn't betray her presence, and then crept back to Graham's driveway. The mayor's car was still there, but he wasn't inside it.

Maybe he hadn't had a chance to take his morning walk before getting the call about Lena's complaint, so he was doing a make-up trek around the subdivision. It still seemed odd though, since he'd been planning to talk to the police chief right away about interrogating Lena more closely.

She did a careful visual sweep of the subdivision and saw no one on the sidewalks. The road bent out of sight eventually, but not in the distance the mayor might have traveled in the last two or three minutes.

What if he'd decided to get the clippers and bring them to the police, despite the risk of contaminating the scene? Mabel trotted up the driveway and found the greenhouse door propped open. That shouldn't have been possible. She knew it had been closed securely before she left. She checked the doorknob, and there was no obvious damage from the door being forced, so someone other than herself apparently had a key. Or had found one, if Graham had kept a copy hidden outside in case he was locked out. Lena probably knew where it was from seeing it get hidden while she was snooping. Or the mayor might have guessed the hiding spot, since in his role as a broker, he'd probably experienced all the places where a homeowner might leave an emergency key. But Mabel couldn't think of any good reason for either the mayor or Lena to be on Graham's property. Maybe it was someone else. Sam Trent, perhaps, having finally remembered the clippers and how incriminating they would be if the police found them?

Except no one was visible in the main greenhouse. Why would anyone break in unless it was to get those clippers? With Graham's journals safely locked up at Quon Liang's office, there was nothing else worth stealing, not even by another rhubarb breeder like Sandy Faitakis.

Mabel grabbed one of the discarded metal sidewall supports from the pile of debris near the door, just in case it wasn't the mayor and she needed to defend herself. As she stepped inside the greenhouse, she heard what sounded like a door closing in the distance. It seemed to come from where the second greenhouse led into the back yard. She considered calling the police to report a break-in, but then thought it might be the mayor out there. Perhaps he'd changed his mind about going to the police station and had instead called and arranged for the detective to meet him at the scene of the crime. She would look like an idiot if she called the police on the mayor, and she didn't need that kind of attention from them right now. She was trying to stay under their radar until the killer was caught.

She'd just check to see if she was right about the mayor being in the back yard, and then leave before the detective could arrive.

As she headed down the central path of the greenhouse, she wondered why the mayor would wait in the back yard instead of in his own car. Maybe he was there more in his role as the only real estate broker in town, sizing up the property for describing it to potential buyers, assuming Lena didn't buy it from the estate before it could be listed.

Mabel hadn't really thought about it before, but Danny would benefit doubly from Graham's death. As the only real estate broker in town, he might get paid for selling the property. Even if he didn't get the listing, he would profit politically as the mayor by taking credit for removing a blight on the community. A new owner, whether Lena or someone else, was bound to keep the place in better condition than Graham had. Danny would also have one less set of hassles as mayor, since Lena would have less to complain about to the police who in turn complained to him.

But was any of that a reason to kill someone? Graham hadn't seemed to think so. He'd mentioned worsening relationships with the Enforcer, the Salesman, and the Brother—Lena Shaw, Sam Trent, and Rob Robinson, respectively—but not with the Broker, Danny.

Mabel could see why he'd take both the Salesman and the Brother seriously in their escalated pressure. They both had considerable financial leverage over him, either in terms of causing him to lose his license to practice law or having his property foreclosed on. But the Enforcer couldn't do anything she hadn't done before. Graham could continue to thumb his nose at her, as he'd apparently been doing for years. So why had it even registered on him enough to mention it in his journal?

Unless Lena Shaw wasn't the Enforcer.

Mabel paused on the threshold between the main greenhouse and the smaller one where Graham had been killed.

Who else could be the Enforcer? Someone who could make good on whatever leverage he was using to put pressure on Graham. Someone who could enforce zoning regulations and get the board of health to condemn the property?

The mayor could do that. As the chief executive of the town, he was, by definition, an enforcer of laws. He could even have invoked eminent domain powers to take the property if necessary.

What if Danny was the Enforcer and Lena was the Broker? Graham hadn't even mentioned the Broker after that dream about a relationship between that person and the Enforcer. The Broker hadn't bothered him enough to write about, but he'd clearly been worried about the Enforcer making good on threats.

Had Mabel gotten it backward, and Danny was the Enforcer and Lena was the Broker? The selling of real estate wasn't the first thing that came to Mabel's mind when thinking about Lena, but she had been a broker when Graham first met her and she was selling the houses in the subdivision.

If Danny was the Enforcer, then he was a solid suspect for the murder, much more likely than Lena was. Danny certainly had the physical ability to kill Graham, probably more so than any other suspect except Sam Trent. While not as muscular as Sam Trent was, Danny was a large man, and a sufficient match for Graham, who, despite his size, hadn't been in the best of health.

As to motive, Danny could benefit both financially and politically from Graham's death. And finally, Danny had had the opportunity to commit the murder. Unlike Lena and Sam Trent, Danny was a morning person who took early walks in the subdivision, which potentially put him near the scene at the relevant time. The detectives might not have collected any eyewitness evidence that the mayor had been in the subdivision on Monday morning, but she suspected no one had thought to ask about him specifically. No one would think to volunteer that they'd seen him that morning if it was a frequent event. People tended not to notice things that happened repeatedly, so even if he'd been spotted, it wouldn't have made much of an impression, and the witness might not have made the connection between the murder and seeing him in what appeared to be a routine activity.

Danny was probably elated that Mabel had found some solid circumstantial evidence pointing to someone else. If Trent were convicted, then the mayor wouldn't have to worry that his own guilt would ever be brought to light.

It all made sense, but Mabel needed more evidence before she could take her theory to the detectives. Danny had thought Lena knew more than she was saying. What if she knew he'd been at the greenhouse around the time of the murder, possibly overhearing them arguing? She probably wouldn't have been close enough to see the actual knifing, but she could at least place Danny at the scene. She might be willing to keep quiet as long as no one else was arrested and blamed for the murder, but would she really let an innocent man be convicted? It hardly seemed consistent with what Mabel thought was Lena's true commitment to upholding even the tiniest rules as part of an overall belief in respect for the law.

Lena might well be the only thing standing between the mayor getting off scot-free and being convicted of murder. Danny couldn't afford to let Lena talk to the police, not now that there was a credible suspect who could take the fall for him. And now was the perfect time to silence her, before anyone could question her about Sam Trent's supposed presence at the scene of the crime.

Mabel started to dial 911, but then realized she didn't know what to say to make them take her seriously. Jeff Wright had always taken care of that sort of thing, but now she was on her own.

What would get the police to act? They wouldn't care if she said that someone had broken into a greenhouse that had nothing of obvious value in it. What if she explained she thought the town's mayor might have committed murder and was planning to do it again? No, that wouldn't work, even if it was true. Not only would they be dismissive of her, but they'd think she was crazier than Graham had been. And if it turned out she was wrong after she made that kind of slanderous accusation against a popular mayor? In that case, even Rory and Emily would have to admit Mabel couldn't live in West Slocum any longer and should go back to her home in Maine.

Mabel dropped her phone into the barn coat's oversized pocket with the key, switched the piece of sidewall support to her right hand, and headed across the smaller greenhouse and into the back yard.

A woman's scream from the back yard caused Mabel to pick up her pace and grip her makeshift weapon more tightly. Once she reached the back door, she paused to look through the glass walls to prepare herself for whatever was outside. Danny was a dozen yards away about halfway along the rhubarb beds that took up most of the back yard. He was dragging

Lena toward a small shed attached to the house, from which wisps of smoke emanated.

Lena, to Mabel's surprise, was resisting with considerable success for someone who looked like physical battles, as opposed to legal ones, were completely foreign to her. She alternately kicked, twisted, and dug in her slippered heels with more skill than Mabel herself possessed.

Mabel raced through the door, shouting, "Hey!" in the hope that the mayor would give up now that he knew he had a witness. He turned to look at her, and his expression wasn't that of someone who knew he'd lost. He almost looked pleased to see Mabel. With barely a pause, he merely adjusted his grip on Lena's wrists and resumed dragging her toward the shed where the smoke was thickening.

"I already called the police," Mabel lied, even as she was dialing 911 surreptitiously, her hand inside the voluminous barn coat pockets. "It's over."

Danny laughed. "They won't respond to a call to this address. You can thank Lena for that."

From her pocket came the distant sound of a voice saying, "Fire, police, or ambulance?" Mabel gave up on hiding what she was doing, pulled the phone to her face and said, "All three. Graham Winthrop's house is on fire and there are people inside." A slight exaggeration, but she was confident they wouldn't take the risk of not responding to something that serious.

Besides, if they didn't hurry, her words would come true.

Mabel dropped the phone and raced to intercept Danny before a second person died on Graham's land.

Chapter 25

Mabel skidded to a stop just out of Danny's reach. She raised the length of broken sidewall support to her shoulder like a baseball bat. "Let her go. You can't fight us both."

"I don't have to," Danny said. "I just need to make sure Lena can't talk to anyone about what she saw on Monday morning."

"Why bother?" Mabel asked, "You said yourself that no one ever believes her."

A look of outrage crossed Lena's face. "Why wouldn't anyone believe me? I'm the president of the homeowners' association."

Danny laughed. "Only because no one else wants the job. But the thing is, thanks to Mabel's meddling, I've got a totally credible scapegoat in Sam Trent. As long as you two don't give his attorneys any information that would raise reasonable doubt."

"That's ridiculous," Lena said. "I'm well-respected in this community. More than you are, certainly."

"I know people only tolerate me for my father's sake," Danny said. "I'm okay with that. It's better than being a laughingstock."

Lena struck out in rage, elbowing him in the stomach and then turning to kick him in the shin. Startled, Danny loosened his grip and Lena was able to pull free. She stopped beside Mabel to say, "You're done, Danny Avila. We'll see who the laughingstock is now. Your father is going to be rolling in his grave."

Danny slumped, and Mabel lowered the scrap of sidewall support, saying, "It's over, Danny. Let's go out front to wait for the police."

"I don't hear any sirens," he said uncertainly.

"They're on the way," Mabel said, although she wasn't entirely confident. There was a long history of calling wolf at this address.

Danny closed the distance between them to grab for the hand holding the length of sidewall support. He missed, but on his second try, he caught her other arm.

What was he up to? He couldn't control both her and Lena.

And then the sound of the greenhouse door slamming shut made her realize that Lena wasn't beside her any longer. Lena wasn't anywhere in sight.

"I'm not outnumbered now," Danny said. "I'll just lock you in the shed and then I can find some other way to get rid of Lena."

"You don't have to kill anyone else," Mabel said, swatting at Danny with the length of sidewall support. He grunted and pulled the makeshift weapon out of her grasp, scraping her hand as she tried to hold onto it.

"I can't take the risk that one of you will talk."

"You could run," Mabel said, dropping to the ground to curl up in a ball so she'd be a dead weight and harder to drag. "You still have time before the police arrive. Just disappear. Make a new life for yourself."

He caught her other wrist so he had both of them and dragged her about six feet, despite her resistance, before he had to stop for a break. Apparently his exercise routine of morning walks hadn't done much for his upper body strength.

Mabel felt a glimmer of hope that her ploy to delay him was working. If only the police would hurry up and arrive.

"I can't leave West Slocum," Danny said while he adjusted his grip on her wrists. "If I could have, I'd have left as soon as Graham provoked me into killing him. But I belong here. It's my destiny to be the mayor, just like my father. I can't let anything get in the way of my destiny."

"I totally understand that," Mabel lied. "I'm destined to be an app developer, and I would never give that up."

"It's not the same thing," Danny snapped. "The work I do is important. Not just being a mayor, but the history books I write too."

"Of course," Mabel soothed. "But what I don't understand is why you'd risk your destiny by killing Graham."

"It was his fault," Danny said. "You know how irrational he was. Wouldn't listen to anyone. I had to do something about the mess he'd made of his house. Everyone knew Lena had asked me to take care of it, and she was telling everyone how incompetent I was since I couldn't even handle something this minor. She was even going to finance a campaign for someone to run against me."

"You could have used legal means to deal with him," Mabel said. "You didn't have to kill him."

"I didn't mean to. I was there to tell him he'd been given his last warning, and I was going to have the board of health inspect the property, which would undoubtedly lead to its being condemned. But then he started talking about when he represented my mother when she divorced my father, and I couldn't let him live. Not with the way he'd been spilling secrets lately."

"What could have been so bad that Graham needed to die?"

Danny dragged her another foot. "It would have destroyed me."

"No one would hold your parents' actions against you."

Danny laughed. "Of course they would. I know I'm only mayor because of him, because of the respect everyone had for him. I'd be voted out if anyone found out he wasn't really my father. I couldn't let that happen."

"Is your job really worth a man's life?" Mabel asked.

"It was self-defense," Danny insisted. "My job is my life. Without it, I might as well be dead. So it was him or me."

Mabel loved her work, and she'd miss it terribly if she had to give it up to keep her aunt's farm going, but she wouldn't consider her life to be over. She wanted to tell Danny it was crazy to think that way, but now wasn't the time for her usual bluntness.

"If it was self-defense," she said, "why did you make it look like he'd eaten the rhubarb leaves? That seems more like something done in anger, not in fear."

"I was angry. If it hadn't been for Graham's stupid obsession with rhubarb and then his foolish experiments with eating the leaves, he never would have lost his mind and threatened me with the disclosure of secrets that should have been protected by attorney-client privilege. In retrospect, it was also useful in confusing the police. Just like your dying in a fire will, and Lena's dying in an accident."

"But if Graham's death was self-defense, you can explain it to the police. You don't need to kill anyone else."

Danny shuddered. "I can't do that. To prove self-defense, I'd have to explain about my father not being my father." He adjusted his grip on her arms. "I'm sorry, but now you're the threat, and I've got to defend myself."

He resumed dragging her, and she tugged and twisted against his pull until her arms felt like they were going to pop out of the shoulder joint. At least it was slowing him down and tiring him out. He'd only gone about three feet before the next time he had to stop.

Mabel considered twisting around and kicking at him while they were stopped, but she wasn't sure it would actually get him to release her. He'd be prepared for an attack after Lena had surprised him into releasing her. But if she could lull him into complacency and wait for the right moment, he might drop his guard. For now, all she could do was to distract him from time passing by getting him to talk about what he'd done instead of dragging her closer to the shed. Every second they stayed in one spot was more time for the police to arrive.

"What about the fire at my aunt's farm?" Mabel asked, lying still to conserve her own energy until she had a chance of escaping. "I thought it was Porter, but now I'm wondering if it was you."

"Of course it was me," Danny said with a distinct note of pride in his voice. "Porter gave me the idea, talking about how he'd bought up other farms that had experienced fires. It was supposed to get you motivated to sell. And as a nice side benefit, I thought it would distract you from investigating Graham's death."

Mabel heard distant sirens and could only hope they were responding to her call. Danny looked in the direction the sound had come from before adjusting his grip on her wrists.

She had to distract him, focusing his attention on her words and not on the approaching police. Making him angry might work. "You're as bad at arson as you are at being the mayor. Your father would have revealed that you're not his son himself if he knew how incompetent you'd be."

He let go of one wrist to slap her face. Her head snapped to the side and she felt blood dripping from her nose. Perhaps she'd gone a little too far in provoking him. She'd better be right about imminent help from the police.

Her ears were ringing, but over that sound, she heard the sirens, which were definitely heading toward her. Even better, she heard Lena Shaw shouting to someone, "They're in the back yard! Go through the greenhouses."

Danny redoubled his efforts to drag Mabel toward the smoking door, while she screamed once and then twisted to kick at the man's shins. She managed to land a solid blow finally, startling Danny into releasing one wrist, right before her peripheral vision caught movement at the back door of the smaller greenhouse. Charlie Durbin stood there, scanning the back yard.

"Over here," she shouted and kicked Danny again, freeing her second wrist. She scooted away from him on her butt as Charlie raced up to stand between her and Danny.

The mayor tried to go around Charlie to get to Mabel again, so Charlie punched Danny in the stomach. The mayor grunted and fell down.

He didn't stay down though. He got to his feet faster than Mabel would have expected, and reached for Charlie's neck as if to strangle him.

"Stop it," Mabel shouted, trying to think of something that would get through his irrational thoughts. "You're the mayor. You can't kill all of your constituents."

Danny hesitated. "Not all of them. Just you two. And Lena."

Lena's voice in the distance was repeating what she'd said to Charlie before. "They're in the back yard. Through the greenhouse."

"That's the police," Mabel said as she got to her feet and went to stand beside Charlie. "You can't kill your own police officers."

Danny looked over his shoulder to see two officers racing through the greenhouse door. He took a step back and tugged on the bottom of the sleeves of his blazer before waving his arm to invite the cops over to his side.

"Arrest them," he said. "They were trying to kill me."

Chapter 26

The small-town police might not have had a lot of experience with murders, but they had plenty of experience dealing with people telling contradictory stories. They knew better than to let anyone go, even when one of the parties was the mayor, before getting all the facts. They took everyone involved to the police station. Everyone was quietly resigned to the experience, except for Lena Shaw, who seemed to revel in finally being taken seriously. Once at the station, everyone was placed in separate interview rooms. Mabel's was only about ten feet square, with nothing but a metal table in the center, and four matching straight-back chairs.

Detective O'Connor popped in briefly to demand an explanation for why she'd tried to kill the mayor.

"You can't possibly believe I did that," Mabel said. "Have you talked to Lena Shaw yet? Or Charlie? They'll tell you what really happened."

"More likely they'll tell me what you asked them to tell me," O'Connor asked. "You could have coached them before the police arrived."

She'd been too busy fighting for her life at that point, but she doubted O'Connor would believe her. "In that case, I want to talk to the state detective. I'm not saying anything else until she arrives."

"I don't need her help."

He would never admit to his own incompetence, but maybe she could convince him it was to his benefit to have the more experienced detective present. "You don't need to convince me, but wouldn't you like to show the state detective how good you are? Especially with a case that's going to get a lot of media attention with the mayor involved?"

He managed to giggle thoughtfully. "You might be right. I'll call her."

He left, and Mabel wished the uniformed officers hadn't confiscated everyone's cell phones, so she could get some work done while she settled in for what she expected would be a long wait.

It was two long, boring hours later before the state detective, Deanna Cross, came through the door with O'Connor behind her. She looked like she could have been his mother, about thirty years older than he was, short and thin like he was, with red hair that looked natural. The big difference though was what looked like a perpetual scowl on her face instead of the junior detective's false cheerfulness.

"I'm told you won't talk to anyone but me." Detective Cross dropped into a chair on the opposite side of the table, while O'Connor remained standing behind her like a bodyguard. "So what have you got to say about what happened today?"

Mabel gave her a quick rundown of how the mayor had tried to kill Lena Shaw because she had information that implicated him in a murder, and when she'd eluded him, he'd tried to kill Mabel while confessing to Graham Winthrop's murder. She ended with, "The other witnesses will confirm what I said."

Cross looked over her shoulder at O'Connor. "Well? What did the others say?"

"Lena Shaw said pretty much the same thing, but everyone knows she's crazy. Charlie Durbin said he was stopping the mayor, not attacking him, but he's a friend of Skinner's, so of course he'd say they were innocent," O'Connor said. "What the mayor told me was just so much more credible. He's respected around here, unlike the others."

Mabel forced herself not to defend herself and Charlie.

The skeptical expression on Detective Cross's hard face suggested O'Connor wasn't impressing her with the way he'd handled the matter. "So what did this paragon of a politician tell you that was so persuasive?"

"That he was just having a conversation with Shaw, who was always making impossible demands on him, so she became agitated, and then Skinner suddenly attacked him with the assistance of Charlie Durbin."

"Did he say why they attacked him?" Cross asked.

"No, but he's the mayor. Why would he lie?"

"Everyone lies," Cross growled again. "So you've got one purported victim who can't explain why he was attacked. And you've got another purported victim, Ms. Shaw, who has a solid reason for why she was attacked, and she corroborates Ms. Skinner's and Mr. Durbin's statements, right?"

"I suppose, but it's the *mayor* disagreeing with the others," O'Connor insisted.

"All the more reason to get it right," Cross said. "I understand two uniformed officers responded to the scene. What did they tell you?"

"Just that Shaw was waiting for them and sent them into the back yard where the mayor and Durbin were facing off, and Skinner was on the ground behind Durbin."

"So it's consistent with what three witnesses claimed happened, and yet you're determined to believe the one person with a different story, just because he's in a position of power." Cross sighed and turned back to Mabel. "I'm sorry. I'm going to have someone come take your official statement, and once you sign it, you can leave."

O'Connor laughed heartily as if he'd just heard a hilarious joke.

Cross turned and growled at him, and his laughter faded.

"What?" he asked. "Are you serious?"

"I was just about to ask you the same thing about how you've treated the witnesses," Cross said. "I'm guessing you haven't yet asked Ms. Shaw about what she knew that might incriminate the mayor in a murder. I'm pretty sure that when you do, you'll finally understand what a big mistake you've made. And maybe then you'll apologize to Ms. Shaw, as well as Ms. Skinner and Mr. Durbin, for your treatment of them."

"But—"

Cross's renewed growl cut him off. "Go do your job."

O'Connor glared at Mabel, as if it were her fault that he'd handled the matter badly, and his planned moment of triumph had instead turned into humiliation. She'd just made a powerful enemy, but she couldn't see how she could have handled it any differently. She'd be under arrest by now, probably with Charlie in the adjoining cell, if she hadn't insisted on bringing in the state detective.

Cross stood and made a shooing motion before following O'Connor out the door.

As promised, an officer came and took Mabel's statement, and another hour later, she was escorted out to the lobby, free to go home, with assurances that the mayor would be held for more intense questioning about Graham Winthrop's death.

Charlie was in the lobby waiting for her, which she hadn't expected but found incredibly comforting.

He'd arranged for one of his employees to pick up his truck and bring it to the station, so he could drive her back to Graham's house to get her Mini Cooper. On the way, Mabel asked how he'd known to come to her rescue.

"I got your message about going to the greenhouse and called you back, but you didn't answer. Then I left a voicemail, and you didn't respond to that either, so I started to worry and decided to check to see if you were still at the greenhouse."

"I never heard the ping," Mabel said as she checked her phone. Sure enough, he had called. There was not just one but three messages from Charlie in as many minutes, escalating from asking where she was, to whether she was at the greenhouse, and finally why she hadn't called him back already. "It must have been after I turned off the ringer. I didn't want it to go off while I was trying to sneak up on the mayor. Then I was a little too distracted to notice the phone vibrating."

"Good to know," Charlie said. "I thought you were ignoring me, because you didn't want me around."

"I'd never ignore you," Mabel said. "And if I don't want you around, I'll tell you."

He laughed. "Yeah, I should have known you wouldn't be shy about telling me to go away if you wanted me to."

"I don't usually want you to go away," she said. "It was really nice to see you waiting for me in the lobby."

"As long as you like seeing me, how about planning to do something together that's got absolutely nothing to do with work or murder."

"I could definitely use a break from both," she said. "What did you have in mind?"

"How about lunch tomorrow at Jeanne's Country Diner?"

"I'll meet you there at noon if that's good for you."

"For you," he said solemnly, "any time, any place."

* * * *

While Charlie waited to make sure she didn't encounter any more trouble outside Graham Wilson's house, Mabel climbed into her Mini Cooper gingerly, aware of her bruises and the shock of her ordeal. As she pulled away from where she'd parked, muscle memory took over, and she drove the short distance home.

As she entered the kitchen, the residual adrenaline from her fight for her life was fading and being rapidly replaced by exhaustion. She couldn't give in to the fatigue quite yet though. Emily and Rory were seated at the table, waiting for her.

"Are you all right?" Rory asked. "We heard what happened, how the mayor tried to kill you and Lena to cover up his murder of Graham."

Mabel wondered if the grapevine had also heard about what was even worse—in Danny's mind, at least—the lack of biological ties to the previous mayor.

"I always thought there was something off about Danny," Emily said. "He had such negative energy in his aura. I never thought he'd be a threat to you though."

"I'm fine," Mabel said, "but I need to go check on Billie Jean and her babies. I hadn't expected to be gone so long when I left this morning."

"They're fine," Emily said. "I checked on them as soon as I heard you were at the police station."

"Then I need to pack for Maine."

"You can't leave now," Rory said.

"Of course not," Mabel said. "I'll take a nap first. I'm too wired to sleep right now, but I'm sure I'll be ready once I'm done packing."

"But what about the farm?" Rory asked. "I thought you were going to stay until you could hire a manager and get him settled in."

"I am." Mabel swayed a little with exhaustion, and dropped into a chair before she fell over. "But first I need to go to Jeff's funeral."

Emily and Rory both sighed in relief.

Emily said, "We'll take care of the cats and kittens while you're gone."

"Thanks," Mabel said. "I'll ask Terry to take care of Graham's seedlings until I get back. I'm definitely going to plant a field of rhubarb next spring. I'll talk to Sandy about jointly buying them from the estate and dividing them between us, now that we know she didn't kill for them. I might even offer to fund some of her research if she'll agree to name the first breakthrough variety she develops after Graham's wife."

"Speaking of naming, the kittens will need names soon," Emily said. "They could be varieties of rhubarb."

"Until recently, I didn't even know there was more than one variety," Mabel said. "And I'm not keeping the kittens, so they'll be named by whoever adopts them."

"You'll still need temporary names," Rory said. "We'll help with that when you get back. There are lots of suitable variety names. I can think of Victoria, MacDonald, Sutton, Cherry, and Ruby right off the top of my head."

"The farm will need a new name too," Emily said. "Rhubarb is sour, but it doesn't stink like garlic and lavender do."

"You could call it Skinner Farm," Rory suggested.

"I'll think about it," Mabel said before excusing herself to go upstairs and pack until she collapsed in exhaustion.

By the time she fell asleep, she'd already decided her friends were right. The farm needed a new name. One that reflected both its history—a recognition of Aunt Peggy's initial work in starting it—and its future, with a new beginning under Mabel's oversight.

From now on, Stinkin' Stuff Farm would be Skinner Farm, and at least until she could hire a manager, Mabel would be a farmer.

ACKNOWLEDGMENTS

This story was inspired, first, by memories of a great-uncle's two-hundred-foot-long row of rhubarb plants and his sister's expertise with jams. Then a pregnant feral cat showed up in my yard, and I trapped her and kept her (and her eventual kittens) in a dog crate until the kittens were weaned and homes were found for everyone. Her tomcat boyfriends kept visiting my yard, but none of them would admit to paternity, so we named her Billie Jean, after the song. When I was populating the cast for *Rhubarb Pie Before You Die* and wanted to include a greenhouse cat, my experience with feline fostering became a part of the story.

The inspirations for a book, and even the writing of it, are just the beginning of the process though. I am fortunate to have so much help and support to turn the manuscript into a published book. I'm particularly grateful to my editor, Norma Perez-Hernandez, who tells me when I do things right, not just when I do them wrong! Her team at Kensington Publishing, from the copy editors and the art department to publicity and marketing, work so well together to turn a manuscript into a book that people hear about and want to read.

I wouldn't be able to concentrate on creating a story if it weren't for my agent, Rachel Brooks, who keeps a close eye on the business/publishing side of things, so I don't get distracted by it all.

I'm also grateful for the Argh Ink community, who surround me with wisdom and happiness, and Sisters in Crime, which offers education, advocacy, and sisterhood.

RECIPES

Rhubarb Crisp

My mother always used white sugar instead of the more traditional brown sugar when she made rhubarb crisp. I loved the shocking contrast in each bite, mixing the soft, sour rhubarb and the crunchy, sweet topping. The recipe was lost for years, and when I went looking to recreate it by studying crisp recipes, either the topping was too soft and cookie-like or else it used brown sugar, which seemed to blunt the sweet-sour contrast a bit. Finally, I used a basic apple crisp topping recipe from The Joy of Cooking, *and just replaced the brown sugar with white sugar, omitted the cinnamon, and it was exactly what I remembered from childhood! This recipe allows you to make it either way.*

4 cups rhubarb, washed and chopped into half-inch pieces
1/2 cup flour
1/2 cup sugar (white or brown)
1/4 cup butter
1/4 teaspoon cinnamon (only if you use brown sugar)

Place rhubarb in a casserole dish.

Combine the flour and sugar, and then cut in the butter until the dough is crumbly. Sprinkle on top of the rhubarb.

Bake about 30 minutes at 350 degrees.

Blueberry Rhubarb Jam

This is my favorite jam of all time, I think. The rhubarb cuts the potentially cloying sweetness of the blueberries and also thickens the texture nicely. It's inspired by Madelaine Bullwinkel's Gourmet Preserves Chez Madelaine, *although I like to use a potato peeler to remove strips of lemon peel and then cut it into tiny slivers instead of grating it, and I add extra peel, so there's a little burst of lemon in each spoonful. This jam is messy to make, spitting bubbles of blueberry juice all over the stove and counter, but well worth the effort. You can chop up the rhubarb in advance and freeze it until blueberries come into season, which breaks up the work into more manageable bits of time.*

2 pounds rhubarb, washed and cut into half-inch slices
2 pound blueberries, rinsed
1/4 to 1/2 cup water
5 cups sugar
Zest of one lemon, cut into tiny slivers
2 Tablespoons lemon juice

Place rhubarb, blueberries, and water in a heavy pot, like a Dutch oven, at least 4-quart-sized. Simmer on medium heat, stirring occasionally until the fruits are soft and mushy, and the liquid is bubbling softly.

Add sugar, half a cup at a time, bringing the jam to a bubble again each time before adding more sugar. Add the lemon zest and continue to cook for about fifteen minutes until the jam comes to a full boil, stirring with increasing frequency as it gets closer to a boil. It will probably spatter at the end, which will tell you it's almost done, so you may want to partially cover it in the last five minutes or so. Add the lemon juice right before turning off the heat.

For short-term use (within a week or two), simply pour into clean jars, add lids, let cool, and then refrigerate. For longer-term use, it can be frozen in freezer-safe containers or processed by submerging the filled pint or half-pint canning jars in boiling water and boiling them for ten minutes after the water returns to a boil.

Makes about 4 pints. The recipe may be halved for a small batch, but, really, you'll regret it if you don't make all 4 pints!

Stewed Rhubarb

My maternal grandmother's brother and sister both had extensive rhubarb patches at their homes, where I visited frequently as a child. It was used mostly for desserts, although I have a vague recollection of being told it was good for one's digestion, and that it should be served frequently, stewed, as a side dish, more like a vegetable than a fruit (although it would still need some sugar to be palatable). Most recipes for stewed rhubarb today are less medicinal and are intended for use as a topping for ice cream or pancakes or the like, and that's what I use it for too, unlike Mabel's aunt.

8 cups rhubarb, washed and cut into half-inch pieces
1/4 cup water
2 ½ cups sugar
3/4 teaspoon cinnamon OR 1 Tablespoon lemon juice and the zest of one lemon

Combine rhubarb, water and sugar in a heavy pot, like a Dutch oven. Bring to a boil and then simmer until the fruit is soft and has the consistency of jam or applesauce. Stir in the flavoring of choice, either cinnamon or lemon.

Makes 4 or 5 pints. For short-term use (within a week or two), simply pour into clean jars, add lids, let cool and then refrigerate. For longer-term use, it can be frozen in freezer-safe containers or processed by submerging the filled pint or half-pint canning jars in boiling water and boiling them for ten minutes after the water returns to a boil.

Printed in the United States
by Baker & Taylor Publisher Services